This is a 1st edition misprinted
copy of Two: The Tale of Light & Darkness.

Check out @blu_innovative on Instagram
for the final copy, along with the
sequel Three: The Tale of Time, available
now on Amazon!

TWO:
THE TALE OF LIGHT AND DARKNESS

LEVITT YAFFE

authorHOUSE®

AuthorHouse™
1663 Liberty Drive
Bloomington, IN 47403
www.authorhouse.com
Phone: 833-262-8899

Published by AuthorHouse 08/30/2021

ISBN: 978-1-6655-3329-4 (sc)
ISBN: 978-1-6655-3328-7 (hc)
ISBN: 978-1-6655-3327-0 (e)

Library of Congress Control Number: 2021915570

Acknowledgment

This book is dedicated to my parents, Claire and Rick Yaffe, for their boundless love and support.

A very special thank you to my sister, Bebe, and my father, Rick, for their thoughtful contributions, keen eyes, and masterful editing.

I also want to thank one of my closest friends Logan Devitt, for working with me to produce the artwork for the book, including the cover and chapter designs, and my logo.

Jacket Copy

Everyone has a soul.
The soul holds many secrets.
Some are able to unlock the Attributes
of Soulmagic within their soul. The only
way one can harness these abilities
is through the use of a sword that
is either connected with its maker or
bonded to its long-standing wielder.

Brace yourself as you are about to enter
a Tale of a universe built from Soulmagic.
With themes of time, family, the lust for
ultimate rule, peace, and of course a bond
more powerful than anything seen before.

Two: The Tale of Light and Darkness will
unlock each doorway of your imagination
creating a space for you to get lost in
thought, while also cementing you to the
story you are about to embark on.

Table of Contents

Prelude

This was not the first time the Merchant saw Palaleon sway into darkness.

Very clearly, he remembered what others had long forgotten. It was a time of upheaval, of uncertainty. It was a time of madness. Nobody was safe. And yet the Merchant saw people obtain the will and power to rise up against this madness, the authoritarian rule. Life then transitioned to a time of peace and prosperity, where the people from all around the universe united to build a democracy where ideas were shared, and culture prospered. There was no fighting, and no war. Everyone was content. Even the Legendary Beasts had nothing to fear as they traveled throughout Palaleon.

But it was all in vain. A new darkness soon contaminated the universe, one that crushed the people. A new ruler appeared. He was an outsider. The people fell into obedience, allowing themselves to be ruled once again by a despot. Darkness clouded the hearts and minds of everyone. To avoid detection, the Legendary Beasts transformed from their beastly selves to humanoids. Their goal was to survive and guide the future to a better age. Only to make their presence known when the time was right for them to return.

And so, the Merchant went on his way. His only prized possession was a lute that he crafted from a gnarled fragment of rosewood. He continued to travel throughout Palaleon dressed in white rags, his shoes worn down from the miles he walked on foot on the planets he visited. On his back was his instrument. On the planet, Draefast, he found his way to a city, walking along the streets filled with people bustling in all directions. He made his way to a quieter side street and proceeded to sit outside a local bakery. He took out his lute, and began to sing:

> *I come out here daily*
> *Dusk till dawn*
> *To reiterate about our past*
> *Now that it's gone*
> *From times old that which I sing*
> *The Council of Swordmasters will survive again*
> *To reteach us the ways of peace*
> *Unity we had until the Dark Wizard came to be*
> *We had a time like this before*
> *But I doubt you would remember*
> *Since above us there is a Shroud*
> *Corrupting your minds*
> *No doubt*
> *He isn't perfect*
> *He isn't great*
> *Your mind is already his*
> *Wake up*
> *You must wake up*

The Merchant found himself connected to Draefast, more so than the other planets, and so he decided that that is where he would reside. He traveled to the other planets occasionally but did so unseen and would not stay there for long. He had his own personal mission inside the bigger picture of this world. He knew that he played a role in the redemption of Palaleon. It was not his job to interfere with the events unfolding, but it was his responsibility to guide the future to a better tomorrow.

The Merchant sat on a bucket strumming his lute, not bothering anyone, just singing, and enjoying his day. People began to scold him, calling him a liar and telling him to leave. This created a stir, one Hoshek did not need in his city. He summoned his grunts to handle this interloper, by any means necessary. As the grunts descended upon the Merchant, he shouted in protest, but nobody helped the poor old man; they did not want to interfere for the sake of saving their own skins. The people had become complacent, feeling it easier to accept Hoshek as their new ruler. They knew him to be fierce and unforgiving, so nobody wanted to get on his bad side.

The grunts pulled him into an alleyway on the first level of the city. The Merchant tried to fend them off with his lute, thinking he could scare the five creatures. He was wrong. They swung first. The Merchant caught one of the grunt's hands with his own and blocked another with his lute. "Crash!" One piece of the lute was now dangling from the other. The Merchant lost his balance as if a piece of his soul had just been severed. The grunt had started to bleed as one of the lute strings broke. The other grunts decided to step in, and that is when the Merchant realized he might need to do something drastic in order to escape. "Come on you foul creatures, just a little closer," the Merchant said as he started walking backwards out of the alley taunting the grunts. As his lute snapped in two, he realized that it was time to flee. He threw the two pieces of broken instrument at the grunts using it as a distraction to run. He then ran through the crowd of people behind him, and safely made it out of the city. The grunts rushed back to their leader to show him the broken lute left by the mysterious, disruptive man.

Hoshek, a man pale in the face, draped in dark robes, stayed seated. The grunts entered the throne room within Hoshek's castle, and he pointed towards the grunt holding the broken lute. "Bring that here!" The grunt walked over to his master, rested the lute on his lap, and bowed. The grunts were not asked about the man holding the instrument they had just given their master. The grunt that was bleeding also stepped in front of Hoshek. Hoshek tapped the grunts hand with his sword and all of his cuts sealed back up, as if they were never there in the first place. The grunt screamed. It felt a burning sensation as if his blood was boiling. The grunts then left Hoshek's throne room.

Hoshek seemed to have a lot of things on his mind, so they did not need to disturb him. Using his right hand, he placed his sword face down on the right side of his throne, his hand resting atop the pummel. His nails were long and thin. He turned his head to focus on what was in his lap. Hoshek lifted the lute with both of his hands off of his lap and it began to glow. *What is this unusual feeling? Why is this instrument glowing?* Hoshek thought to himself. His hands then started to burn. As Hoshek inhaled the burning feeling went away, he had absorbed his pain into his soul leaving him with no physical scars, but his soul was in pain thus it became a weaker magic source.

He dropped the pieces of the lute on the floor and out of the glow came two swords. The lute was no more. *Did the lute just transform into these two swords?* Hoshek did not know what this meant. He called for the grunt that was standing outside his throne room and said "Bring these two swords to the artifacts room. I will study these later." Hoshek was blankly staring upwards. He was puzzled as to how two swords came from one instrument. *But for now, I must focus on my plan.*

The Merchant felt his connection to his lute fade. It was as if the lute along with a piece of his soul was split into two new forms. "It's gone," he cried out. He made it to one of the villages away from Hoshek City while also making sure he was not followed. The grunts were busy with other tasks, so they did not pay much attention to the Merchant after he escaped their clutches. He knew that he would eventually need to go back to the city, to make sure that he could obtain necessities for his travels: food that will last him a while, some warmer clothes, and water. His goal after going back to the city would be to travel through various village eventually heading to Lightning Hills. The Merchant knew that he would find what he sought there.

I must travel discreetly. Now is not the time for me to be in Hoshek's vision. I will continue my travels, but I will need a new instrument to bring the people Tales from old in the form of song. The Merchant clasped his hands together and then released them. A yellow glow emanated from between his palms. A wooden body of a lute started to take shape. As he twiddled his fingers, golden strings started to take shape. The lute floated in the air and then dropped into his arms. *I will cherish you even more so than my last lute.* He had added even more of his soul, so he felt weaker, especially when he was not holding his new instrument. Nobody around him paid attention to him as he crafted his instrument. The villagers simply thought he was a beggar coming from the city to eat their food. They had yet to learn that they would be enjoying his songs quite soon. His lute was done, now it was time for him to continue his songs. He then sat outside a fruit stand. The fruit above his head did not smell fresh, with flies hovering around it, but it was food for the people, nonetheless.

"Hey you!" a voice cried out from behind the Merchant. "If you're going to sing and play that instrument in front of my stand, the least you could do is entice people here to buy some fruit."

I recognize that voice only this time it sounds more gravelly. The Merchant turned around and noticed that the one speaking to him was his old friend the fruit stand seller whom he met years ago only now he seemed to have aged and with that became the fruit stand owner.

He must have forgotten due to the Shroud that I have played here before. In fact we had already made another deal, maybe the Shroud is making him forgetful. Hmm. Anyway for the time being I should make a deal with him, but I know I won't stay in this village for long.

"Ok I can try to do that with my Tale-songs, but let's make a deal. For each person who comes here to buy provisions, you give me one piece of fruit. That seems fair, doesn't it?" The Merchant's stomach made a noise as he spoke.

The fruit stand owner noticed this, and replied, "Ok, old man, you have yourself a deal." The two shook hands. "What should I call you?"

The Merchant thought about this for a while, *Well I can't go by my Legendary Beast name, as no human would be able to pronounce it unless they were a Councilmember. Since I will be helping this vendor sell his fruit to people from this village, I will tell him an appropriate name.* He replied to the vendor, "You can call me 'the Merchant'."

"Fine by me." he shrugged.

Once I stock up on enough fruit I will be able to leave this village, and head back to the city before heading north.

As their conversation ended, the Merchant started to play his lute and sing:

> *I come out here daily*
> *Dusk till dawn*
> *To reiterate about our past*
> *Now that it's gone…*

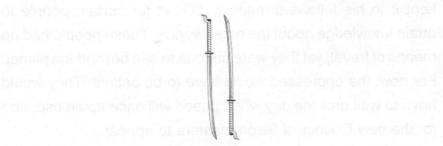

Chapter I

The Family

Deep in the universe known as Palaleon, five young humans were brought together when they each heard a voice in their head. The voices they heard came from the Legendary Beasts telling each of them where to find the pieces to create the Planetary Sword, and form what would be known for generations to come as the Council of Swordmasters. These five people would also be the ones who created the five Attributes and Sub Attributes of Soulmagic, but could only extend their abilities through swords. After creating these Attributes, they passed down their knowledge in the form of Tales.

The universe was not expansive. In fact, Palaleon consisted only of four planets with their moons, all rotating around suns. Before the villainous Dark Wizard Hoshek took over Draefast, the second largest of the four planets, people had heard about planetary travel, but ever since the day the Council of Swordmasters disappeared, only a select few traveled off world and knew about other planets besides their own. Living in a society where the ruler closed off certain information and only kept it to his followers made it difficult for certain people to attain knowledge about the other worlds. These people had no means of travel, yet they were curious to see beyond the planet. For now, the oppressed would have to be patient. They would have to wait until the day when peace will once again rise, and for the new Council of Swordmasters to appear.

With Hoshek's arrival, a Shroud of Souldarkness was cast, stretching across the planet like a thick smog. Most people were affected by it, leaving them in an almost mindless daze. They succumbed to Hoshek's reign and offered no resistance.

From the observatory atop Hoshek's castle, he punctured holes in this Shroud, by focusing all of his Souldarkness Attribute to the tip of his sword. This allowed for his citizens to see the moons and suns, which acted solely as a way to tell time, while still being under the Shroud's stultifying effects. He could not keep the holes open for long, for it was as if the Shroud had a mind of its own. It was too powerful, and every time Hoshek toyed with it he would become fueled with more Souldarkness which amplified his inner darkness, making him angrier and more emotional.

Hoshek's castle was grand, resembling the ancient sanctuaries of his forebears. The castle's interior held many spacious rooms including a Great Hall where Hoshek and his most trusted followers feasted on luxurious meals and consumed great amounts of fermented beverages. Hoshek's chambers were towards the top of the castle, where there was a giant metallic door separating himself from the rest of the castle. To the side of his platform bed was a hand-crafted rug where he would sit and think, getting more and more engulfed in the darkness. Arched windows framed the views in all

2

directions, overlooking his city. Connected to his room was a staircase to his observatory. His throne room was a couple stories beneath his chambers, and under the massive throne room, was a cellar and kitchen, where workers toiled to feed their ruler. The castle led all the way beneath the surface level of Draefast, to a more rustic-looking tomblike area. There was a ruin with a stone archway leading to a tunnel. At the end of this tunnel was a circular room with a portal in the center. The portal had a rock outline around it, and its purpose was to lead to another dimension.

In the beginning, grunts were in charge of constructing the interior of the castle, training one another in the castle, along with guarding weapons and Tales. When Hoshek created them, he brought them into his already constructed throne room regiment by regiment and tell them their purpose. "My beautiful creations, I need you to disguise yourselves while causing panic in the city and around Draefast, distracting my dear citizens. By having you instill fear, and creating a scare for the people, they will succumb even more so to the Shroud of Souldarkness gracing our presence. Thus their minds will be mine." As he said this the area around Hoshek's eyes tinted to a dark purple color showing that he was being affected by the Shroud, and that his own abilities were growing.

There were four different tiers of the city, the bottom was where the poorer subordinates lived. These were the people who worked as Hoshek's staff, tending to the daily needs of the castle's elite. On the second tier was where the entrance to Hoshek's castle was along with the middle-class civilians. The third and fourth tier is where the more important people in Hoshek's eye - the wealthy followers lived. Each tier had entrances to the castle hidden inside them that the grunts used. Before Hoshek's time, there was a castle in this very place, but as time moved on it had become rustic thus a model for a more modern castle. Upon being built the city was named Hoshek City. Most of the civic action took place in Hoshek City and was overseen by him, but there were also villages around the planet that he kept a keen eye on.

Light on Draefast generated from a deep crater extending to the planet's molten core. A beam of light shot into the atmosphere from the crater, spreading heat and luminosity across the world. A majority of the land was filled with dark forests. There was also a waterfall made of light, along with many villages populated with humans who would go about their day, hunting, gathering, trading, and crafting. There were many streams on the planet, but most of the time they were guarded by Hoshek's grunts. Draefast was also home to the Inbetween which was a dangerous land that was surrounded by a desert. The portal to the Soul Realm was found only on this planet.

This story focuses on a family of thieves who lives on the outskirts of one of the dark forests on Draefast: The Father, The Mother, The Son, and The Daughter.

The hut the family resided in was built by The Father when he met The Mother and knew that he wanted to spend eternity with her. He could not afford to build it in a village or close to Hoshek City, so when he obtained materials like stone, straw, and wood, he built the two story hut on an empty patch of land near a dark forest. The Mother helped design the interior of the hut and was able to steal appliances within the city to make the various rooms in their home feel more lively.

They were not thieves by choice. It was a skill that The

Father and The Mother honed since their family was poor and in need of provisions. They knew that Hoshek's castle was brimming with food and supplies, more than enough than he and his supplicants could ever use. All the while, the people of Draefast tried in vain to scratch out a living. The Father and The Mother were no different, except that they took matters into their own hands. They knew they were putting themselves at great risk, but they also knew that Hoshek, the Dark Wizard, was a tyrant with an impetuous temperament, so they felt no guilt when they needed to obtain food. Hoshek starved the planet of its resources including food and other materials. The residents of the planet knew this but were powerless. They quickly lost all hope as they transformed into mindless chattel.

In the villages it was easier to get by, but The Mother and The Father were witnessing what this tyrant was doing to their home. They concluded that since no one else was there to stand up for one another, then they had to do it themselves. That is why they started stealing from Hoshek's castle and giving materials to villagers near their home. As time went on The Mother and The Father decided that they wanted to start a family, so they had to repurpose their criminal activities. They could no longer give poor people materials from Hoshek's castle or else they risked becoming a bigger target for the grunts. The Father and The Mother eventually had The Son and a few years later they had The Daughter.

One night, thunder - as loud as the creation of the Planetary Sword - clapped and Purple Lightning - as bright as The Son's future - struck the family's little hut. The Mother and The Daughter were not in the hut at the time, but instead had been on a quest to find one of the final pure water sources on

5

Draefast. Most of the water on this planet was the property of Hoshek and his most loyal followers. The Mother's and The Daughter's goal was to collect enough water in buckets to last them a couple more moon cycles. Each bucket had a different purpose, whether it was to use the water to drink, bathe, or to cook.

As the Purple Lighting struck, The Son and The Father were in the hut admiring their new swords that they had stolen from the castle the week before. The Father wanted The Son to get something nice for his 10th birthday which was on this day. They were holding onto their swords with a firm grip, as they glanced up and down the shimmering metal.

"Thank you so much for the present, Dad," The Son said with glee.

"Make sure you train with it, so you do not hurt yourself, and are able to defend yourself my son. The Dark Wizard will be looking for the return of his swords, so you must be ready in case I am not around."

The Father and The Son began to reminisce about how they took the swords from a the bottom level of the castle, which they knew how to get to from traveling around the city before. As they walked towards a grate connected to the castle adjacent to the first tier of the city, they noticed this scraggly looking man walking past them playing a lute and singing:

> I come out here daily
> Dusk till dawn
> To reiterate about our past
> Now that it's gone
> From times old that which I sing
> The Council of Swordmasters will survive again

To reteach us the ways of peace
Unity we had until the Dark Wizard came to be
We had a time like this before
But I doubt you would remember
Since above us there is a Shroud
Corrupting your minds
No doubt
He isn't perfect
He isn't great
Your mind is already his
Wake up
You must wake up

They pushed open the grate and walked through sewage, making a left turn down the tunnel to traverse up a ramp to get to the floor that had the artifacts room. If they had gone straight instead of turning left, they would have descended beneath Draefast's surface towards the ruin. Instead, they were on a level of the castle in between the tiers. It seemed to be a part of the many secret passageways. Grunts were guarding the level, so The Father and The Son had to be swift.

Since the Dark Wizard let the grunts watch over Draefast while he was busy conducting his plan, The Son and The Father had an easy time stealing the swords from the castle. The Father grabbed a rock he found outside the grate and threw it as a distraction. The grunts moved trying to locate where the loud noise came from, giving The Father and The Son the opportunity to walk down the corridor of the new level. They did so quietly and with ease.

"I guess the Dark Wizard did not think anyone would be dumb enough to break into his castle," The Son stated brazenly.

The Father replied, "When it's for the sake of survival,

people like us need to do anything we can. Remember - we are not bad people for stealing, we are trying to survive, and make it day-by-day, as we are being tormented by a ruler who has only brought darkness to our world."

"Is this where you and Mom got the Tales from?" The Son asked.

The Father pulled out a map he had made of the castle but more specifically this floor, and proceeded to point. "No, see we are here," as he pointed to the weapons and artifacts room. "The food is over here." The Father moved his finger slightly to the right. "And the room with the Tales is over here." He moved his finger again. Only this time it was to the left down a hall, and then down another one. "Obtaining the Tales was by far our most dangerous theft. Your mother and I wanted to get them so we could teach you and your sister about the past. When I was younger I read Tales and through their knowledge I learned that history has the tendency to repeat itself." The Father and The Son opened the door to the artifacts room.

"It's all clear," The Son said. The Father walked in behind The Son and closed the door gently. As they gazed around the room, both of their eyes caught sight of two swords on a workbench. There were four other swords to The Son's left in a glass container, but The Son and The Father paid no mind to those. Behind the two swords on the workbench rested a third encased in a black sheath. *That sword looks rusted, as if it has seen many years of combat,* The Son thought as he and The Father continued roaming around the artifacts room.

"I will continue examining the swords shortly," They heard a voice say from outside the door.

"I wonder who that could be," The Son whispered. Realizing

8

that they had only enough time to take one thing each, they lunged for the swords. Quickly gripping the hilts, they pierced the floorboards with the blades and cut two holes large enough for them to escape. Beneath them was dirty water that would lead the two back to the grate.

"That's our way out!" exclaimed The Father. "Jump!" As The Father dropped on top of the sewage water, The Son followed, just as the door opened. The man walked into the room, looking puzzled.

"Where did the swords go? Hoshek is not going to be happy about this. I was never here." The man turned around as he spoke to the grunt to his left and walked out of the room, not noticing the holes in the ground. *Maybe he will blame a grunt and dispose of them. I will not say anything, as I value my life.*

The Merchant was back in the village at the fruit stand as The Son and The Father were leaving the castle. He felt a tingle in his chest and thought to himself, *I have a feeling my path will cross with whomever is holding the pieces of my old lute. I feel the two pieces in two separate sets of hands. One of them is worthy of holding it as that person's soul does not feel corrupted by greed or anything sinister.* For now, the Merchant could rest knowing part of his soul was in good hands.

The Father and The Son successfully escaped and had hastened back to the hut. The Son's sword was as white as the fourth moon above their homeworld, and The Father's sword was as black as the dirt beneath his feet.

The Mother and The Father kept the Tales that they stole in a chest in the room next to the kitchen. The Son had learned from one of the Tales early on in life that, "Purple Fire could only be extinguished by the Soullight Attribute or Souldarkness

Attribute of Soulmagic or a Legendary Beast." Neither The Son nor The Father wielded Soulmagic nor any Attributes. They had thought that, along with the stories of the Legendary Beasts, those were just Tales from an ancient time.

The Dark Wizard became even more secluded and rarely made a public appearance. He was distracted with his ultimate goal instead of focusing on the people on the planet. It took him a week to figure out where his two precious swords from his past were. One of his followers told him that they were stolen due to the fact that they noticed two holes in the artifacts room. Feeling enraged, but knowing that there was nothing he could do, Hoshek commanded grunts to repair the floor. After hearing the news about the thieves, he was finally able to track where the swords were as he sat perched atop his castle with his hands clasped around his sword breathing in and out as he pointed it to the north, east, south, and west. Through his connection to his Souldarkness Attribute and his own sword he found the general direction as to where his property was. His intent for the Purple Lighting had been to kill the thieves who robbed him of his swords and Tales. The bond he had with the Tales had weakened so when they were stolen, the problem he was running into was that he did not know where they were. It was like a part of him went missing, and his Souldarkness was directing him to where he could find it.

From the top of his castle, he was able to see past the dark forest all the way to the family's hut. He had pointed his sword at the hut and then to the sky. Through this motion, he generated Souldarkness, creating the Purple Lightning from the sky. The metal within the swords acted as an electrical conductor, which attracted the Purple Lighting to strike through the roof. As the roof collapsed around The Son and The Father, they were both struck by the Purple Lightning which decimated the ground of the hut. This lighting created a Purple Fire that slowly engulfed the hut.

Both The Father and The Son laid on the floor of the hut severely injured but not dead. They were both badly bruised and scarred. The Father had indentations in his arms where the lightning passed through his skin, and The Son had two half star-like shapes etched into his palms. The Son foresaw his future and what he was destined to become right before he hit the ground unconscious. All The Father saw was darkness. They were surrounded by the Purple Fire, which was very slowly consuming the hut, as the third sun passed for its cycle.

The Mother and The Daughter returned.

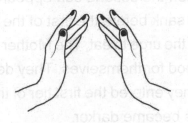

Chapter II

The Ones Struck By Lightning: Enter The Old Wizard

The Mother and The Daughter could not get to The Father or The Son since the Purple Fire, which reached the top of the dark forest tree line, blocked their only way in. While the embers below glowed in brilliant purple, the flames above danced menacingly above the ring of Purple Fire. Only someone with a connection to the Soullight or Souldarkness Attributes could burst through the ring. They knew nothing about the Attributes and had no connection to them.

Overcome with grief, The Mother and The Daughter just sat on the dirt with their eyes fixated on a distant point. Their legs were crossed, and arms bent in towards their bodies, with their hands close but not touching. They were able to keep track of time by watching the suns and moons through holes in the Shroud. The two of them watched the first sun move early in the morning, then the second sun appeared before midday, then the third sun sank before the first of the moons appeared.

When they felt the urge to eat, The Mother and The Daughter needed to steal food for themselves. They decided to go to the city together. As they entered the first tier of the city, the Shroud above their heads became darker.

"Mom, why is it so dark here?" The Daughter asked.

"Look up, this is not normal," The Mother replied.

They continued to walk around the first level of the city, their usual thieving grounds.

"Don't look now," The Mother said, "but there are beings attacking those poor people over there. It looks like nobody's fighting back, they are just giving in. I have heard of the Dark Wizard who rules over these lands. Why is he not doing anything?" The two of them walked by a home watching grunts pull the family out and knock them to the street as they went inside and stole valuables. There was a crowd of people watching the family's home get raided, but nobody did a thing. They continued walking down the newly cobbled street, glancing around at the homes to their left, some with broken doors as if what happened to that poor family happened to others. On their right side were little stands consisting of various foods, leather, drinks, and home goods. The Shroud above them got darker, The Mother and The Daughter were starting to feel the air get thinner and could see their breath every time they exhaled.

The Daughter held tightly onto The Mother's arm. "Is there a reason that nobody is helping? Why is everyone so scared? Why are we the only ones noticing that there is something wrong in this city?"

The Mother replied, "I cannot answer that, my child, let us

just get what we came for and go home. I hope you memorized the route since the next time we do this we should take turns. I will watch over our family and you can go and then we can switch."

"Ok mom," The Daughter responded.

The two of them successfully stole fruits, some uncooked meat, and fresh water. They stole from horse-drawn carriages containing shipments meant for Hoshek and his inner circle. They stored these items in a homemade leather satchel that was slung around The Mother's shoulder. They then dashed out of the city so they would not be seen.

Without looking behind, the two ran through the entrance to one of the many forests on the outskirts of the city, traveling further and further away from the castle. The Daughter was lagging behind. The Mother turned and shouted, "Honey, you must keep up if we are to make it safely home."

"I can't, mom. My stomach is hurting me. I'm so hungry."

"Just a little farther, and we'll be home. I hear your stomach and will prepare food after we get the fire started. Can you help me with that?"

The Mother knew they were close to home since she started to see the Purple Fire from atop the little hill they traversed over. "I wonder why nobody has come to see what is on fire." The Mother thought to herself, *Maybe people think it is cursed so they wouldn't go near it. Anyway, that's good for us since we can then eat without being disturbed.*

"Yes mom, I will lay down this wood and start the fire." The Daughter stacked the wood in a pile and took a kindling stick to the Purple Fire surrounding her home. It ignited.

15

"What are you doing near that fire, and with that stick?" The Mother shouted.

"I was being resourceful. I thought since there was a fire already here we could use…"

The Mother cut her off. "You will do no such thing ever again. Do you understand, your father and brother are in there, and we have no idea if they are alive or dead? Do not use this fire to cook our food. I have taught you how to make a fire. Do it that way."

"Ok mom, sorry." The Daughter then quickly threw the stick back into the Purple Fire. She noticed two sticks underneath her left foot and bent over to pick them up. She then rubbed them together the way The Mother taught her until a spark ignited thus creating fire. The Daughter then brought this flame to her pile of wood and soon there was a roaring fire.

As The Daughter was overseeing the fire, The Mother removed the raw meat from her satchel. Quickly realizing that the kitchen knives were beyond her reach, for they were sealed off by the Purple Fire, The Mother used her hands to tear away the meat from the bones. She then put the meat on two sticks and then placed them into the fire. While the meat was cooking, she prepared lettuce which they would use to cradle the meat. When the meat was golden brown, The Mother and The Daughter removed their sticks from the flames and placed them on the beds of lettuce.

After dinner, The Mother said, "I am getting drowsy, so I might retire soon. I think we should sleep near the fire since the nights are getting colder. Tomorrow, as we wake, we will pray for our family to return to us unscathed."

"I will do the same. Have a good night's sleep." The Daughter replied as she watched her mother curl up close to the fire and close her eyes.

As The Daughter woke the next morning, she saw her mother already beginning their daily routine. She walked over and sat next to her to copy the motion. They were praying to the Old Wizard, for him to conjure his connection with Soulmagic in order to breathe life back into The Father and The Son. He was the only wizards rumored to have the ability of returning life to the dead. It was said that he did this by combining both the Soullight Attribute and Souldarkness Attribute of his Soulmagic. This form of magic passed through his sword and then into his hands. Both the Attributes had to be in perfect balance in order to bring a life back from the dead. Since the Old Wizard was known to be in hiding for many years, people came to the assumption that his connection to his Soulmagic had diminished.

The Mother had heard about the Old Wizard from other villagers. When those villagers needed aid, they would call out to him to heal their wounded or ill family members. But that was before the Shroud of darkness clouded the villagers' memories. Some people in the villages while corrupted still found a way to believe in the Council of Swordmasters. They prayed to them for guidance and to be free from what felt like a curse on their minds and bodies. The Mother wondered if he actually existed, and if he did, whether or not he ever came to their aid. Regardless of this confusion, she needed something to hold onto, to know that she would soon have her family back, that they would be whole again. She found hope believing that he could help.

They continued this routine for seven days, when suddenly,

the ground shook, and inside the hut the two swords began to rumble. As the swords inched towards one another, a wave of the Soullight and Souldarkness Attributes kept the swords demagnetized allowing them to float upwards cutting a white glowing doorway in the thin air. Through the blank void of its center, a man's brown boot emerged, followed by the rest of his white-robed body. He was an old man, with a weathered face. The blank stare from his eyes was evidence that he had seen death and despair a thousand times over. His nose protruded outwards from his face a little and then drooped down towards his all-white mustache. He did not look clean. He had a mixture of scruffy grey and white hair beneath his lower lip creating his beard. His arms were thin but covered in his robes. One would not know when the last time this man ate.

As the doorway retracted, Draefast went quiet. The two swords that created the entryway fell. Their physical appearance changed. The energy of the doorway had melted each down to their core elements: a white shard made from pure light, and a black shard made from pure darkness.

The flames of the Purple Fire still continued to dance around in a ring shape now entirely consuming the hut's walls.

The Old Wizard had a device in his hand and pressed a button on its right side. A ship then flew down to the planet cloaked in Soulmagic so it would not be sensed or seen by Hoshek. The ships in this vast universe looked like giant metal wings with vessel-like structures in the middle. The size of the ship and size of the planetary hopper engine depended upon one's wealth and status in the universe. Due to the family's lack of wealth, they had no ship. Life beyond the sky was never even a thought. Hoshek kept that knowledge to himself and his wealthy supplicants on Draefast.

Even though the Old Wizard's ship was concealed, Hoshek started to feel that something or someone had entered his planet's domain. It was as if the Shroud was whispering to him. "He is here, the one who will ruin you. You must find him before he finds you and ends everything you have worked so hard to build and maintain." He could not taste the dullness of the air that typically surrounded him on a normal day. He felt full, but he could not pinpoint what he was full of. Was it emotions, anger, power? There was a presence, he knew that for certain, the kind that only appeared when his plans were about to be foiled. His goal is currently unclear, but to understand why he is the way he is; one must look into his past.

Chapter III

Hoshek

Hoshek was not always the disturbed Dark Wizard with hatred boiling in his blood. He grew up in a loving family, his mother being a nurturing woman with darkness in her past, and his father being the leader of the fifth Council of Swordmasters.

This Council helped keep the peace throughout the universe. Hoshek and his brother were the eldest of the Councilmembers' children. The children would meet and train whenever their parents would gather for Council meetings. Hoshek was the most skilled sword fighter of the children and the most connected to his Soulmagic and Attribute.

Before the fateful night in which Hoshek changed the course of Palaleon, he used to go on many different adventures with his father. Even though Hoshek felt closer to his mother, he appreciated every lesson his father taught him. His mother would watch from the Sanctuary on Aestercrat as his father taught him skills, such as how to craft a sword, and how to use a sword in a fight.

During their most recent journey Gathran, his father, took

him to train on the planet Vastrilio. As the two got off their ship they found a spot to begin Hoshek's training of the day, outside a city in one of the few green areas on the planet. They noticed a traveler walking by, alone. Hoshek looked at his father and asked, "Aren't there beasts in this forest? I recall being taught that when Baraka's mentor was giving us the geographical lesson of Vastrilio. That traveler should not be walking alone, especially at this hour." The sun was setting. Gathran replied, "There seems to be no threat. If I sense something amiss, we are close enough to intervene if we need to." As Gathran finished speaking a bear jumped out from behind a tree and tackled the traveler. The bear was about to kill the villager with its claws, but Gathran stepped in. He cut the bear's arm off, so it could not hurt the traveler. As the traveler got out of the bear's loosened grip Gathran delivered the fatal blow. "Thank you so much for saving me. How do I repay you?" the traveler asked.

"Just be more cautious when you're alone in the forest. Always watch your back. You don't know what else is out here," Gathran replied tersely.

The traveler then ran back towards the village outside the forest.

"Dad, why did you save him? I thought our job was to let nature run its course and not to get involved. That is how the people will learn isn't it? Bears are fiercer than humans so we should either let the circle of life occur or train the people to fight, right?" Hoshek asked, confused as to why his father just got involved. This was the first time Hoshek verbally stated his concerns with how the Council presented itself. He had had these thoughts on previous adventures with his father.

"Well, our job is to protect people. We give them lessons

22

and advice through protecting them thus keeping peace and unity between all. Don't forget. Everyone on Palaleon has a soul, and each soul holds many secrets. Some people like us are able to unlock the abilities held within their soul to access the Attributes of Soulmagic. Not every human is like that, and this is why we have been chosen to protect the people who are different from us. Not lesser, just different."

The two of them then went back to their ship and traveled back to Aestercrat, where the next Council of Swordmasters meeting was soon to be held.

Hoshek was a loyal child, always willing to help his peers, training with them, and showing them how to unlock certain Soulmagic abilities specific to their Attributes. He was a prodigy. But there was something off. Every night his dreams turned to nightmares in which he envisioned his friends dying around him. After having these dreams for over a week Hoshek went to his father to tell him about them. "Son you must learn to ignore your inner feelings and these 'messages' in your dreams. They will only get in the way of your greatness. I do not need you to worry about this as there are more pressing matters to attend to such as your training." As Hoshek looked back at his father he replied, "Understood. I will try to suppress these dreams so much so that they won't affect me anymore." Hoshek then walked back to his bedroom, leaving his father alone in his chamber. Hoshek never wanted his dreams to become his reality, so he decided to follow his father's instructions by trying to ignore his nightmares but night after night they became more intensified. One night Hoshek got up to get water and found himself pondering as he was walking to their well. *Why does my father not want to help me figure out the root of these dreams. Why is he only focused on his view of what I need to become. I listen to him and do the best I can at everything, but he only acknowledges me when I show progress with my Attribute training or my studies of the Tales. Why does he not care about how I feel. I guess I will talk to mom about it as I usually do. I can't show weakness in front of...* Hoshek returned to his chamber, jumped on his bed, and fell asleep.

His mother taught him kindness and compassion, but due to Hoshek staying by his father's side for weeks on end, his temper started to shift. He became angry at the littlest of things. His mother knew his heart was in the right place. She believed that at the end of the day that he was just under a lot of stress and pressure for being a role model to the other students.

The day had finally come when the Council of Swordmasters along with their successors, traveled to the Sanctuary on Aestercrat to gather together. Each successor challenged Hoshek to a sparring match, but he did not even have to use his Attribute to knock down his opponents. With sheer skill of the sword he was able to best one at a time. They trained all day only stopping for meals in between. Then nightfall was upon them.

During the night a Council meeting was occurring, Hoshek had gone to his chamber to sleep. Upon closing his eyes, he became haunted - haunted by a vision of the council's destruction - and watched his family burn in dark purple flames. He started to feel warm. Sweat ran down from his forehead and over his eyelids. Upon feeling the water run down his cheeks, Hoshek opened his eyes. It was as if something within him was amplifying this nightmare using Souldarkness to affect his body physically instead of just his mind. Hoshek did not understand how or why this was happening.

As Hoshek got up from his bed he began to run to his door. As he reached for the doorknob his body turned into a shroud and he moved through the door. Before his body materialized he glanced at where his left hand was. The hilt of his sword which remained in his sheath was being held tightly by his shrouded right hand. Hoshek's sword glowed in a dark purple color through the sheath and as his body materialized his hand let go, and the glow subsided. Then the tint of dark purple completely disappeared. Hoshek did not know what just happened. All he wanted to do was go to one of his parents to tell him what he saw in his nightmare. In the nightmare, Hoshek was watching an older version of himself become taken over by a shadowy figure that told him that in order for there to be true peace and unity in Palaleon he must destroy the Council of Swordmasters and create a new one using his Souldarkness. This figure introduced himself as a family member of Hoshek's who was betrayed by Gathran, his father. Hoshek was speaking to this figure in his mind while standing on top of a castle in black robes watching over a planet as it fell into complete darkness. In the nightmare, he clenched onto his heart with his right hand. He knew that this was not his goal, but it was too late for him, for he had no living family and no one to consult with besides the voice in his head. He was alone and scared. Hoshek went into his father's Council room thinking both of his parents would be there, but it was just his father. Hoshek told his father about his nightmare and when Hoshek finished speaking, Gathran aggressively dismissed the significance of the dream telling his son, "My Council defeated the strongest

Dark Wizard long ago, so there is nothing to worry about. You, your brother, and your mother are all safe. Now go back to bed, I have more important business to attend to." Hoshek left his father's Council room disquiet that he was not taken seriously. He then went to find his mother, Malikaya. She was in her and Gathran's bedroom. Hoshek ran in and told his mother about his nightmare. She then comforted him by showing her attentiveness and hugging him telling him that "Everything will be ok." Deep down she became worried and believed that Hoshek was sensing a darkness that was similar to one she had sensed when she herself was a child. She told him to get his brother and stay with him in his sleeping chamber. Hoshek was twelve years old, and his brother was seven years old. Hoshek nodded and left the room. Malikaya went to speak with Gathran.

"You shouldn't be so hard on your own son, the one you are training to be the next Council leader. We never told him about my father, so this is concerning."

"Malikaya, the darkness has been gone for over a decade. You were the one who defeated it," he stated, relieving the stubborn side of himself as he spoke with his wife.

"I know Gathran, but I am worried for our son," she replied.

"He is just imagining things."

"What if my father's essence is in our son?"

"Nonsense, he is my son, but if he continues to act this way, I will stop his training and instead will train his brother to be the next Council leader. I get to choose who takes my place. Now learn your place and only enter this office again if there is true urgency!" As quickly as Gathran's presentable and comforting tone appeared, it then vanished.

26

Gathran raised his hand to his wife, not realizing that Hoshek had heard this quarrel and went to see what was happening. This was not the first time Hoshek had witnessed his father being cruel towards his mother, but he made it so it would be the last. Engulfed in anger from being lied to his entire life, his physical appearance started to change. His eyes turned purple, and his hair turned from blonde to black. It was as if two people were watching a loved one be abused, and they could not take it anymore. He ran into the room, holding his sword that he picked up off the side of his bed frame. Right before his father was going to strike his mother, Hoshek unsheathed his sword and swiftly slashed his father's arm off. After realizing what he had just done, Hoshek's grip on his sword weakened, and it then fell to the ground. He felt betrayed since his father had kept his mother quiet about his family history. Hoshek's anger was fueled by the fact that his parents did not tell him about his grandfather, but what finally broke him into unleashing his inner Souldarkness Attribute was watching his father mistreat his mother. Denying his son the knowledge of his family's past and belittling his feelings and questions made it easier for Hoshek to let go of his feelings towards his injured father.

Gathran was hysterical, screaming in pain from the loss of his arm. "Help me. Someone please help me!" His son, the one he helped bring into this world, the one he trained, the one who was now his downfall just stared at him. Hoshek's intent was not to kill his father but to injure him. He never realized that by cutting off Gathran's arm, he had left his father to die. Nevertheless, Hoshek stood motionless.

"What a coward you have become," Hoshek said as he gazed upon his father. Gathran had just then come to terms with the fact that he had become weak in his Attribute. Gathran fell to the floor. While bleeding out, Gathran came to the realization that he was the problem and that he had failed his son. The last trace of his heart finally broke down, and he succumbed to his mortal wound. He loved his family, and did anything he could to protect them, but in the end his own way of protecting them was his demise.

How could I not be trusted by my own father? Hoshek thought to himself, *The man I looked up to. The man who raised me. Who trained me. Who put me on a path following his footsteps. Does that mean I am destined to be as cruel as him? I don't want that.* The other Councilmembers heard Gathran scream and ran past of Malikaya who was already in the room to see what had just occurred. Their fate was decided the minute they stepped into Gathran's office as Hoshek laid his eyes on them. He then bent down and picked up his sword.

Using the element of surprise, Hoshek moved towards his next targets. The Councilmembers realized this, but it was too late. They had become overconfident and thought that they were the only ones strong enough to be considered saviors of the universe. They could not see the growing anger and interest in the Souldarkness Attribute that Hoshek possessed. They had become lackadaisical throughout their years in which they believed that training was not necessary in order to maintain peace and their power, thus Hoshek was able to easily outwit them and strike with fatal blows. Although he was just a boy, Hoshek honed his skills every minute of every day striving to be the best. He was able to appear from the shadows, create phantom copies of himself and kill each Councilmember. *I believe I just unlocked my inner Souldarkness Attribute as no*

28

other Attribute allows user to create shrouded phantom copies of themselves. With this new power I will create a more fair, just, and peaceful universe.

Malikaya started screaming, "Stop!" She raised her hand, and with a blast of wind, shot her son back. This woke up the other children as they ran into the room trying to corner Hoshek, using their Attribute swords and Soulmagic abilities. They were not strong enough to hold him back. In his fit of anger and rage he killed each of them by plunging his sword, which was surrounded by bursts of Purple Lighting, into their hearts. He did not let any of the successors land a single strike towards him.

Malikaya ran to her younger son and put her hand on his forehead. She thought that she was erasing his memory since that was a Soullight Attribute ability she had, but she did not have enough Soullight energy for it to be effective. She put him on their family ship with a satchel filled with provisions and Tales that would help him to survive. She sent him away while telling him, "My son, I wish for you a new..." Malikaya paused. "A better life than the one we have given you. Forget all that you were, become someone new and eventually you will find your calling. I, we, believe in you. You are destined for greatness but for now I need you to survive, and by doing so you must stay out of sight."

All of a sudden, the Sanctuary fell silent. A giant blast of Purple Lightning struck the Council building knocking Hoshek's brother's ship off the platform. Malikaya was startled. She used the Soulwind Sub-Attribute from her hand, which was scarred years earlier, to keep the ship steady. As Malikaya's scar began to glow, she used her final ounce of Soulmagic to conjure a blast of Soulwind to shoot the ship with her son on it into orbit and away from the planet. "Goodbye my son," Malikaya mouthed as the council building was becoming immersed in darkness.

Hoshek laid in the center of his father's office surrounded by the corpses of his fellow Swordmaster successors, who were once his friends. They were all dead along with the Councilmembers, including his own father - all by his hand. Hoshek's eyes opened as he saw his mother slowly walking towards him.

"I am so sorry for everything. Your father and I wanted nothing but the best for you and your brother. We wanted to protect you from the evil that is inherent from my side of the family. But now I realize that we should have taught you the true nature of yourself so that you would be prepared to use your powers for noble causes."

Hoshek seemed to be unmoved by his mother's words. She continued, "I don't blame you for feeling this betrayal, and acting out in this hideous manner, but I hope you can find your own peace." With this final word, she exhaled her last breath. Her soul exited her mouth forming an apparition that quickly dissipated into thin air. With her lifesource gone, Malikaya's body collapsed right next to her son's feet.

As Hoshek knelt down his face sunk into his cupped hands. Tears streamed from his eyes finding their way through his fingers and dripping onto his mother's face. Hoshek then kissed her forehead. As he arose, he took his mother's sword and sheath and tied it around the right side of his waist. He noticed the other swords strewn about the Sanctuary floor. He scooped them into his hands. "I will make it my life's work to make amends for everything I have just done. I am sorry. And yet I believe that good can come from this." As these words trickled out of his mouth, a Shroud of Souldarkness appeared over Hoshek's head. It started to expand, growing from his anger, his regret, and his sadness. The Shroud eventually covered Aestercrat, and then enveloped the remaining planet's atmospheres.

Hoshek dragged the swords to his ship and prepped it for take-off. He entered the coordinates to the center of the universe, but froze before taking off. He knew he wanted to go there before heading to a planet he had yet to see but read about in Tales from previous Councilmembers. He was now on his own. He had to survive in order to make his desire come to fruition. Hoshek thought to himself, *Time to start a new venture, one without Palaleon's pitiful Council of Swordmasters.*

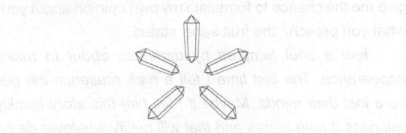

Chapter IV
Council Origins

While Hoshek succumbed to his inner darkness the Merchant was on Draefast in a village singing songs of old. He sat down at his usual spot which was in front of the stand of a young fruit seller.

"Hey you! How about instead of singing to the people today, you tell me a story from the times in which you sing about? You seem to know a lot as if you were there," the fruit seller asked the Merchant. The two of them had made a prior agreement where if the Merchant brought business to the vendor he would be given free food. Since the Merchant's song was bringing business to the fruit stand owner for the past couple days the vendor thought it would be fair to give the Merchant a little break.

"Would you believe me if I told you, I was alive when the first Council of Swordmasters was created?" The Merchant replied.

"Maybe, but you have brought business to my stand so how about today you tell me what you know. When I have heard you sing in the past, your stories sound far- fetched, so this will give me the chance to formulate my own opinion about you and what you preach," the fruit seller stated.

I feel a soul tempted by darkness about to make its appearance. The last time I felt a dark presence the people here lost their minds. Maybe if I tell him this story quickly he will pass it onto others and that will nullify whatever darkness is about to pursuit them.

"Where do I begin, Ah, yes. The original Council of Swordmasters was made up of three men and two women. They were the same five called upon by the Legendary Beasts to find the Planetary Sword. The Legendary Beasts were the original guardians of Palaleon. They birthed each of the four planets along with the Soul Realm and created people to start inhabiting each of them. The five humans were special compared to the rest of humanity since they were born from a portion of one of the five Legendary Beast's souls on their specific planet. The Legendary Beasts' souls contained a unique magic, granted to them from the universe. This magic would become an intense version of Soulmagic, and this was the reason why these five were very special humans in Palaleon. The Legendary Beasts looked over each of the five as they grew, acting as their conscience. From a young age, the five were advised by the Legendary Beasts on how to survive on their own in a new environment. They were taught key concepts like how to maintain peace, in order for them to teach the other humans these concepts. Through their time alone, the Legendary Beasts judged their progress to see when each of the five were ready to meet one another. The goal for their first meeting was to create the Planetary Sword - a sword that acted as a symbol for peace and unity. It would become the strongest weapon in Palaleon."

"Wow that is insane. So, you're telling me there are these beasts out in the universe that have these special abilities, that were passed down to people like me." The young fruit seller stated.

"Yes, but the Legendary Beasts played a bigger role than just containing Soulmagic. Let me continue. The Legendary Beasts created conflicts on the planets that acted as training exercises for the five pupils. Each task helped to develop real life skills, such as arbitration, conflict resolution, and protecting other humans. When villages, towns and cities were first formed, conflicts invariably arose. These disputes between neighboring villages and towns needed a solution. But more than that, the people needed guidance. They needed someone to teach them how to coexist peacefully, without spiraling into war. Each of the five humans taught the values of peace and unity, so the people could pass these concepts down to their descendants."

The Merchant continued to tell the detailed story of the original Council of Swordmasters to the fruit stand owner. After the Legendary Beasts created the five humans, they also left shards in a part on each planet. The shards were hard to obtain becoming a task in itself. Eventually when the Legendary Beasts deemed them ready to find the shards, they contacted them. Each Legendary Beast whispered into the mind of one of the five humans, 'There is a shard, a very sacred object here and I need you to find it for me.' They began traveling across the land looking for it. On Aestercrat the shard was atop the tallest mountain. As Shalal, the human who was put on Aestercrat, learned of this special object he became intrigued. "I will find this shard. It is my duty." He relied on his gut throughout the journey. When there was a fork in the road, he thought to himself. *Where should I go?* As he raised his hand, his finger pointed in a direction and that is where he went. He was a very free-spirited man, who communed with nature around him. He eventually made it to the bottom of Mount Calasmic the tallest mountain in all of Aestercrat. "Well, my guess is that the shard is at the top. Time to climb." He gripped the first rock and pulled himself upwards. The journey only took seven days since he resided near the mountain, but while he was climbing, he could not afford to stop or look down. He just kept propelling upwards. Eventually he decided it would be quicker to leap from boulder to boulder, while maintaining his dexterous sure-footedness. Once he made it to the top, he dropped to the ground, hungry and thirsty. Luckily for him there was a berry tree and a little pond only a few steps away. He picked the berries, quickly devouring them. He bent down towards the pond, and scooped handfuls of water into his mouth. He then noticed something shimmering beyond the pond. "This must be the shard." He got up from the pond to take a closer look. It was indeed the shard. "I guess I proved my worth by being able to climb this mountain. Now comes the fun part traversing all the way down." Yet as he reached for the shard, it began to glow.

On Vastrilio, the shard was embedded in a fire, but the fire looked more menacing than it was. Forgia, the woman placed on Vastrilio, was tasked with finding her shard. At first, she did not care for this task. All she wanted to do was to continue helping people and entertain her love of fire. The voice in her head continued to gnaw at her. *You must find this shard. It will make you whole - a better person - and someone with a support system to count on when times become tough.* Finally, she caved. *But I do not even know where to look,* she thought.

I can help you with that. What is your truest love that can be both calm and fierce? the voice answered.

Fire, Forgia replied.

She continued having a conversation in her head when she noticed in the distance something burning. There was no sign of a fire started, and she knew this was not one of hers. *Where did it come from? I must investigate.* As she drew nearer, she noticed an object in the flames. *Should I grab it? I do not want to get burned. That fire looks like it will be out of control. Maybe I should just get water and put it out.* Forgia ran back to her home to get a bucket. She then ran to the closest pond and filled the bucket. She ran back to the fire and tried to extinguish it, but the fire continued to rage. *You must believe in yourself. Reach out. It will not hurt you. Do not be scared,* the voice in her thoughts stated. Overcoming her fear, she reached into the fire. Astonishingly, her arm was fine, she felt no pain. As she gripped the shard, it started to glow.

On Crateolios, the shard was in the depths of the icy cold water. Glida was the best swimmer. It was a skill she picked up from a very young age. Nobody else on Crateolios dare swim in the freezing waters, they just went about their day ice fishing. The way Glida got to visit each ice village was by swimming. One day as she was swimming to the western ice village, she noticed a glow from an object under the crashing waves. It then disappeared. She decided to follow it. The object sank to the dark depths of the water, but as it touched the ground, she noticed it again. The object was calling to her. *This must be my shard.* She went to pick it up, bringing it to the surface. It glowed.

Finally, on Draefast, one of the shards was atop Lightning Hills while the other was in a cave in the main dark forest. Ohtav was a natural born leader. He helped create government systems at a young age with most of the villages on the northern side of Draefast. When he heard the calling to find the shard, he immediately jumped at the task.

Where should I even begin? Ohtav thought to himself.

Well, what scares you the most, replied the voice in his head.

Being useless. Dying when I had so much more to live for.

Travel to Lightning Hills. It is there that you will find what you seek.

Ohtav packed a bag filled with food, and a canister for water. He put the bag on his shoulder and went on his journey. He traveled during the day and set up camp near villages at night. He eventually made it to Lightning Hills. As he entered the village, he heard a young boy say, "Mom, how are we going to eat when all of our cows run towards the top of Lightning Hills. Who knows if they will return? Plus, none of us can go there since every time a villager does, they do not come home."

"Excuse me young boy, can you point me in the direction of the entrance to Lightning Hills. I believe I can help solve your problem." Ohtav lived to help others so he knew this was his task. The boy pointed to a gate and beyond it the clouds were dark, and a flash of light beamed from the sky.

"There it is."

"Thank you," Ohtav replied.

He ventured onwards. Ohtav found the shivering cows

surrounded by bolts of lightning. As he ran towards them to scare them into coming down, he was almost struck. He marched forward, showing no fear. As the cows moved, the shard appeared. He dove to touch it, and as he did, it glowed.

Hosra lived for obtaining new knowledge, so when he was told about the shard, he wanted to find it to learn about it and all of its secrets. He resided in the dark forest on the southern side of Draefast. He kept mostly to himself as people were scared to come to him for advice. He enjoyed his solitude; it helped him clear his mind in order to fill it with more knowledge. As he traveled through the dark forest, he heard of a man named Ohtav who was sent on a similar journey to find a shard. He became enraged. *I thought I was special, and that I would be the one finding a shard.* As his anger grew, he noticed something sticking out of a tree. *It is not wood. What is it?* He began to walk closer. *My emotions must have brought the shard to me. I truly am powerful.* As he gazed upon the shard his ears reacted to it and all he could hear was horrific screaming and crying. He tried to cover his ears, but that did not stop the sounds. He lunged towards the shard and as he touched it, it glowed a dark purple.

The glowing of each of the shards occurred simultaneously, for each of the five found their respective shard at the same time. The energy from their souls formed a bond with the shard, transforming the shard into a unique sword.

The Legendary Beasts, who were on each planet at the time of the glowing shards, decided the five were ready to finally meet. They called out to their human telling them *It's time.* Each human climbed upon the back of the Legendary Beast who appeared before them, and the two set off into the atmosphere. They flew so fast that they cut through the air, opening a teleportation portal to Aestercrat.

One by one the Legendary Beasts appeared with each human on the lush and verdant planet. Shalal's journey was the quickest since he was already on Aestercrat. They all met at a Sanctuary that the Legendary Beasts had built for them years prior. Each human dismounted their Legendary Beast. While walking into the Sanctuary they all turned around to notice that the Legendary Beasts were not following. "This is where your journey truly begins. If you need us, we will be here," the White Lion said to them. The five continued onward.

As they all convened in the rotunda of the Sanctuary, they saw five chairs surrounding a table fabricated from Counterrock. As each of them took their seat they began telling one another about their adventures on their homeworlds, bonding over their stories and how they found the shard. There was an immediate connection. They had already begun to trust one another. They all introduced themselves and through their conversations came to the realization that each member would have an equal vote, but one of them should oversee the Council actions.

"Hey everyone, I'm Forgia. I was brought here by the White Ocelot. I found my sword on Vastrilio which is where I am from and I am ready to help in any way I can."

"I'm Shalal. I am from the planet we are on now which is called Aestercrat and was brought to this Sanctuary by the White Warbler. I am here to learn more about who I am, and why I am here much like the rest of you. I hope we can all get along, as I feel this is the start of something greater."

"Hi guys, my name is Glida. I come from the icy planet Crateolios. I was brought here by the White Manta Ray. I want to help out in any way I can. I believe that we all play an equal role in teaching the humans of our worlds the differences between right and wrong, and how to live coexisting with one another in a peaceful and just society."

"I agree with you Glida," both Shalal and Forgia replied.

"I'm Hosra, and I am here to gain all the knowledge about everything I can. I came here on the back of the White Hyrax. I need to know more. I want to know more." Hosra spoke quickly as he believed he did not want to waste his time with a silly little introduction.

Finally, Ohtav spoke. "I am so grateful to meet all of you. You all sound like such wonderful people, and I can't wait to build a better future for the people with you. I am Ohtav. Hosra and I are both from Draefast. I traveled here on the back of the White Lion. I want what is best for everyone and will do everything I can to ensure that we do our job in order to achieve total peace and unity. We will learn through our practice and our failures so remember not to become discouraged. Everything we experience together will only tighten our bond and further us to our goal. Our reason for being here."

"Thank you for introducing yourself, Ohtav. I believe that you are meant to be our leader," Glida replied, as Forgia and Shalal nodded in agreement. Hosra shook his head in disbelief. "Are you certain we need a leader. Why can't we just do what we want?"

"Well, somebody needs to make sure we are doing our best for the people of Palaleon, and Ohtav seems to be the best one for the job," Shalal replied to Hosra. "Our leader does not have to be the strongest, but has to be someone brave, and someone who is willing to fail and through their struggles be able to continue onward," Forgia said.

This act formed the tradition that the one who made decisions based on the good of Palaleon and the people should become the Council leader. That person was the Soullight Attribute Swordmaster. Ohtav's personal mission was to never let anything sway or cloud his judgement. He vowed to put his life at risk before losing his fellow Councilmembers. He was honorable and kind. After their discussion, they each removed their swords from their sheaths, and laid them out onto the table for all to see. Each sword fit the individuality of its bearer, enhanced with hilts made from special materials only available on their homeworlds. A colored gem formed the pommel, representing the connection to their soul. The colors were brown, black, blue, red, and white. All of a sudden, their swords started to glow. Aestercrat started shaking. They all watched as their swords acted as if they had a mind of their own sliding towards one another. As the swords touched, the glow stretched across the entire room. When the glow subsided, a larger, more magnificent sword laid in the center of the table. Each member went to touch it. Almost instantly, each sensed a transformation within their bodies. They felt an immense power but started to feel as if they had aged a millennium.

The meeting quickly adjourned as each of the five looked up at one another noticing a physical change in their appearance. The Planetary Sword sensed an imbalance among the Swordmasters since it was connected to their souls and deconstructed back into each member's original sword. They picked up their swords which then transformed back into shards. Tucking the shards into their sheaths, they left the Sanctuary.

There was a pond nearby that the Swordmasters traveled to in order to analyze their appearance and come to terms with what had just occurred. Each of them looked down at their reflections and noticed that they looked elderly, and not youthful anymore. The Councilmembers had grey hair and wrinkly faces, their bodies looked shriveled, but their minds were still crisp, along with their connections to their Attributes. The strangest part about this experience was that each Swordmaster felt fine, even though they were significantly slower. They had obtained a power nobody else had which eased their mind for future conflicts. Consequently, they vowed to only wield the Planetary Sword when it was truly needed, since using it will bring each one of them closer and closer to death.

Ohtav then took a blank piece of parchment out of a tube connected to his belt and started to write. "Whoever wields the Planetary Sword, could also wield Time." This confirmed that there was a famed Attribute of Soulmagic - the Time Attribute. This Tale would be one of the very first that he wrote. He then rolled the scroll back into the tube and clipped it to his belt. He later summoned his Legendary Beast who was still waiting outside the Sanctuary to go to Draefast and hide this scroll in one of the trees in the dark forest. Ohtav tasked the other Councilmembers with keeping all their knowledge for future members in Tales.

They all had the ability to conjure Soulmagic and in doing so they created the core Attributes, and Sub-Attributes. An Attribute is a special form of Soulmagic, that turns soul energy into a physical form through a conductor, a sword, like shooting fire from a sword. Since Ohtav, Hosra, Forgia, Glida, and Shalal were connected to the Legendary Beasts, the bonds with their souls were enhanced. Through this bond they were able to make Attributes and then master them in order to pass them down to future generations. They were only able to use their Soulmagic and Attributes through the extension of their swords.

On top of creating them each Councilmember controlled an Attribute through their Soulmagic. Glida controlled the Soulwater Attribute thus also being able to conjure the Soulice Sub-Attribute. Forgia controlled the Soulfire Attribute and Soullightning Sub-Attribute. Shalal controlled the Soulrock Attribute, and Soulwood and Soulmetal Sub-Attributes. While Hosra controlled Purple Fire, Purple Lightning, and Poison, his connection with his Attribute Souldarkness was not to its full potential. There were still abilities within his Attribute that were unknown to him, so he became intrigued by finding out what they were, devoting his life to attaining more knowledge.

Ohtav controlled the Soullight Attribute and Soulwind Sub-Attribute and was tasked with learning a basic knowledge of the other's Attributes.

As for their personal lives, all of the Councilmembers had fallen in love and had become parents - even Hosra. Their children also displayed a special connection to their souls; thus, they became the second Council of Swordmasters. They would meet as successors during their parents Council meetings. Hosra had asked Ohtav to train his son since he was too busy studying. Ohtav had agreed thus taking on two pupils instead of one. Since Ohtav knew how to wield the Souldarkness and Soullight Attributes he trained his son to be the next leader of the Swordmasters and Hosra's son to be the next Souldarkness wielder. Each of the children beyond having the urge to protect those around them also had a thirst for knowledge about the universe.

As time went by, the original Council of Swordmasters continued passing their knowledge to the next generation of Swordmasters - the five children of Ohtav, Forgia, Glinda, Shalal, and Hosra. The training was rigorous and intense, but also calming and peaceful. They needed to be ready for anything, so the original Council put them through many different scenarios to help each of them get a better understanding of what their purpose was now. Overtime each of the successors grew into their roles, they were not just children anymore.

The Council had helped govern the planets in Palaleon by teaching humans how to go about their lives in a just and fair manner. They had instilled peace, making all inhabitants feel protected. To the people, they seemed godlike. Many began to pray to the Councilmembers for good fortune and healing. However, this interpretation was incorrect. The Councilmembers were real people. They chose not to interfere in human troubles unless it was truly necessary or affected the universe as a whole.

Each sword, Attribute and Sub-Attribute of Soulmagic played a vital role in securing everyone's safety, since they were the source of unity. Everyone has a bit of Soulmagic in them, but only a few are able to connect to this magic and conjure one of the five Attributes. The Souldarkness Attribute can only be unlocked in a person tempted by to their inner darkness. That person also has a tendency to crave more knowledge of the different Attributes of Soulmagic. By having Souldarkness manifest in their soul and in their mind that person will also be able to create techniques that in they deemed unstoppable.

There was only one person known in each generation to become tempted by their inner darkness, and that person would become the Souldarkness Attribute sword wielder on the Council.

Like all humans, all of the original Councilmembers but Hosra had succumbed to illness, and eventually died. At such time, the Legendary Beast that was associated with the Councilmember, took the lifeless body, and was able to transform itself into a human form guised in the body. The White Lion now looked like Ohtav in human form, the White Ocelot looked like Forgia, the White Warbler looked like Shalal, and the White Manta Ray looked like Glida. Hosra was now a living relic. Their names had become stories, but their bodies were still present in Palaleon. Only a few knew what the original Councilmembers looked like making it easier for the Legendary Beasts to travel around each world.

As they passed away the Councilmembers children, who were all grown up now, officially became the second Council of Swordmasters. After forming their new Council each of them furthered their training through the teachings of their parents. They would eventually pass these teachings down by Tales to their pupils. There was no visual representation of what their parents looked like so as the second Council grew older, they had forgotten their parents' faces thus concluding the spoken memory of them. Everything now had become written.

Hosra and Ohtav's grandchildren had adapted souls just like their grandparents and became a part of the third Council of Swordmasters. The other Councilmembers were not related to the original or previous Council; they were children with special connections to their souls. The second Council of Swordmasters had kept an eye on these individuals and helped the future leader of the Council and future Souldarkness Attribute Swordmaster, recruit the three other members as a part of the upcoming Council of Swordmasters. They would all train and become strong in their Attributes together. As the second Council grew older they retired, leaving their duties to their successors. The third Council of Swordmasters was now official. They began studying conflicts occurring throughout the planets, making sure that no conflict was too drastic that it would impact the shape of the universe. When their masters died, they knew it was time for them to find their own successors. It came to a surprise when Ohtav and Hosra's great grandchildren were not born with the same connection to their souls as their ancestors. This meant that while the rest of the Council went to find successors, so did Ohtav and Hosra's grandchildren. They knew they would find their pupils back on Draefast.

The children of the leader of the third Council and Souldarkness Attribute Swordmaster were dropped off on Draefast and were handed over to their mothers to be raised amongst the other villagers.

While traveling the Souldarkness Attribute Swordmaster met a young boy named Nahvel in one of the southern dark forests of Draefast. Nahvel lied and told the man, "I have no family, I see you are a sword wielder. Can you train me?"

The man replied, "Do you know how to wield a sword?"

Nahvel reached for the man's sword. He gave it to Nahvel, and as Nahvel grasped it, Purple Flames appeared from the edges. Instead of getting scared, Nahvel was fascinated by this. The man had seen no other person, let alone a child, able to conjure such Purple Fire besides himself due to his mentor's teachings. "I will train you to control this Purple Fire as I can conjure it too along with many other abilities," the man said.

Nahvel replied, "Thank you, mentor." He was already showing his gratitude towards this man he deemed strong. As the man continued training Nahvel, he became jealous. His mentor had so much power and potential to do great things but was overshadowed by the leader of the Council, someone Nahvel resented for seemingly holding his own mentor back. This hatred for his mentor's Council brewed a hatred he held for his own Council. He did not want to be viewed as weak, so he began engrossingly reading and rereading the Tales his mentor gave him, studying and surrounding himself with his Souldarkness Attribute. Within a relatively short period of time, his insatiable thirst for knowledge had completely corrupted his mind. Nahvel's inner darkness was granting him access to untapped abilities unimagined by others. Nahvel's training had begun at his mentor's two-story Sanctuary in the southern region of Draefast. Nahvel and his mentor would spar outside in the forest behind the Sanctuary and then take the ramp up to the building where Nahvel spent his time reading and rereading Tales.

The leader of the third Council found his successor in the northern regions of Draefast. The boy was bright-eyed, and talented in using wind blasts from his sword. It was as if he had already trained for years before the leader of the Council arrived. He was a natural. The "perfect" pupil, in the leader's eyes.

While the training of the fourth Council was underway, Hosra and Ohtav's descendants met in a village and fell in love. After going on multiple dates around the forest, Hosra's great-great-grandson proposed to Ohtav's great-great-granddaughter. They were soon married and set up their home in a village on the other side of the planet's southern hemisphere which was still surrounded by a dark forest. They continued living their normal life as collectors of books and other scriptures eventually coming across some Tales.

While continuing the training of the fourth Council, the third Council noticed something wrong between their students. There was a disconnect, and it started when Nahvel, the next Souldarkness Attribute wielder, started to ask too many questions about Darkness Tales. The others thought in the beginning that he just wanted to know more about his abilities and what he could achieve. The Souldarkness Attribute Swordmaster of the third Council saw nothing wrong with what Nahvel was doing so he left him alone to train. The Council did not fathom his true intentions and dark thoughts until it was too late. After training on his own for so long, he gathered the second Council in the Sanctuary by asking his mentor to bring them since he had questions about how the Council should maintain peace and prosperity throughout Palaleon. This was just a cover up, as Nahvel really wanted to test out a new ability he nurtured. As the second Council gathered, Nahvel struck like a viper, as if hidden in a bush. He was able to mind corrupt the entire second Council of Swordmasters and pin them against the third Council. Nobody saw it coming and nobody could do a thing about it. He was more powerful than the rest of the successors, even the leader of the successors was scared to fight him alone and did not want the rest of his future Council to get injured. Instead, they stood frozen in shock staring at what Nahvel was able to accomplish. They watched as their mentors struggled fighting their predecessors who were significantly older than them but eventually were able to overpower them. Nahvel had committed one of the greatest atrocities, he made children kill their own parents. Nahvel then took command of his mentor's ship and flew to the upper atmosphere, but not before he heard the leader of the third Council's booming voice scream, "We are banishing you to Draefast. If you leave that planet, both of our Councils along with the Legendary Beasts, will hunt you down and kill you." Realizing that he could not defeat the third and fourth Councils on his own, he listened to their command. Now he would solely focus on taking over Draefast. As the members from the third Council died, the fourth Council excluding Nahvel decided to live out their lives on their homeworlds and train successors in hopes that one day they would be the ones to defeat Nahvel.

Back on Draefast, even Hosra, who had learned how to extend his lifespan living in the shadows, could not stand up against Nahvel's wrath. He attempted to take over Nahvel's body to learn more secrets about Souldarkness, but was outwitted. Nahvel was stronger and more connected to his Attribute than Hosra. He was able to turn his predecessor's soul into pure Souldarkness and rip it from his body using one of the many forbidden sword techniques he had read about in a Darkness Tale. Nahvel found on Draefast written by a devout follower of the Souldarkness Attribute Swordmaster of the second Council. Nahvel sealed Hosra's Souldarkness into the Attribute sword resting on the ground by tapping his sword to it. *This Attribute sword is now made of pure darkness I can feel the Souldarkness within it in my own soul. Even though this sword may have new abilities hidden within it, I doubt it is as powerful a conductor to my Souldarkness Attribute as my own sword.* Nahvel had thought to himself as he threw it into the Soul Realm. The portal to the Soul Realm was in the back of his predecessor's home. *He must have opened the portal right before I got here.* After the sword entered the portal it immediately closed. Nahvel knew of this portal and its significance since he had heard stories about it as a child. The stories he heard did not mention what was in the Soul Realm. Nahvel only learned about it after reading about it in a Darkness Tale. He went on to sheath his own Souldarkness Attribute Sword thinking that one day it could become the famed Planetary Sword and lead him to his goal.

After Nahvel left Hosra's home, the White Hyrax appeared in front of Hosra's lifeless body and transfigured into it turning the body into its own human form. The White Hyrax had to lay low on Draefast, since it knew that if Nahvel saw and recognized its body then each Legendary Beast would be in more danger than before.

Nahvel lusted for ultimate rule and the means to make his vision a reality. By banishing Nahvel to his own planet, the Council thought it was doing the people of Palaleon good, but did not think of the future consequences. Nahvel had immediately started working on his plan to become the ultimate ruler. He traveled around to the different villages and persuaded the villagers to listen to him and promised them a better life under his rule. Eventually he made it back to a familiar place, his mentor's Sanctuary. There was a ramp built prior to Nahvel's move that lead to the second story as that was where the entrance was. Nahvel viewed the ramp as a power dynamic displaying his ideals of ruling over everybody beneath him. The first story had several grates around it that expelled sewage water and other waste. This Sanctuary was where he perfected his mind corruption technique by hosting villagers and nonlethally stabbing them in the soul, corrupting and swaying their minds. These poor people were forced to become his followers. Nahvel then started to have his subordinates build a city around the Sanctuary, and move the Soul Realm portal from Hosra's home to a ruin beneath the surface level of the ground floor of the Sanctuary. The people reconstructed the Sanctuary to look more like a castle, even though it was rustic. It was there that Nahvel invited more and more villagers to meet him in his home and then he mind-corrupted them the same way he did to the second Council of Swordmasters. The city had become very popular with Draefast natives, and many people began moving there. Nahvel planned to add another more story to the castle and create an extension of the city that would surround the entrance to the castle. If more people were coming to him, he would just mind-corrupt them to do his bidding.

Nahvel became infatuated with one of the most beautiful women he had ever seen in a nearby village. He decided to spare the village from mind corruption since he fell for this woman. He traveled to the village often to see her. The two went on walks through the village, and that is when he displayed his scorn towards his "subjects". During these walks she wrapped her arm around his and allowed him to discuss his day to her. Nahvel found this comforting, and was starting to let his guard down. He soon realized, however, that her presence was dampening his connection to his Souldarkness.

As he returned home after one of their dates in the city, he had to come to a decision. *Do I forgo everything I have worked for? Everything I can achieve for this woman? Or do I corrupt her mind, making her follow me and continue on with my plans? She will never truly love me if I do this, but for the sake of my vision I must.* On their next date, a nice candlelit walk through the city, Nahvel noticed the woman's distance from him, as if she was not fully present and attentive to him. She displayed her care and love towards him at the start, but like a candle in the wind it soon faded. This made his decisions even easier. Towards the end of the night, they walked up the ramp going back to his castle. As they entered Nahvel showed her around the castle and showed he his blueprints for the add-ons that he wanted to make. As they were sitting in his study, Nahvel proceeded to get up and walked behind her. He stabbed her in the back touching her soul. His mind corruption was complete, but something was different about this. Tears were falling from his face; he did not enjoy this feeling, but he also felt stronger at the same time. "Why am I crying? She is mine now." He quickly wiped away his tears, and went about his evening with his companion. During some nights while in bed with Nahvel, she began to ponder if she was any different from the people around her, but she was in love with the man next to her, so those thoughts left her mind as quick as they entered.

As he continued corrupting more and more people, he told them to build ships. He knew that he could not take over the people of other worlds since he was banished by the Council to Draefast, but that did not mean he could not send his followers to persuade people to join his way of life. Much like the other people that Nahvel corrupted, his wife's scar over her chest started to disappear over time and she had no idea or questioned the story behind it. She had overheard while going into the city one day that other people had the same scar, so she believed that everyone obtained it at birth. During this time, Nahvel and the woman had a baby girl named Malikaya. Before Malikaya's birth, Nahvel burned the village that her mom was from using a blast of Purple Fire from his sword so that everyone on the entire planet could see since the fire rose all the way to the atmosphere. It was controlled by his anger. He had to show the rest of the planet that he was not a force to be reckoned with. He knew he had not corrupted everyone on Draefast but by displaying his power, he reasoned that he did not need to. People followed him either due to his strength or out of fear. To Nahvel, it did not matter. In reality, his connection to his powers were subsiding. Mind corruption exhausted a great deal of his Souldarkness Attribute. There was yet to be a Tale written or ability through Soulmagic created that could replenish someone's soul, the source of one's power.

As the woman gave birth to Malikaya, her mind became freed from his grasp. Nahvel's mind corruption passed on to the baby girl she held in her arms. The next night after putting Malikaya to sleep, her mother stealthy left the castle and ran into the dark forest. Nahvel woke up the next morning and did not see her anywhere. He checked Malikaya's room and thought to himself, *Where could she have gone?* He then summoned a meeting with his most loyal followers and said, "Find her at all costs."

The morning after Malikaya was born, another baby was born on Draefast. It was the child of the two great-great-grandchildren of the original Council. They had a son and named him Gathran. When he was born, the White Hyrax came out of hiding and acted as a decoy for Nahvel to focus on. It transformed into its human form looking like Hosra and walked into Nahvel's castle thus startling him. Nahvel noticed him and began chasing him. *Was that who I thought it was? It can't be... He is dead.* Nahvel thought to himself as he followed the Legendary Beast. "Hey you, stop at once! I command you to stop!" Nahvel shouted. The White Hyrax continued, unconcerned. Then as he turned a corner, he transformed back into his Hyrax form and ran through the castle wall without leaving any trace. As Nahvel turned the corner he bumped into a young boy who was working as one of his chefs. He looked at the boy's face then thought to himself, *I must have imagined that.* This gave the White Lion enough time to take the baby boy and fly out of Draefast towards Aestercrat. The White Lion then left the boy on the Sanctuary steps. He was found after the leader of the fourth Council came back from one of his morning strolls and after raising the boy as his own was tested to see if he was connected to his soul. Gathran was, and thus his true training to lead the next Council of Swordmasters began.

For years Nahvel scoured Draefast looking for Malikaya's mother, but he never found her. He began not paying much attention to his daughter and that is when she started to break free of the mind corruption. Malikaya was different from others. Since her soul was tainted by the circumstances of her birth, she adapted her mother's kindness but also her father's distaste for others. These qualities made her a manipulative child who was aggressive yet understanding and empathetic towards others. To her this was not a character flaw but something that Malikaya carried with her throughout her life making her emotionally stronger than most.

As Malikaya grew up, the White Hyrax would come visit her in its shrunken Hyrax form and play with her almost as if it was her pet outside the castle walls. The White Hyrax kept a close eye on Malikaya as it wanted to protect her. She would never tell her father about the Legendary Beast as she feared he would have it killed.

Years passed and Nahvel's plans were slowly starting to become reality. He created the Obsessors of Souldarkness by using a Souldarkness Attribute curse that bound humans to a leader. It was an ability that he taught himself while studying his Attribute in the heart of a dark forest. The Obsessors of Souldarkness used to be humans with no connection to any form of Soulmagic, but Nahvel had cursed them, unlocking a falsified version of the Souldarkness Attribute within them. He did this by cutting through each of their soul's. As the Souldarkness poison leaked from their wound, it would generate this falsified Souldarkness that moved through the rest of their bodies from their damaged decaying soul's. Since he was able to grant them this new power, they devoted their lives to him. Nahvel's reasoning for creating them was that he felt soon he would be betrayed and needed a devout set of followers to come up with a back-up plan. He commanded the Obsessors of Souldarkness to travel sneakily throughout Palaleon to study more secret techniques of the Souldarkness Attribute. One of the Obsessors had a vision through their falsified Souldarkness about Nahvel's grandson. When they all returned back to Draefast, the Obsessor who had the vision had a private meeting with Nahvel. He told Nahvel, "Sire, I had a vision about a young boy from what seemed to be the future, lost in his way. This boy was destined to wield the Souldarkness Attribute, and is in your bloodline."

"Thank you for telling me. You have proven to be very loyal. I will have to start to plan my manipulation now. Do not worry this act will not go unrewarded." Nahvel replied. He brought Malikaya, who had displayed abilities through the Souldarkness Attribute which he had never been seen before, to open up the portal in the ruin. Once Malikaya opened the Soul Realm portal, Nahvel communicated with the other Obsessors to go to the Soul Realm. There they would find their reward for doing his bidding. He found a way for them to be rulers of time, if they were able to absorb souls in this realm and use them to corrupt the timeline, it would split into various timelines. Years prior Malikaya informed her father of a Tale that she found that informed her of a three-minute time limit in the Soul Realm before whoever is in there becomes taken over by their inner darkness. Nahvel interpreted this as a gift of his power which would be used by the Obsessors to break time. Nahvel knew that the Soul Realm was huge so his plans along with the existence of the Obsessors would never be compromised by the Council of Swordmasters.

Nahvel continued to neglect the people of the planet, as he only sought more knowledge from Tales he found. Since he spent so much time creating the Obessors of Souldarkness, he had lost his touch with the people. They had started to regain their minds as their souls slowly repairing themselves. The villagers from around Draefest started gathering together to formulate a plan to take down Nahvel.

Nahvel had some of his followers take their ships to other worlds to spread the word of his ruling. These people were not very secretive about being mind-corrupted. In fact, the Council of Swordmasters found out about these people through overhearing villagers' conversations and had their successors kill them, as they could see no other way to solve the problem. As the successors did what they were sent out to do, they also used their Attributes and destroyed the ships along with any evidence of planetary travel. Nahvel had lost contact with the people he sent out on the ships; he knew something went wrong so now he just had to stick to his plans on Draefast. Nahvel had sent all of his followers who built ships off-world so now there were no more on Draefast. The people who were under his mind corruption then reverted back to believing that there was no way off their planet and that if they were to find a way to leave there was nothing beyond the moons.

On Aestercrat, Gathran was reading Tales of old, when he asked his mentor, "Where is your fifth member?"

"We banished him to a planet no one should go to. Not until you and your Council are ready to face him."

"But how can we possibly defeat him when neither you nor the previous Council could. We also are missing a member; don't we need all five in order to stand a chance."

"My Council has trained you since you were very young for this exact task, but you do make a good point. You might require a fifth member. Let me discuss it further with my Council."

Upon holding a meeting, the fourth Council came to the conclusion together that they would allow Gathran to travel on his own to Draefast to scout out a fifth member, and to spy on Nahvel. Gathran departed on a ship that he had spent time building on Aestercrat, and cloaked it in his Soulmagic to breach the atmosphere of the northern part of Draefast. While traveling through a village on his mission he met a beautiful woman. He did not know it then, but this woman was Nahvel's daughter, Malikaya. She was on the northern side of Draefast where she would find and read Tales about how to further her connection to her Soullight Attribute. These Tales were written by Ohtav. As she traveled she saw the effects of her father's rule on these people and how they could do nothing to break free. She tried to aid them but knew that if she did so during all of her ventures her father would find out. That was when she met Gathran. They bonded over food and some drinks and even spent the night together under the stars. The next morning, they both confessed to one another who they truly were. They had fallen in love. The fact that they had their own lives filled with complicated pasts did not matter to them, but Malikaya had to hide this love from her father. She told Gathran to stay in the northern regions of Draefast since her father believed he already controlled the people on this side of the planet, so he never traveled there. She would handle her father since she knew it was time for a change on this world.

Nahvel had plans to take control of the Council in the coming years using what he believed had become the Planetary Sword. He had a vision in which a Shroud-like figure told him that someone in his bloodline was destined to rule this Council and all of Palaleon. Nahvel took this as a sign that that person would be him.

Nahvel could not even fathom the idea of fighting his fellow Councilmembers in his current state, so he decided to stay hidden in his home and continue his studies on Souldarkness. He wanted to teach himself new techniques as his mind corruption ability was fading throughout Draefast. He realized that his grasp on his homeworld was fading day by day. He looked out from his window and saw flames moving closer to him. People were carrying torches as they headed towards his home. He understood that his time was soon coming to an end, but he still had a will to fight. As he continued to glance out of his window he saw the failed attempt he had at creating an even larger city and castle. There were columns built with a concrete slab resting on them, but the area was barren. There was a bridge built from that area to the castle as the sole point of entry.

Nahvel never took into account that his own daughter, a person he tried to convert to darkness, was the one who turned on him. During her journey she broke free of her father's mind corruption after learning through interactions that the people on her homeworld were corrupted to obey her father's every word. As her mind reverted back to her control, she seemed to be one of the only ones untouched. There was a light inside her, she was connected more to the Soullight Attribute and Soulwind Sub-Attribute of Soulmagic than her father's Souldarkness Attribute. She was different from anyone else who was connected to Soulmagic, but she had to hide her abilities and act as if they were unreal. She was able to manifest both the Souldarkness and Soullight Attributes without the use of a sword.

Malikaya was an avid reader, consuming all of the Tales her father had collected along with finding ones on her adventures through Draefast. Malikaya had written her own Tales about this but kept them hidden throughout her life.

She returned to her father's city as the people who were

marching began lighting the castle on fire. She ran up the ramp, entered the castle and made her way to her father's chambers where he was pacing back and forth. "Father you should leave this place if you want to be able to enact your master plan. I think I have a way for you to survive in the Soul Realm until you gather enough strength to take over Palaleon," Malikaya said. "Thank you Malikaya. Even though I disregarded you throughout your life, you have always shown true loyalty to me", Nahvel replied as the two of them rushed down the stairs and to the Soul Realm portal just as the villagers broke through the castle doors. Malikaya and Nahvel heard the villagers above them rampaging through the castle looking for their "ruler". *I could just give them my father and see what they do. But he could have come up with a new technique to permanently control them. If he did why was he pacing in his chambers looking frightened. That does not matter now, I know my plan will work.* Malikaya knew of this portal from her childhood days of exploring the castle. She always felt drawn to the portal as if it spoke to her. The two of them stopped in front of the portal where Malikaya stated, "I learned how to enhance the effects of Souldarkness in the Soul Realm. May I show you?"

"Yes of course you can."

Malikaya knew she had her own destiny lying in front and she had to extricate herself from his abusive ways. She pretended to open up the portal. She conducted the beginning of the ritual the same way she had always done before. She had previously shown her father this method by placing her hand on the sigil, but instead of using Souldarkness to open it, she used Soullight. This meant that the portal would not open to the Soul Realm, and as he stepped through Nahvel's body became encased in Purple Flames. Malikaya was the one who found the Tale that depicted the ways to open the Soul Realm and after reading it she hid the Tale from her father. As his flesh started to burn, he thought to himself, *I must live. My plan is not done yet and neither is my time in this universe. But how do I survive? Ah, yes, the forbidden soul attachment technique that Hosra conceptualized. Let me try it.* As his left his body, his body burned to a crisp. Malikaya thought that her father was now dead. She said to herself, *he is no longer a threat.* The truth was, however, that he was an apparition, a soul that needed a place to reside. He decided to latch onto his daughter's soul and wait until she had her first child. Then he could use the remainder of his soul to corrupt the child's mind in utero becoming its conscience.

Malikaya then left the ruin holding onto her father's sword. She escaped the castle as it continued to char. She went north and upon meeting with Gathran told him that, "My father is no longer a threat." Tears ran down her face, and Gathran knew exactly what that meant. Gathran took his ship and flew back to Aestercrat but before he left, he said to Malikaya, "I will come back for you so we can leave this wretched place and live out our lives in peace. But first I need to inform my Council of something." Gathran was off on this adventure when his mentor, along with the other members of the third Council, died. As he arrived on Aestercrat to tell everyone his good news, he noticed his fellow Councilmembers standing around the newly dug graves of their predecessors, mourning their loss. Gathran told them that he, rather than Malikaya, had killed Nahvel. After hearing what Malikaya did, Gathran felt he wasn't worthy of the title of leader of his Council, so figured that he would elevate his position by stating that he had killed Nahvel. "We do not need a fifth member. We will change the Council of Swordmasters to only have four members from now on. That should stop future tyrants. We will have a Soullight Attribute wielder, a Soulwater Attribute wielder, a Soulfire Attribute wielder, and a Soulrock Attribute wielder. There is no need for a Souldarkness Attribute wielder anymore."

One of the other Councilmembers looked at Gathran and asked, "Are you sure that is a smart idea?"

"I believe it is smart. Do not question my methods. I alone ended our problem along with the previous Council's problem once and for all. Don't forget that I am the leader of this Council. The fifth Council of Swordmasters." The other Councilmembers nodded in agreement. They believed in Gathran.

When word spread throughout Draefast that Nahvel had perished, the people cheered. They started to rebuild their villages and the city for a better tomorrow. They left the castle in its burnt state to symbolize their revolution, but they did not destroy it. The mind corruption had fully faded, and life was back to a form of normalcy for now.

Gathran came back for Malikaya and brought her to his homeworld Aestercrat. They chose to raise a family on Aestercrat since it was peaceful there, and the children could have more space to train under Gathran's guidance. Gathran had always believed that Nahvel had a tyrannical intent, and was overall a bad man. This added to the reasons why Gathran chose never to reveal to his children the identity of their grandfather. Gathran told Malikaya that he informed his fellow Swordmasters of her father's defeat by his hand. She was fine with that; she did not need people knowing that she was the one who killed her own father. Malikaya chose to hold onto her father's sword, but would never need to use it.

While pregnant with Hoshek, Malikaya kept having dreams where her father was calling out to her from Draefast. One morning after this recurring dream, she woke up in pain from the baby kicking her. She took this as a sign. She must return to Draefast to the site where her father died. She sneakily left Aestercrat by taking Gathran's ship. She flew all the way to Draefast where she landed the ship by a forest next to the castle. Malikaya got out of the ship, and walked into the city. She walked with a purpose so nobody around her stopped her from entering the castle. Before entering the castle, she turned around and noticed that the people completed the second tier of the city, but built their homes and shops closer to the edge than the castle. Malikaya closed the castle door behind her then walked down the stairs and into the ruin. As she entered, she felt cold. She was dressed in warm clothes not only for her sake, but for her unborn baby's health as well, and still she had this feeling of a silent chill. Malikaya continued to walk through the ruin, until she got to its center where the portal was located. The portal doorway had survived the vagaries of time, and looked the same as the day Malikaya used it to kill her father.

On the side of the portal, was an emblem that resembled an eye with poison within it. After she touched it, she immediately felt a sharp pain and her hand started to bleed. The proper ritual had begun, she infused Souldarkness from her palm into the portal. *This will be the last time I ever use Souldarkness.* This technique was one of the two known ways someone could open up the portal to the Soul Realm. She looked out into the vast dark plains of the Soul Realm only to see nothing.. *As I suspected he burned when I place my hand on the insignia the last time I was here. There is no way he made it through to the other side. He is truly gone, and this feeling is just a product of my nightmare.* As she continued to peek into the realm, she heard a whisper in her thoughts but could not make out what the voice said. It sounded like her father. Frightened, she pulled her head out of the portal as it began closing. *I guess that was his last warning to me so I would not get severed into two pieces as the three minutes were up. Should I be grateful for that?* Suddenly, Malikaya's hand felt like it was on fire. Malikaya screamed in pain. She gazed at her hand to see that the wound she obtained moments earlier was cauterized by a Purple Fire which then vanished in her palm leaving a scar. Malikaya then turned around and walked back towards her ship. She got to her ship, turned on the engine, activated the thrusters, used the steering device to angle the ship upwards and took off.

"Back to Aestercrat," Malikaya whispered as she looked down towards her belly. The cold feeling had gone away once she left Draefast's atmosphere. "Your family's history lies on Draefast, but I hope one day, I will be the one to explain everything to you, my son." Malikaya said aloud as she entered Aestercrat's atmosphere then landed the ship outside her and Gathran's home.

"Where have you been?" Gathran asked.

"I just needed some fresh air, but now I am tired, so I am going to get some sleep," Malikaya replied as she covered her scarred hand with part of the sleeve from her robe. She found ways to hide this scar for years to come even until the day of her death.

The Merchant concluded his story as the first sun started

to rise. He had been talking throughout the day all the way into the night.

"How are you so sure that all of this happened?" The young fruit seller asked.

"Would you believe me if I told you, I was there?" The Merchant replied.

"That's a tricky question. Whether or not it is real, I do appreciate you telling me. Maybe we could have days when after you are done singing in front of my stand, you can continue telling me these stories. I quite enjoy them," the fruit seller stated as he prepared his goods for his boss for the day ahead. The Merchant replied, "I am heading to the city for a little while as I want to travel a little bit more, but when I return I would be happy to take you up on that offer." The Merchant then got up tied his lute to his back and began walking out of the village. *I forgot to ask that man his name. Oh well, maybe when he returns I will ask him,* the fruit seller thought to himself.

Chapter V

Hoshek's Plans

A figure stepped out of his ship midway through the take-off sequence, standing alone on the docking bay of the Sanctuary. He breathed in the Aestercrat air for what he deemed would be the last time. Clad in a black shirt and a grey shawl wrapped around his torso with his two sheaths tied to his dark purple pants extending down to his leather boots, he cut a stirring image. As Hoshek unleashed his Souldarkness, a dark Shroud began to loom over Palaleon. The Shroud was increasing his power, but in doing so amplified his anger. Hoshek was becoming corrupted by his inner darkness, granting the Shroud a larger form. He was about to unveil his Souldarkness techniques to the people residing in this universe.

Leaving Aestercrat, the home planet of the Council, Hoshek traveled to the various planets before landing on Draefast, a planet he discovered after stealing Tales from the ruins of the old Council. Draefast is the planet where his mother grew up. While reading Council Tales years ago he learned that this was the place where darkness rose and fell. When Hoshek flew past the other planets the Shroud followed him only to grow bigger, hovering over the different planets.

The Shroud was everywhere. People all over the universe felt uneasy; they had never experienced anything like this before. Their thoughts were fleeting rapidly as if they were becoming blank slates. With each breath, the Shroud flowed right into their brain, obnubilating their minds, leading them to despair. Memories of the Council had evaporated. With no hope but an inescapable future, the people had lost all control of their lives. From that point on, everyone was living in Hoshek's universe - pawns to be manipulated to serve his own plans. It was as if the Shroud hurled shadowy daggers into the soul of everyone underneath, leaving a larger yet similar scar to what Nahvel did to his people.

While on Vastrilio and Crateolios, Hoshek came across some people tried to resist the numbing effects of the Shroud. Those who were successful noticed that the scar on their chest had shrunk in size. These few were educated in the study of meditation and restful breathing, giving them insight into their souls while monitoring their air intake. Through mindfulness, they were able to keep an assemblance of individuality, but only for a short time. Hoshek quickly put an end to each resistance by stabbing the people in the soul with his sword. He then extracted their souls leaving their bodies in places never to be found on their perspective planets. Those souls journeyed to the Soul Realm awaiting a new life one far bleaker than they would have had if they chose not to resist. When others heard about people vanishing, they quickly decided to keep their thoughts to themselves and bade time until this darkness passed. For now, however, nobody was able to help the people.

The Swordmasters vanished, neither to be heard from nor seen. The knowledge of what Hoshek had done to the previous Swordmasters never left the Sanctuary on Aestercrat.

The Shroud made people believe there was and will only be Hoshek, the Dark Wizard. He ruled over all now.

As Hoshek walked through the villages and cities before getting on his ship to leave both Crateolios and Vastrilio he heard the people talking about people vanishing. He was glad that people were obeying him by not following the others who tried to resist. He did not want to harm anyone else but knew he had to if people started to think that they could rise against him.

Before Hoshek's grand entrance, it had been years since anyone from his bloodline had been to Draefast. The planet and its people had been able to restore itself from the previous tyrannical ruler. They had instilled a system, where no one person was a ruler, but they had a Council that would make decisions that would be beneficial for most people on the planet. This system was destroyed as the exit ramp from a sleek black ship was lowered onto the ashen soil and out walked a shadowy figure.

"A man has appeared," a villager said.

"Look above, why is it becoming dark, what should we do?" Another villager replied.

The villagers had left an eatery along with others as they noticed the sky change color during midday.

The corruption of the people's minds had begun. People watched as this hooded figure entered the old city square. He opened his mouth and in a booming voice stated,

"I am taking over this planet, and all of you will help by refurbishing this castle and adding more stories to it." Hoshek was pointing up at the two-story castle that the city was built around.

"How do you want us to do this?" one person replied.

"Like I just said, I want all of you here to build on top of that ruined castle," Hoshek said as he pointed in the direction of his grandfather's castle, "while also vertically expanding the surrounding city. Once that is complete, everyone around here will begin to live lavishly under my rule, and your old looking city along with the neighboring villages will combine in the form of layers around my castle and turn into my city."

"Understood, my ruler," the villagers said in unison as they dropped what they were doing in order to create Hoshek's vision. Villagers from around the planet heard his call, and came to be a part of something greater. More and more people started to show up, making Hoshek City become a reality. The people who could afford to, packed up their lives to move to this up-and-coming metropolis. As people started to move, some villagers stayed put at home since they enjoyed living far away from the city in their own secluded village. While his city was a priority to start his rule, Hoshek left the construction of the castle and layers of the city surrounding it to his subjects so he could continue on his journey.

Hoshek wanted to learn everything about the Souldarkness Attribute since he believed he had already learned everything about the Soullight Attribute. He wanted to create balance, but through his studies of Souldarkness he pushed himself further and further from that reality. He never realized that he was the cause of the imbalance in the universe. He yearned for the ability to go back in time and learn from his ancestor who controlled the Souldarkness Attribute, in order to stop what he had done to the Council.

Seven years had gone by since Hoshek had murdered his father along with the other Councilmembers. During that time, he had gained followers and his city was near completion. Hoshek had found Nahvel's blueprints for his add-ons to the castle and used that as a guide when designing a more modern version of the interior while constructing two more tiers of the city and castle. When Hoshek had arrived nobody was living on the second tier, but that changed once the construction of the city and castle started. People were living and working on each tier now. Hoshek was now too far gone from the light to figure out how to restore life to the dead. Hoshek sat atop his throne in his castle and used the old Councilmember swords to generate enough Soulmagic to start the process of opening a SpaceTime portal. He poured his Souldarkness into this portal so that he would be able to enter the exact time and place that he wanted, but it was not yet time for him to enter the portal. Hoshek wanted to make sure there was no risk in him going through before he put his body to the test. While maintaining concentration to keep the portal open, his Souldarkness Attribute had started to deplete from his soul causing Hoshek to feel exhausted. His arm fell over the pommel of one of the Councilmember's swords, his body went limp, and his head drooped down. While he sat in this unconscious state, he had a similar vision to the Obsessor's years ago. Only this time a Shroud-like being spoke to him telling him, "You are the one destined to find an Attribute

Sword, and use it in combat against the leader of the Council of Swordmasters, once you defeat this leader it will turn it into the Planetary Sword, and you will be able to rule over Palaleon." This is not entirely what he wanted, but if it was truly his destiny why stop himself from achieving this future.

He awoke realizing he was still not ready for this journey and needed more time to prepare. Throughout the rest of the day, Hoshek scoured his castle searching for Darkness Tales that he had brought from Aestercrat. He left his castle to go to his docking bay where his ship laid. He looked there as well. Nothing. He could not find what he needed.

The knowledge and thoughts of planetary travel and ships died the moment the Shroud took its effect on the people. Hoshek had told a few followers about how to build ships in his city, but he wanted the knowledge to be scarce, so he kept those he told directly under his thumb.

As he left the docking bay which was on the south side of where the fourth tier of the castle rested, Hoshek decided to clear his head and walk through one of the dark forests on the outskirts of his city. He walked through the various floors of the castle but instead of heading to the bottom level he exited on the second tier. He exited the city and hiked along an unmaintained path, he noticed something engraved into one of the trees. *This must be centuries old,* he thought to himself as he took out his own parchment and quill to copy down the etching. He conjured Souldarkness at the tip of the quill as a way to write down the words. Hoshek then returned to his castle and read what he had written. It did not make sense. The words were not in his spoken tongue he could not formulate what they meant. Hoshek proceeded to strike the wick of the candle next to him with his sword thus creating a flame out of Purple Fire. As he lit a candle next to his bed in his chambers with Purple Fire, the parchment started to react and the letters from the words started to rearrange to become the true meaning behind this Tale. "The only known way one can travel through time is by leaving his or her body and becoming their soul to enter the portal. - Hosra". Hosra was not strong enough to transcend time, but he found ways for others to do it. He felt it was important to write down his findings for generations to come.

Hoshek realized in an "aha" moment that he could attain that ability through enhancing his own Souldarkness with the essence from souls.

Hoshek created a gourd imbued with his Souldarkness. He went on to store all the souls he planned to collect in it. The more souls he obtained in his gourd, the closer he was to breaching the gateway to SpaceTime. If he were to be successful in opening the portal, he would be able to travel to the past.

Before he entered the portal to travel back in time, Hoshek declared to his citizens that the city be named after himself. The people did not object, for due to the mind-controlling effects of the Shroud, they believed that Hoshek was a benevolent ruler. The people in the city all served Hoshek, as they thought him as man of the people. They envisioned him as someone who would protect and care for his people.

This was a mirage, however, painted in their head by the Shroud looming above. People went about their daily lives doing what they thought was normal. They appeared to see the world the same and functioned the same way as before: eating, drinking, carousing with friends, walking through the streets. Yet their minds were almost paralyzed in a shell. They fought their own conscience which ended up taking control, telling them what to do and how to act. Each person's own inner darkness was now in charge of them. For some people, their darkness took the commanding seat of their soul all of the time. For others, it was a sporadic loss of control.

These were the people who from the day of Hoshek's arrival, dropped what they were doing to work, day-in and day-out on building what their ruler wanted the city to look like. They received their instructions on where and how to build parts of the city from the Shroud which was connected to Hoshek's soul. The entrance to the city was on the east side of the castle. A total of four tiers were built around what became the four-story castle. Each tier of the city had a ramp that allowed the people to move between the various layers. Streets were built radiating out from the wall of the castle, and then branching out into many little streets where people had their homes and shops. The ground layer was an area not connected to the castle but surrounded it with fortified columns to hold up the second tier. The second tier was built wrapping itself around the castle with a bridge to the entrance. There were columns all around the second tier that supported the next level. Another ramp was built on the second tier for people to traverse to the third. The third tier mimicked the design of the lower level. Tier three was the last tier that had fortified columns since the final tier was built upon it. The final tier started from a ramp from tier three leading to the north-west side of the castle. The fourth tier was the smallest of them all, as only select people lived there. With each rising tier the level of one's status increased along their importance and loyalty to Hoshek.

Hoshek conferred upon his four most devoted followers, who had happened to be the democratic council on the planet before he arrived, the title of High Ranking Officials. They became his most trusted advisors. He even promised some of them that they would rule over other planets. This promise also ensured that Hoshek was able to rule through his High Ranking Officials and do whatever he needed to do on the other planets without being disturbed. Before Hoshek told his High Ranking Officials about where he would be sending them via ship, they all thought that the only humans in the universe lived on Draefast.

The people who lived in villages on the outskirts of the city and in other regions around Draefast were not as harshly affected by the Shroud as the people in close proximity to Hoshek. These were the people who sporadically fought their inner darkness and lost having it take control of them for up to a few days. The darkness resided back within the persons soul only to come back a few days later. It was an endless cycle. Throughout Hoshek's early reign over Draefast, villagers had tried to revolt, but failed time and time again. Hoshek jailed the agitators in his dungeon on the level of his castle above the artifacts room but beneath the first tier. He did not want to kill them just yet. They were chained to Counterrock, a material native to Aestercrat that was indestructible. He personally saw to feeding them scraps from his meals every three days. One of his kitchen staff members heard screams from the dungeon but never left her post since she feared that she could end up like someone down there screaming if she did. Hoshek knew he would have a purpose for them, and that purpose became clearer after studying Hosra's Tale. He went to the dungeon where these people were barely clinging onto their own lives, and took their souls as punishment the same way he did to the people on Vastrilio and Crateolios. Those people were named the "Vanished" by other citizens and villagers who feared that if they tried to rise up, they would be next to disappear. No one dared speak of the Vanished. People saw cases where their friends or family members talked about the Vanished, then disappeared. Anyone who questioned it or called out Hoshek for being an inattentive ruler to his people also disappeared.

What nobody suspected was that Hoshek was collecting souls of the Vanished. Hoshek then began targeting the young in certain villages since their souls had more energy than those of the elders. Their souls were still filled with hope.

Hoshek started to become gluttonous with power and began Soul-taxing everyone around the planet. The Soultax worked by having each family relinquish something meaningful in their lives. That item had raw soul power emitting from it. The penalty for not abiding by this decree was to be subject to disappearing. Once Hoshek absorbed the soul energy from the item he put the energy in his gourd and destroyed the object. He created his first battalion of grunts through the Soultax, and continued the process to create a bigger army. These grunts were not his finest work and Hoshek knew he could make stronger battalions, so he came up with a new idea. Hoshek called to his followers to bring him the sick or anyone who was unhealthy and on death's doorstep. He promised their families that he would heal them. The grunts would use the grate on the side of the lower level of the castle as a way to travel undedicated with the people that they kidnapped. No civilian who walked by this grate ever thought that it was odd being there as sewage was expelled from it.

Hoshek had a stone table in a room across from his chambers. There he laid each of the sickly people on the stone and operated on them. He cut them open using his sword fused with his Souldarkness Attribute and they died in the process. He then took their dying soul, absorbed it into his gourd and replaced it with the Souldarkness imbued soul energy from the Soul Tax. By adding this new falsified soul made of pure darkness, the body of the person became conscious but lacked free-will. These bodies would become the new grunts and were controlled by Hoshek. Their bodies transformed into the prime look of the sick or old person they were before. He did not even need to speak for them to do his bidding. Anything he thought they did. He tested that theory by asking one of his grunts to stab another without saying a word and it did. They recognized Hoshek as their master since he created them.

Hoshek implemented this tax for years, and barely left his castle. His grunts did all of the work. All of the grunts wore dark black cloaks to cover up who they were and what they looked like especially while they were conducting Hoshek's bidding. Hoshek knew that they could not be seen outside especially by former family members as he informed the families he tried to help that his efforts failed and that he was deeply saddened that he could not save each of the people that he secretly turned into grunts.

Hoshek's tax ensured people that they would be safe as long as he was their ruler. The people of Draefast didn't know better. Nobody ever questioned his methods when dealing with the sick or old after the first time since he would send an

77

advisor to inform the family that Hoshek could not revive their relative but to never speak of it again. An advisor went door-to-door to the relatives saying "I'm sorry for your loss my, I mean our ruler Hoshek tried his best but could not save them. We cannot speak more on this since the last time someone did, they disappeared, and I would hate for that to happen to you." Each citizen nodded at the advisor and agreed to never speak of it, not even in their own home since they had no idea who could be listening.

The grunts played their part perfectly. After a new batch of them were created they kidnapped citizens and brought them to Hoshek. At first the people were scared, but when they saw Hoshek, and the food in the Great Hall they believed that they were being commended for a good deed. Hoshek said to them "Please sit, enjoy some delicious food my staff has prepared." As they started devouring the food Hoshek walked around the table and stabbed each person with his sword using his Souldarkness Attribute to rip their souls out of their bodies. They became limp and fell face first into their bowls of soup. Hoshek carried a gourd with him to store the souls in. As the last few people at the table were done eating, they noticed their fellow citizens thoroughly enjoying their soup, so much so they had fallen asleep in it. They got up franticly running as they saw that the others were not breathing, but they were too slow. Hoshek became enraged, they never thanked him for their meals so as the rest of his guests ran away, he had his grunts corner them. "Thank you for attending this feast. I hope you enjoyed it. You will now be a part of something bigger than your meaningless lives." All of the remaining guests were lined up as Hoshek swung his sword against their arms grazing their skin. Each of them fell to the floor poisoned. "Now for the main event." One of the guests tried to speak, but could not, he was so focused on the pain caused by the poison coursing through his veins. Hoshek stabbed each guest in the gut, absorbing their soul. With each act of Souldarkness Hoshek committed, his own soul was being ripped apart piece by piece he believed he was getting closer to fixing everything he had done, but it was the opposite his Souldarkness Attribute was further corrupting him tempting his mind for more bloodshed. The Souldarkness poison did not affect the souls of the guests, only their bodies, so Hoshek could still use their souls as energy for his plan. He had most of the citizens of Draefast at his fingertips since their grandparents had stories from their youth of Hoshek's grandfather being a great ruler, even when Nahvel was a cruel ruler. With these thoughts settled into everyone's minds the Shroud had an easier time invading their thoughts, corrupting each person it could even more by their own inner darkness. After Nahvel's disappearance, most of the citizens did not know how to go about their daily lives. Children had watched their parents get brainwashed by Nahvel and his dark abilities, and now those children were the parents of the next generation and were the same people being corrupted by a far greater power than Nahvel. Most of the children grew up thinking Nahvel was a great ruler since that's what their parents told them to believe, so when Hoshek came to rule the same people who were now parents to the next generation, had no problem with becoming subjects again. This is only how some people on Draefast felt, mostly the ones who migrated towards Hoshek City as it was being built. Hoshek did begin to lose some followers though when the people started noticing that their children and other people's children were going missing. The difference between Hoshek and his grandfather was that due to the Shroud created by Hoshek he was able to unite all the weak-minded people of Draefast from each region by manifesting their inner darkness, so they had no time to even conceptualize standing up against him. He had true followers everywhere so it would be foolish for people to fight his rule.

Hoshek had gathered the corpses of his old Council friends on his ship before leaving Aestercrat. Now that he was settled on Draefast thought it was the best time to experiment on them to make stronger grunts. At first his experiments did not seem so fruitful, so he continued studying different Souldarkness Attribute techniques in order to perfect his craft. It was as if he was missing a mentor for this, or someone who knew of different Souldarkness Attribute methods that he could learn. Before he had his grunts stealing families and children, he had loyal followers doing it since he corrupted their minds with Souldarkness making them believe they were doing it out of their own free will, but that was not the case. To everyone else on Draefast, these people were the true threat and only Hoshek's protection could help them. Hoshek made his citizens believe that there was a cult living in a nearby village that was responsible for the kidnapping and disappearance of children and families. Hoshek made an announcement across his city from his castle lookout. "Through the Soultax I implemented I have created an army to protect you, my people. You shall no longer live in fear. Let me demonstrate to you just how powerful my grunts are." He then sent his grunts marching out of the city towards the village to burn it down along with the people who lived there. Hoshek believed there to be no survivors. This proved his strength and trustworthiness to the people. This act furthered the grunt takeover of villages on Draefast, and continued the reason for taxing the people. After the grunts returned victorious, Hoshek started to hear people in his city chanting, "Hoshek!" and "Our ruler does care about us." He decided in order to keep this facade afloat he would not order his grunts to kidnap people for the next two days. After that he instructed his grunts to continue on but to be even more stealthy about it.

He was persuading people using his Souldarkness in the exact way that his grandfather took control of the planet decades earlier but on a greater scale. Hoshek wanted to gather as many souls as he could to generate enough Soulmagic for his goal. He threatened the unity of Palaleon, due to this the Legendary Beast traveled to the center of the universe and upon this gathering emitted a light that made all knowing lifeforms on each planet lose the knowledge of the worlds other than their own. Hoshek's act had corrupted Palaleon and destroyed everything that previous Councils of Swordmasters worked so hard to create and maintain.

After years of Soul-taxing, Hoshek collected enough souls so that he was able to successfully enter the portal and traverse through time. For what was three decades to the outside world, Hoshek had projected his soul into the past. He was trapped in a loop starting from watching what his grandfather did when he took over the universe in darkness. As he watched his grandfather reign over Draefast in terror he screamed, but nobody heard him. He soon learned that he could not do anything in the past to change the present. He was but a phantom. A bystander. A soul. The time loop continued as

Hoshek's soul was then shot forward to the time when his father met his mother and defeated his grandfather. He watched each event unfold. Nahvel, who was connected to Hoshek's soul at this time, was altering his grandson's view of the past. Nahvel was also ensuring that his grandson's own inner darkness in his soul did not overpower himself thus erasing him from existence. Nahvel created the illusion that he had won all those years ago, thus making Hoshek believe that he had done the universe a great service, by eradicating the liars who called themselves the Council of Swordmasters. Even though Hoshek had no material body here he started to get shivers down his spine. *Was my purpose to only eradicate the existence of the Council? Was I put in this universe in order to reset Palaleon?* He started to question everything around him. He was vulnerable.

While Hoshek was in the time loop the four High Ranking Officials were ruling over Draefast in a council-like manner. One night while the High Ranking Officials were gathering for a meeting, they noticed that Hoshek's body which was above them sitting on a throne was glowing purple. Suddenly the High Ranking Officials were encased in the same purple glow. They could hear their ruler's voice, telling them "You have done this planet a great service in my absence and for that I grant you your own world in this universe. Remember you will become the ruler, but you will report to me and continue my way of ruling on these planets." Then the voice disappeared. The High Ranking Officials were confused, but felt that they should just continue on with their work since they still had an entire planet to keep in order while Hoshek was gone.

As the following night's meeting between the High Ranking Officials occurred, one of them took to the floor to speak. "After much thought upon hearing our master's voice last night I believe that you three should go to the other worlds while I remain here to rule in our master's absence. We do not want to make him angry when he returns. Plus, you will be able to rule over your own planet, from north to the south and east to the west. What could be a grander offer than that?"

The other three High Ranking Officials looked at each other and nodded in agreement. "We will leave at the first sunrise tomorrow," one replied.

The following morning the three left Draefast on separate ships that Hoshek had made for them. Each journeyed through space, ultimately landing on either Aestercrat, Vastrilio, or Crateolios. Along with the High Ranking Officials Hoshek sent grunts to conquer the various worlds as well as the High Ranking Official's staff of trusted loyalists. The loyalists' job was to listen to the High Ranking Official then come up with a plan and review it with him or her. The grunt battalion consisted of grunt sub-leaders. The grunt sub-leaders leaders took orders from the loyalists who took orders from the High Ranking Official, who did everything Hoshek wanted them to do.

As Hoshek's soul traveled through time he finally made it to his last destination. It was the night when his life changed forever. The moment he killed his father, he saw darkness surrounding his soul. It created a purple aura around his body. As Hoshek further inspected this aura, he noticed a shadow of a being other than his own. It was Nahvel, whispering deception in his ears.

Hoshek was angry, angrier than he had ever been before. He then heard a new voice only this time it was not coming from his younger self's consciousness but his own in his soul form.

"My child look at how you have grown. The darkness has treated you well. Would you like to learn even more power? I can help you change events from the past."

Intrigued by his grandfather's offer, Hoshek replied, "I thought that was impossible. Plus why should I listen to you know weren't you the one that caused me to commit such horrible acts."

"It is impossible if you deem it so. Through the power of Souldarkness, anything you dream of can become reality. Yes I guided you but as you saw they needed to be dealt with. I never forced you do kill anyone; you did that all on your own." Since Nahvel became a part of Hoshek's consciousness he was able to show him a future that Hoshek did not know he could create. One where there was peace and unity throughout Palaleon, one where there was a new Council of Swordmasters that was led by Hoshek. He also knew that he had no one to turn to for help anymore, so when his grandfather offered his guidance, Hoshek felt obliged - and even relieved - to take it. *Since he is willing to help me I feel like a weight has been lifted off my shoulders. With his guidance and training I will be able to achieve my dream*, Hoshek thought to himself unbeknownst that his grandfather could hear his thoughts. He brought Hoshek to the very first time he met the Council of Swordmasters so Hoshek could witness how they had not changed even in Nahvel's youth.

"Let me show you how I was betrayed by two Councils - the one prior to mine and my own. Then you will understand why a new Council from a new perspective must be created." As Nahvel finished speaking the two of them traveled back in time to witness Nahvel as a young boy. Nahvel described the scene they were witnessing as they watched from afar. "I was but a young boy playing with my friend in our village when two men appeared. One used Purple Fire to burn homes in my village while the other created a wind tornado from his sword to fan the flames. My village was destroyed. Then these two men enticed my friend and me to learn from them, this power that as the two survivors of our village would use to eventually go back in time and stop our mentors from conducting the atrocity that they created. We followed them to Aestercrat and trained with them. They had broken their promise and corrupted my friend's mind. He forgot about our true goal and left me alone to figure everything out myself. Then I got banished for studying too much Souldarkness. It was unfair. That is why I will train you to actually change the past, something my own mentors lied to me about. Nobody deserves the same fate as me, especially not my grandson."

As Nahvel concluded his theatrics, he had gained more of Hoshek's trust, even though what most of he said was a lie. Now Hoshek further believed that his father was a liar and was holding back the truth for no reason. Hoshek recalled how highly Gathran spoke about his mentor's Council. This stood antithetical to what Nahvel conveyed to Hoshek.

He taught Hoshek that without darkness there can be no light, but twisted Hoshek's beliefs into making him think that he was the one meant to create a new more powerful and fair Council of Swordmasters.

Little did Hoshek realize that Nahvel just wanted to use him so that he could conduct a mind-body-soul swap with his grandson using his dormant Souldarkness Attribute while also defeating any opposing threats to his rule in the process. This ritual could only be done in the presence of the Soul Realm, so Nahvel told Hoshek, "The Soul Realm must be conquered in order to achieve your dream of creating peace. In order to properly affect the past, you must bring the future Council of Swormasters to the Soul Realm under their own will, corrupt them and steal their souls. With that much soul essence you will be able to travel to any time and unlock the Planetary Sword making you able to change time to your favor."

"How do you know there will be another Council, and how do you know that will work?" Hoshek asked.

"The Council of Swordmasters always seems to appear, especially when one is so close to their goal. I have been trapped in the past for so long I have learned from various Darkness Tales. Our plan will not fail."

"Ok, once we return to my time, I will pursue your idea. Thank you, grandfather."

"You are most welcome."

The Soul Realm is a vast plane where the essence of Soulmagic is skewed due to what is happening in Palaleon. It was also a place where Hoshek could store all the souls he collected from the gourd, so he could continue to collect more. The souls became tainted by the imbalance of Soulmagic thus swaying some that Hoshek collected to become dark souls and others to become pure souls. Both versions had stronger light and darkness energy within themselves. Once contained in the Soul Realm these souls amplified and multiplied in Soulessence, so the more that Hoshek collected and stored there the more control over time he believed he could gain, and over a greater number.

Nahvel was the first person to be fully consumed by their

inner darkness thus he was able to use the full power of his Souldarkness. Little by little, he went on to teach Hoshek about the Souldarkness Attribute, but did not show him every ability since he had his own plan for the future. One of the first techniques Nahvel passed down to his grandson even before they met was the ability to use the Souldarkness Attribute through his sword to rip a soul out of a body. Hoshek had become proficient with this technique over the years that he used it.

If Hoshek could get the Planetary Sword and go back in time, then he would be able to fix his family's past, all the way up to his dark deeds. He has learned that in order to achieve his true goal he needs to delve deeper into his inner darkness, fully let it embrace his soul. Hoshek thought to himself, *I must find a way to master my Attribute so that I can not only travel back in time again but also change the past.* The fact that he was unable to alter the past when he went back in time frustrated him and only drove him more earnestly into wanting to study more about the Souldarkness Attribute and listen to what his grandfather had to say. He needed to find a way to hide his true intent from his grandfather who was occupying his mind. *I must study more about Souldarkness so that I will find a way to control my grandfather's soul and use it to siphon more power to create the Planetary Sword. I need to find a way to conceal these thoughts, though. Perhaps if I write them as Tales, my thoughts will escape my mind, and Nahvel will have no chance to perceive them.* Hoshek believed that if his grandfather found out what he was truly up to then Nahvel would try to corrupt his body since he was in his mind. Then Nahvel could use it to take control of the Time Attribute to go back to his time. After that he would be able to make himself the ruler of Palaleon since he would have the knowledge of how to win and survive.

Nahvel did indeed know of this, but he believed that by using the Soul Realm and his old sword, he could create his own version of the Time Attribute. Nahvel thought to himself, *I wonder where my sword could be. If I find it the I will be able to bend tome to my will without any repercussions. Hmm, I like the sound of that.* He was also unsure if his inner thoughts were heard in Hoshek's mind so he had to be conscious of what he was thinking. That is not how time works. Nahvel's goal was to create a time where he existed without a Council of Swordmasters. He did not fully realize that since the dawn of time itself whenever there was a tyrant there would always be a Council.

If Nahvel managed to erase this cycle the humans of each world could potentially wage bigger more terrifying wars with each other and destroy all that is in their path including Nahvel. The humans goal would become ultimate rule over the universe since greed, wrath, and lust were poisoning their minds. It was for that reason that the Council taught the first humans the meaning of unity and peace and showed them how to go about life's doings incorporating these techniques, which were then passed down to the next generation of humanoids and continued. Inversely, if Palaleon became completely corrupted in a Shroud of Souldarkness so would the people, creating the same result as if there was no Council. This is why the Council of Swordmasters existed so that could never happen.

This was only Nahvel's back-up plan since his goal to take over Palaleon was coming to fruition. During his time as Draefast's ruler and Council of Swordmasters member, he told the Obsessors in the Soul Realm of his second plan and to find a way to bring him back to the past if he loses his future fight. While in the Soul Realm they were tasked with finding a way to transport themselves through time. They spent the rest of their lives battling their inner darkness and studying more Souldarkness Attribute techniques to see if this was possible.

The life and existence of one man is the reasoning as to why Hoshek's and Nahvels' plans currently could not come to fruition.

While Hoshek was stuck in the time loop, Ohr was on his own multi decade long adventure. He felt that this was the perfect opportunity to learn more about his Attribute and Soulmagic. Ohr had a sword with him since the day he was put on the ship by his mother. That sword had never left his side, and he trained with it every day, so he was able to protect himself and others if they needed his protection. When he flew off Aestercrat his ship burnt out and he was stranded in space for what seemed to be a few days to him. There was enough food on the ship for him to survive but he could not leave his ship to make the necessary repairs. Ohr risked his life by jump starting his ship with a Wind Sub-Attribute blast. He was able to make it to the planet Vastrilio where he crash landed. He explored his new surroundings, maintaining a low profile, since he was new to this planet. Upon his adventure through the torched terrain, he found Tales from the Soulfire Attribute Councilmember. He also learned that apparently during her lifetime she was the best mechanic there was, so he used some of her knowledge applied to the new age he lived in and recrafted a working engine. He spent years repairing his ship where he had become friends with a fellow blacksmith on the planet. The blacksmith helped Ohr and abided by the rule of not asking about his past and Ohr would do the same.

"I need you to melt this down. Cut these pieces in half and stick them in the engine compartment. That should get the rotor working."

Ohr nodded, "Thank you for your guidance."

The blacksmith watched as Ohr used a Soulfire Attribute technique he learned from one of Forgia's Tales to be able to cut through solid metal and leave burn marks but never show a flame or seared effect. This technique had to do with channeling little bursts of the Fire Attribute through Ohr's sword enough to cut the metal perfectly. Ohr ate, meditated, studied, and slept in his broken ship never going into town unless he needed to. He promised the blacksmith, "I will repay you with this knowledge. I fear a great evil will be coming soon. Practice these meditative techniques and your body and mind should not go through the harsh effects of what is coming. Also never tell anyone I was here, for that will make your chance of survival less likely." Ohr had asked the blacksmith to help me make a communicator device since he had a feeling, he would need one in the future. "Just so I never forget you and what you have done for me what is your name?" Ohr asked the blacksmith before he left to go to his ship. "My name is Azure. Good luck on your adventures, and hopefully we will meet again," the blacksmith replied. Ohr then walked away. As Ohr entered his ship he started the take-off sequence and in no time was already above the planet's atmosphere and was heading back to Aestercrat. He was not the best pilot, but he made it to Aestercrat in one piece. Time had passed tremendously from when Ohr was on Vastrilio. When Ohr landed near Mt. Calasmic he used a Soullight ability he created called soul-search. While using this technique Ohr noticed a new presence in this world, not human and not animal. It was Hoshek's grunts. They had noticed a ship landing near the mountain range and went to go investigate. Ohr was able to sneak past grunts when exiting his ship, and used a Soullight Attribute ability he read about that allowed him to cloak his ship so it was unseen to anyone but himself.

Ohr stole supplies from loyalists and gave them to villagers who took it upon themselves to revolt against the grunts. Unfortunately, the villages were besieged by grunts due to the people's lack of training in self-defense. This made it more difficult for Ohr to help villagers, so he ended up leaving. He couldn't afford to become a captive for the grunts to bring back to their leader. After collecting enough supplies from Aestercrat Ohr went back to his ship and flew to Crateolios. He was able to aid people from Crateolios on his journey to find the next Councilmembers, but again had to flee fearing that he would be captured. Ohr felt horrible every time he had to leave a village that wasn't fully restored but he knew that eventually he wanted to come back to each planet and free the people from the control of the grunts.

During his travels, he could not train the people from the different planets and fight off all the grunts alone. He needed to try to defeat the tyrant taking control of the planets on his own anyway. *I have a feeling that the one who is causing these people to have so much turmoil resides on Draefast. I must head there and defeat the source of this darkness. Since I have trained my entire life how hard could this really be?* Ohr then flew his ship to Draefast, his final destination, as this is where he could do the most damage to Hoshek. However, all that changed once Hoshek's soul re-entered his body and he opened his eyes. After decades of his soul and body inhabiting separate planes, the Dark Wizard sat on his throne, his breath and heartbeat returning to their normal rhythms. He continued looking around his throne room until he glanced at his hands which aged. He needed to go to his chambers, to a mirror to see his new appearance. He stood up; it was too quick his body had not yet adjusted to a non-sitting position. His blood flowed throughout his body to his legs in order for him to walk. He almost tripped but caught his balance. He felt older. As he made it to his chambers and his mirror, he noticed his appearance changed. He had a dark brown mustache and a long beard, and his hair had some grey in it. He started running back and forth in his room to see if his body could handle it. He went on to grab his sword and swing it. He was still agile which was good. His body aged but his mind seemed sharper, and since it was enhanced with his Souldarkness Attribute due to everything Nahvel taught him, he felt like a new version of himself. A more powerful version. He was 52 years old. He returned to his throne to await the arrival of his High Ranking Officials including the one that had stayed on Draefast. The other High Ranking Officials were informed of his arrival due to how swiftly the sky went from a dark grey to absolute black across the universe. They all flew back to Draefast and landed in the docking bay of his castle. The four tiers of the city had been completed along with the exterior and interior of the castle. They paraded through the backside of Hoshek's castle only to look around his throne room and see an older decrepit body. Yet Hoshek's eyes remained sharp. Hoshek did not feel it, but the Souldarkness that was enhancing his abilities and perception was also making him weaker, and he would have to find new strengths in order to be balanced with the fact that he lost his youth.

"Continue ruling over the worlds as I take on a more important task," Hoshek stated to them.

The High Ranking Officials were confused. One looked up at the man who had just spoken and said in a dissenting tone, "Where is our leader?"

"Do not misjudge my powers by the way I look. Appearances can be quite deceiving."

Standing at attention, the Officials awaited their orders.

Hoshek continued, "I am your ruler, the one who left you was naive and knew nothing about his true potential. I am stronger than he was. Now bow before your true ruler!"

Hoshek did not like that one of his Officials spoke up against him, so he waved his arm, and grunts opened the great doors to the throne room and grabbed the shoulders of the High Ranking Official. The grunts then pushed him to the ground as Hoshek stood up grasping his sword to the man's throat. "Don't you ever defy me again!" Hoshek was angry that he had to make an example of this man. He genuinely thought that the Shroud made the people blindly obey, and this was the first time he was proven wrong by his thoughts. *This man is supposed to be someone who full heartedly believes in me and someone I trust. How could he speak to me in such a tone*, Hoshek thought to himself. "If you ever think of speaking up, I will remove your soul from your body, then do it to the rest of your family." Hoshek said angrily.

The High Ranking Official replied sheepishly, "I am sorry my lord. It won't happen again."

"Let me send you all off with some important advice. I might look weak due to my advanced age, but the wisdom I have now obtained makes me the most powerful person here and you all should truly fear me." As he turned his back to the High Ranking Official who spoke up against him, the same one who ruled over Draefast in his absence, Hoshek quietly unsheathed his sword. With the speed and precision of his younger self, he plunged the blade into the man's torso. The High Ranking Official dropped dead. Hoshek grimaced, "I did not need him anymore. If you really did not think that you should fear me before, this is what will happen if you defy me." The other High Ranking Officials watched as the man's lifeless body hit the floor. Hoshek then signaled to his grunts, who were still in shock seeing what just occurred in front of their eyes, to escort the High Ranking Officials out of his throne room, back to their ships and then back to their worlds.

With the knowledge he obtained from the teachings of Nahvel, coupled with the Tales scribed by Hosra, Hoshek embarked on a new mission. Even though he was armed with strategies to further his plans, this would take time since each step needed his utmost attention in order to be perfect. By generating Souldarkness-infused souls, he would create the most efficient peace-inducing Council of Swordmasters, along with siphoning dark and pure souls from the Soul Realm. The reason for siphoning souls was due to the fact that he was meddling with abilities greater than his own which were affecting his own control over his own Attribute along with his lifespan. Hoshek needed the Council in order to create the Planetary Sword so he could cut through time and make it malleable to his desires. This Council would adhere to all of his wishes and visions making it the "perfect" one in his eyes. However, by creating his own Council, the universe would be without balance since only one Council can operate per a certain time period. If two Councils coexisted, they would need to fight for the sake of the universe so it would not implode.

As Hoshek was exiting the time loop, Ohr was meditating in the canyons east of the Waterfall of Light, on another side of Draefast. Ohr knew that dark feeling in his soul was being generated by someone close to him. *They must have read many Tales about Soulmagic in order to produce this much darkness*, Ohr thought to himself.

Through Ohr's Soulmagic, he was able to detect where Hoshek had kept Tales in his castle. Hoshek kept them close to him, so that he could study their dark roots and so no one else could get to them. *I believe that I will not be able to stop this darkness own my own. The amount of soul energy around me is too much for me alone. I have to find people worthy of being the new Council of Swordmasters, and train the one that will lead them. In order for me to do that I need to get my hands on some of these Tales.* Ohr unsheathed his sword and gently sliced into his hand. His blood dripped along the edge of the blade as he stuck it into the ground. A flash of white light appeared and from it rose the White Lion. Typically, Legendary Beasts can be summoned when a Councilmember's blood is on their sword then thrust into the ground. Although Ohr was not a part of the Council, he relied on his known lineage to Ohtav to be able to perform the summoning. When a Councilmember summoned a Legendary Beast using their blood, they did not feel pain, but due to Ohr's current standing, his hand was throbbing.

Ohr, now 47 years old, climbed atop the White Lion's back. As it roared, the echo reverberated through the canyon walls with such force that the matter making up the bodies of Ohr and the Lion turned invisible. The White Lion then exited the canyon and as Ohr blinked his eyes he suddenly appeared in front of Hoshek's castle. Charging into Hoshek's castle, the two passed by the grunts, undetected. They made it through the various secret passageways in the castle but stopped on the lower tier as Ohr felt that they were close to the Tales. Ohr dismounted the White Lion and said, "Stay here". Ohr opened up the door and saw multiple grunts protecting the Tales. Ohr conjured up his Soulmagic creating a gust of wind from his sword that distracted the grunts as he slipped by and grabbed as many Tales as his hands could hold. All of a sudden, the door slammed shut. "I know you're here, intruder! I can feel your soul essence." Ohr thought to himself, *This must be a variation of my ability, but the difference is that he can do it through Souldarkness.* Ohr tried to run quickly past his foe, but Hoshek sensed him and swiftly unsheathed his sword. The outer edges of the blade glowed from the presence of Souldarkness poison. As Hoshek sliced the sword through the air, specks of poison flew towards Ohr's face. He felt the poison move throughout his body latching to his soul but had made it to the White Lion. The White Lion was now visible since it had to pick up Ohr who was becoming weaker and weaker by the second having to fight this poison inside his body. The White Lion knelt and put Ohr on his back. Clutching his writhing body, barely holding in the pain, he dropped his sword while getting on the White Lion's back. The poison had absorbed most of Ohr's Soulmagic, and transferred the essence to Hoshek. Hoshek thrust his sword at the Legendary Beast with the intent to kill, but the White Lion evaded the blow. The White Lion charged at the side of the castle, flowing like wind through the cracks of the wall and leaped onto the ground. Ohr's eyes closed as the White Lion whisked both of them away, back into the forest from where they came.

Hoshek pointed his sword at the one that laid on the ground and summoned Purple Fire to annihilate it, thus further damaging Ohr's connection to the Soullight Attribute.

The White Lion dropped Ohr back where their adventure began. Ohr was laying underneath the Waterfall of Light, healing from the poison, but it had already absorbed most of his Soulmagic. Now that Hoshek knew someone was after him, Ohr's body had become strained with the idea that he had just failed the universe. This stress on top of being poisoned was blocking him from achieving his former Soullight Attribute Soulmagic abilities. He knew for certain now that he needed to create a new Council of Swordmasters to help him defeat Hoshek, and by doing so also free the people from grunt control. The Tales he stole would be necessary in order to triumph over Hoshek.

Hoshek was indeed shrouded and corrupted by Souldarkness making him more powerful as a sword fighter and Attribute wielder than Ohr now. Ohr then spent the next ten years training, and mastering each of the Attributes to the best of his ability especially since now it was more difficult due to his connection to his own Attribute was dwindling. One night, he got a vision of Purple Lightning striking a family's hut. He learned from this vision what his purpose was and what he must do. He took up the name Old Wizard, so that his brother could never recognize him.

The Son was born the night Hoshek and Ohr fought, 10 years earlier. Ohr had been Palaleon's protector but now that his Soulmagic was diminishing day by day he could not help anyone. Ohr thought to himself, *If I cannot save everyone by defeating my brother now, then I am not meant to be the Soullight Attribute Councilmember. Which means I am not mean to be the leader of this Council. I must find and train someone more connected to Soulmagic than myself, as they must be the true leader of the next Council of Swordmasters. That must be The Son in my vision.*

98

Chapter VI

The Adventure Begins

Back to the Present

Through the flames of the Purple Fire, the Old Wizard shouted to The Mother and The Daughter to stay outside. Sensing that Hoshek felt his presence on the planet, the Old Wizard commanded, "Enter my ship when it lands so you can escape this place." The Mother and The Daughter were very confused.

"Are you the famed Old Wizard we have been praying to?" The Mother asked, looking through the Purple Fire at the old man. He turned his focus from the two laying on the floor to stare at her saying nothing, as if he had not seen another person or heard a voice in years. "Answer me! Who are you? If you are not him, then get away from my husband and my son!" The Mother shouted.

The Old Wizard finally exited the Purple Fire since he felt he had to handle the situation outside. He replied, "Forget this, forget who you are, who you were. For your own safety, you will forget all about this and live the rest of your lives on this ship. For now, your one goal is to never be found or noticed. Do not stay on Draefast. Leave this planet now since you are safest on my ship."

As he approached The Mother and The Daughter, he tapped their chests with dagger, and they fainted. This was a Soullight technique the Old Wizard learned through reading Tales that he could alter or erase people's memories. The Old Wizard proceeded to put them on his ship, it was still cloaked from Hoshek and the grunts since the time he used it to evade them all of those years ago. His demand was the last statement he thought that The Mother and The Daughter remembered. The Old Wizard destroyed the device that summoned his ship with his daggers so only those on the ship could control it.

The Mother and The Daughter woke up on the Old Wizard's ship with no recollection of their life before this moment they only remembered that they were related. Just like the lightning splitting their hut, the ship took off and they disappeared into the night. In their soul's they had this feeling that they should not return to Draefast. The Mother and The Daughter had enough food and clothes on the ship to last them for a while, along with a glowing device labeled "communicator" next to the steering wheel on the main deck. While sleeping aboard the Old Wizard's ship, visions came to both The Mother and The Daughter. It was a new mission from the Old Wizard. He needed their help with something.

The Old Wizard, now without his ship, dropped a bag on the floor of the hut. He then walked back through the Purple Fire demonstrating how powerful he was even with a weakened connection to his soul and Attribute. Now the Purple Fire had inched closer to The Father and The Son to the point where it looked like they were about to be burned. He gazed at them both, and through pure instinct, moved towards The Son. He recalled his vision about The Son from almost a decade earlier. *This has to be the boy in my vision. I must save him. He is the key to our universe becoming safer and peaceful once again.* The Old Wizard knelt down beside the boy. As he pressed his pointer and middle fingers against The Son's forehead, he took in a deep lung-filling breath. As he slowly exhaled, the Old Wizard's arm glowed white. A bit of his soul transferred to The Son. That same white iridescent glow emanated from The Son's forehead. Then as the Old Wizard looked at him, The Son's hair started to turn from brown to white. By this point the Old Wizard had parted a bit of the Purple Fire to help pull The Son out. As The Son lay on the dirt outside he opened his eyes. His pupils were now red. The Old Wizard now looked even weaker than before. In order to save The Son's life and help his soul heal from the Purple Lighting the Old Wizard needed to give him a piece of his own soul.

As The Son arose, the Old Wizard said to him, "Slowly, my boy, do not get up too quickly."

The Son sternly asked, "Who are you old man? Do not touch me."

His kind face peering through his light grey shawl that was wrapped around his head and slung down past his knees, the Old Wizard did not give the full truth when explaining who he was.

"I saw an enormous flame - not the color of one I am used to - so I was drawn to it. As I approached, I saw two figures on their knees outside the flame and came to the assumption that something sinister had happened. I jumped through the fire thinking that if I did it quick enough, I would not get burned, and there you were laying on the floor. I knew I needed to get you out of there, and when I did your mother and sister had vanished. Maybe they thought you died, maybe they started a new venture. All I know is that you would not be living if I did not intervene when I did, but also there is something special about you. I want to help you explore that and teach you everything I know about this universe and the gifts you possess in it."

Taking in all the information he just did, The Son nodded. "Thank you for saving me. Will you mentor me in these mystical ways?" The Son asked then continued to speak. "You were able to jump through a fire far greater than I have ever seen before. I want to learn how to as well."

Before the Old Wizard replied, he looked at The Son confused. He thought to himself. *He did not even ask about his family. I wonder if he remembers them or not. That just means I do not need to use my memory altering Soullight ability on him then. Maybe for right now that is for the best so he can focus on his training.*

The Old Wizard looked at him and said, "I can teach you a lot more than just how to jump through fire. Let's go begin your training."

The Son's hair was glistening due to the embers from the fire. The sleeves of his grey shirt had been singed by the Purple Fire, while his dark pants were covered in soot.

The Old Wizard thought to himself, *I do not want to start off my relationship with my pupil by hiding the full truth. I think I should give him a more in depth reason as to why I am here.* He began to tell The Son more about his journey prior to meeting him, "I came to the hut after seeing Purple Lightning in the sky. I am from another planet, but was on Draefast collecting medicinal herbs.

Confused, The Son asked, "Planet? There are other planets? Where am I? Who am I? All I remember is..." The Son's words drifted to a murmur. His memories were fading. He wished this feeling away as he closed his eyes, but upon reopening them, he still could not grasp them.

The Son started to hyperventilate. He tried to scream. He needed to form words to communicate with the Old Wizard. With the last ounce of his awoken energy, he was only able to mutter, "Tales! Tales my father used to read to me." The Son then pointed towards the hut. He was battling his amnesia every second he could, but he let his guard down after relaying the message. The Son only became more enraged. The words were on the tip of his tongue, but he could not digest them to remember what he was talking about.

The Old Wizard tried to calm him down. "Everything will be ok. You are going to be fine, just breath. I will get the Tales when I go get your father."

"My father? My father?" The Son could not handle all of the information. He let it go of all of his memories before meeting the Old Wizard in order to remain conscious for just a little a while longer.

The Old Wizard thought to himself, *I believe you were meant to do something greater than to be a thief's son. I will train you in the art of Soulmagic, Attributes, and swords.*

The Old Wizard opened up his bag, took out a little dagger and cut his hand. The Son turned his head and asked, "Why are you hurting yourself?" As he finished the last word of his question The Son then passed out.

The Old Wizard replied, "It is to summon a friend of mine who will help you leave this place." The White Lion Legendary Beast then appeared. "I will teach you this ability when you are ready, and maybe in the future you will learn to summon Legendary Beasts like this one." The Old Wizard then look at the Legendary Beast and said, "Bring The Son to the edge of the forest where it meets the Waterfall of Light."

In a flash, the Legendary Beast and The Son were gone along with the Old Wizard's bag which the White Lion held in its mouth. All that was in front of the Old Wizard was a paw print. He then kicked dirt over the print, so it disappeared.

"Now to see what's wrong with The Father," the Old Wizard mumbled to himself as he walked back through the Purple Fire. He recollected; *The Father should have been laying right about there.* The Old Wizard's eyes focused on a spot depicting the outline of a human body, but nobody was lying there. The Old Wizard bent down to touch the area. *What trickery is this?* The Old Wizard was thinking to himself, *I must find The Father, since without him being present next to The Son while they are conscious, I cannot attempt a mind restoration using what little Soullight Attribute I have left. I have never tried this ability before, but if it works then I will be able to train both of them, but more importantly, The Son with his mind being his own distraction.*

Upon realizing that he had no idea where The Father could have gone, the Old Wizard looked up. A tornado of Purple Fire appeared in the center of the room knocking him backwards. As his body hit the last remaining wall of the hut, a wooden beam from above shook loose, and collapsed on his torso, temporarily immobilizing him. From the inferno, an older man covered in a dark cloak appeared. He paid no mind to the Old Wizard. The figure picked up The Father's near lifeless body by his armpits and began dragging him through the Purple Fire. The figure stopped next to the black shard and stuffed it into his pocket. The figure was unaffected while walking through his own flames but that was not the same for The Father, whose body caught fire. His skin was peeling, and flakes were falling on the ground while most of his clothes melted into his skin or burned off entirely. "This man is broken and burned to a crisp; he will be perfect for the first ever successful Dranstor transformation. He was a nobody before now, just a thief with no purpose. Well, I will give him a purpose now," the shadowy figure whispered to himself. "Nobody will come looking for him either, making him the perfect subject. My servant. Hopefully I can unlock the Souldarkness Attribute within him equal in strength to the famed Legendary Beasts' Soulmagic abilities. I need him to help my dreams become reality and make it so nobody ever has a chance of confronting me."

The Old Wizard overheard the dark figure's nefarious words. Maybe it was intentional or maybe it was not. Now more than ever, the Old Wizard knew that he needed to train The Son not just to rid Palaleon of Hoshek, but if they acted quickly, they could try and prevent the figure from transforming The Father into a Dranstor. If The Father were able to equal a Legendary Beast in strength who knows what could become of the universe's fate. The Old Wizard thought to himself, *The Son must become stronger than a Legendary Beast. Is it even possible for me to be able to train him to reach such a potential? I have no clue but this all must have to do with The Son's destiny.*

As the Old Wizard concluded his thoughts he watched as the shadowy figure pierced his sword into the ground and rotated it around The Father and himself creating a circle around himself and The Father that emitted a dark glow then they suddenly disappeared leaving behind a thick cloud of black smoke that filled the room. *If I inhale this smoke my lungs will be poisoned much like my soul. I can't have that since The Son will need me and I must always be there for him.* The Purple Fire tornado dissipated and the Old Wizard using all of his might pushed the beam off of himself. He needed to act swiftly in order to not be burned by the Purple Fire or poisoned by the smoke. The Old Wizard motioned both of his hands sideways parting the smoke. *How did I do that? Well even though my soul and connection to the Attributes feels weak I keep amazing myself with new techniques especially without a sword. I have only seen one other person able to do such a thing.* There was no time for him to figure it out, he needed to get back to The Son as soon as he possibly could. His plan to restore The Son's memory was no more but he still needed to train him.

The Old Wizard looked around the remains of the hut. He was confused as to why a figure wanted The Father. Perhaps it was the same reason that he wanted The Son. The family's hut was crumbling down completely and the Purple Fire smoldered. The Old Wizard noticed that on the ground there was a white shard from the remnants of The Son's sword. He then found a box in what used to be The Son's room. He opened the box and saw all these old pieces of parchment. As his picked up the box it crumbled into ash and the Old Wizard noticed that some of the parchments were burned at the tops and bottoms from the Purple Fire. *These are the Tales the Son was referring too. I will use their knowledge to train him.* Holding the parchments under his left arm and the shard in his right hand, the Old Wizard walked out of the Purple Fire. He then turned around only to see the trees around him burning with purple flames. He thought to himself, *now it is time for me to train The Son, so he can become the one destined to lead the Council of Swordmasters and bring the universe back to a peaceful time. After training him, The Son will be able to defeat Hoshek along with the Dranstor if it is created.*

On the other side of the planet, the White Lion wiggled his body to knock The Son off of his back by the banks of the Waterfall of Light. As he hit the ground The Son awoke and got up, his eyes were wide as he was looking at his surroundings. He was in a place he had never been before. The Legendary Beast then disappeared from The Son's vision and reappeared in front of the Old Wizard. With a great roar, the Legendary Beast extinguished the Purple Fire through the intensity of its breath. The Old Wizard hopped on the back of the White Lion and they traveled to the Waterfall of Light where The Son had sat in a cross legged position next to the pond beneath the Waterfall.

The Son still had a confused look on his face. The Old Wizard sat next to him and started telling The Son the true purpose of his being on Draefast.

"I am here to create a new Council of Swordmasters to defend Palaleon from the likes of Hoshek."

The Son tilted his head towards the Old Wizard in confusion.

"Who is Hoshek, and what is the Council of Swordmasters? And why did you lie to me?"

The Old Wizard replied, "I lied since I needed to make sure you are the one from the Tales. It is your destiny to defeat Hoshek. He is the Dark Wizard who controls this planet along with others. This planet that we are on is your homeworld."

Grateful that the Old Wizard started telling him the truth, and was seemingly helping him remember things, The Son decided to trust him. *After all, I would have been left for dead if it weren't for the Old Wizard,* The Son thought to himself.

Chapter VII

The Council of Swordmasters

The Old Wizard began The Son's training by showing him the Tales written by previous Council of Swordmasters. He had stored the Tales that he took from The Son's home in his bag that was with The Son at the Waterfall of Light. He told The Son, "All Tales are written in third person, to direct focus upon the teachings and lessons, rather than upon the author. Each Tale has lessons from the past about various topics such as how to manifest the various Attributes including the Souldarkness Attribute, which we do not need to get into just yet. Different sword techniques. The key to inner peace. Soulmagic." The Old Wizard was afraid of losing The Son the same way Hoshek became lost.

The Old Wizard and The Son were sitting around a fire they just made right outside one of the dark forests when the Old Wizard continued, "To understand your role now, I must teach you about the past. The Council prior to the one I am training you to lead had to also deal with a threat like Hoshek. They had defeated this threat only because the tyrant had let his guard down during their final battle. Before the Dark Wizard this man was the most powerful in the Souldarkness Attribute. The battle lasted for many days and nights. The Council eventually emerged victorious from this fight, but then lost against an unforeseen foe decades later." The Old Wizard was referring to what his own father had told him about the days before his birth, but included his own knowledge about the rise of the Dark Wizard. The majority of the story was just a lie, a bedtime story that the Old Wizard's father told him when he was younger.

"Who was this foe?" The Son asked in astonishment.

"It was Hoshek, the heir to the Council of Swordmasters."

The Son asked, "Why did Hoshek turn evil?"

"To my knowledge he was corrupted by his abilities and his own thoughts."

"Wouldn't that mean that somewhere there is still a light inside of his soul?"

The Old Wizard replied, "I believe his soul was corrupted by his own affinity for Souldarkness. I was never able to help him, since by the time we fought he was too far gone. I almost died by his hand and that is why my mission is to create a Council that will be strong enough to end his reign of darkness."

The Son was fascinated by all of the Old Wizard's teachings from the Tales, and other stories he learned from the Old Wizard's past. *I guess for now, my place in this world was to get rid of all evil, and help create and be an integral part of this new Council*, The Son thought to himself. The Son never fathomed that he could be a vital member of the Council, but then again, he still had no idea of who he was. The Old Wizard went on to tell him the Tale of how the Planetary Sword was created along with their universe Palaleon. "On top of the Tale of the creation of the original Council of Swordmasters and Palaleon, I feel that I must remind you that this universe is made from darkness and light and that you cannot have one without the other. The key is to have balance."

The Son replied, "So if there is darkness in light and light in darkness how do we know that what Hoshek is doing is inherently bad?"

The Old Wizard looked shocked at what The Son had just asked. "He is taking control of the universe and the people who live here. He is no god. There is no person who controls the linear path of another's life. Each person's decisions will decide their own future and fate."

The Son then stated, "I understand. Sorry if what I said upset you, I just want to make sure that we are doing the right thing. Which we must be since people should not be held against their will and that is practically what Hoshek is doing."

Continuing his teaching, The Old Wizard told The Son the Tale of restoring life to the dead using Soulmagic. "This Tale is known to be one of the earliest Tales written, but nobody knew who composed it. Since this ability has never worked before, the previous Council of Swordmasters believed it to be a myth." The Old Wizard was never able to fully understand the Tale since it was lost after his childhood.

The Old Wizard had cloth and needles, and taught The Son how to make his own clothing. This technique involved patience and was the perfect way for The Son to clear his mind from his training. It was important that The Son made his clothes since they only had enough money for essentials like food and hilt materials for The Son's sword.

During his first year of training The Son also made new articles of clothing for himself, since all he originally had was a black t-shirt and pants when he laid unconscious in the hut. Making his clothes continued to teach him a sense of mindfulness, connecting him further with his soul. He had made black pants that were breathable so it was easier for him to run, along with a dark grey overcoat for when the nights got cold. Every task the Old Wizard gave The Son was equally as important as the last.

The Son spent the following two years crafting his sword, using the white shard that was next to him in the hut years earlier. The Old Wizard thought that if The Son could tap into his inner Soulmagic while manipulating the shard then it would turn back into the sword that The Son stole years ago. This would not be the case. Every morning The Son woke up, drank water, ate some food he hunted for or picked the day prior, then stretched. After he stretched, he went to rekindle the fire he started with tinder. As he added logs, the temperature of the bonfire rose to the point that he continued to forge his sword. Upon spending hours intently focusing on crafting his sword, he sat with the Old Wizard asking about Tales from the olden days, and learned more about his place in this fight for peace and the freedom of Palaleon. He also took time to learn sword-fighting techniques every other day, to ensure that once he was done making his sword, he would become ready to wield it. He finished crafting the sword by the Waterfall of Light.

"Should we go into a village so that you can buy a sword to

spar with me?" The Son asked the Old Wizard, as he sheathed his sword.

"We can't go into any villages at this current moment as they are either occupied by grunts, or the people residing, who have been mind-corrupted by the Shroud, will inform Hoshek of our whereabouts. If that were to happen our mission would end fairly quickly. We will find other ways for you to train successfully." The Old Wizard replied.

"I understand." The Son stated.

The Old Wizard continued, "While you train with your sword, you must also understand Soulmagic and where it comes from."

"Well, where does it come from? I thought Soulmagic just lives in one's body. I thought everyone has it, but there are just a few people who can unlock it. Isn't that what you told me?" The Son queried.

"Well, what I told you is not wrong, but to add to that lesson I have more to say. Soulmagic, and in turn the various Attributes, do emerge from one's soul, but the reason a sword is so important to the equation is that Soulmagic needs to find an outlet in order to escape one's body when it is being conjured. It moves through one's body to their hands and through the sword. Soulmagic is what makes one connected to an Attribute. Soulmagic is not an Attribute and an Attribute is not Soulmagic, but they are intertwined within the soul of the sword wielder."

The Son didn't know his own name, was unaware he had family, and had no backstory to his knowledge. All he had was his dreams, the lessons the Old Wizard taught him, and the shard of light. Once he had fully accepted his role and crafted his sword from the shard, he was ready for the next part of his training. The Old Wizard was not the best sword fighter, so The

Son had to learn how to wield his sword by practicing basic sword techniques. Ohr dueled with The Son using branches he found on the ground as his weapon, and when The Son was not training with Ohr he was shadow sparring.

There were a few villages around the Waterfall. The Son bought materials to further enhance his hilt using the currency that the Old Wizard had. This currency was known as Zagrad, it was a blue gem-like object. The Old Wizard looked at The Son and said, "When we eventually make our way to other planets to find the rest of the Council of Swordmasters recruits you will notice that different planets have different currency. This was instilled back when the original Council taught people on their homeworlds about currency and the value of different objects." The Son replied, "That is amazing. The first Council did so much to help people I aspire to have my Council be as great as theirs once was." While in the village, The Son also went to buy parchment and a quill so he could record everything he learned from the Old Wizard, along with each of his adventures. "The way to write a Tale is by using your Soulmagic through a quill to produce the words on the parchment. This technique will make it so time will have no effect of the parchment." Ohr stated to The Son who was copying down what he was hearing. Once The Son mastered wielding the sword, he tried to learn how to use Soulmagic, which the Old Wizard conveyed in his teachings. They sat on rocks near the Waterfall trying to create small bursts of energy from the life water. The goal was for The Son to learn to wield Soulmagic, properly duel with his sword, and to eventually fuse his sword with Soulmagic creating his connection to the Attributes.

"Breathe in and out. Control your breath and have it flow like how you hear the water flowing through the Waterfall. This is how you will become in tune with your inner Soulmagic."

The Son replied, "Ok I will. I need to focus first." The Son sat on the ground trying to focus, but nothing was happening.

"This might take time. You are new at finding your Soulmagic, do not be afraid." the Old Wizard said. The Son stood on his feet.

"Ok how about we get some food." The Son stated. The two of them found fish swimming in the pond beneath the Waterfall. The Son jumped in the water, disturbing the fish, but was quick enough to catch one in each hand.

"Wow your reflexes are quick, especially against an animal in its own habitat."

The Son exited the pond and replied, "Thank you mentor." The Old Wizard was pleased The Son used the word mentor, and then started a fire to cook the fish. The Son found two sticks by the edge of the Waterfall, whittled them into skewers, and stabbed the fish with them, making it easier for them to be cooked. The Old Wizard reached into his bag and removed a vial of spices. He rubbed the contents into the raw fish, as if trained by a master chef. Within minutes, the meal was ready.

"This is some good fish, thank you," The Son said, smacking his lips, "Now back to some more training."

"I admire your attitude towards perfecting your abilities, but do not rush the process. You will get there; I believe in you." The Old Wizard replied. He then started to set up camp. "I am going to bed, you can stay up and train, but remember - rest is important too."

The Old Wizard then laid down, and closed his eyes. The Son was now sitting underneath the Waterfall trying to concentrate on each drop of water hitting him. He found peace in this. He closed his eyes, and felt something. His soul was calling to him. The Son then opened his eyes, he felt exhausted, but now believed that everything the Old Wizard told him he could become was true. Knowing that information comforted The Son. He then set up his sleeping bag, laid down, and fell into a deep slumber.

The next morning the Old Wizard saw The Son admiring his sword and said, "I have heard that many swordsmen name their swords. Do you have a name in mind?"

A name?" The Son replied. He did not even know his own name, so how could he name his sword? The Son then swiftly got up and started to run into the forest. The Old Wizard tried to follow him but could not keep up. As The Son turned to see if the Old Wizard was following him, he tripped over a rock, tumbled down a hill, and fell onto a patch of grass. He thought that by having the forest surround him he would be in a more meditative state to envision a name for his sword.

As The Son landed in the patch of grass he began to think. *Do I have a name? Would the Old Wizard know it? Maybe he does not, but maybe he does and he is not telling me. I wonder if he is lying to me. He is my mentor. Why would he lie? What is my name? Am I truly destined to be everything he wants me to be and defeat Hoshek?* All of these thoughts were racing in his head. He kept thinking about the last one. His brain and body could not handle it. All of a sudden, his eyes rolled to the back of his head. His once-red pupils disappeared and blood ran down his face. It seemed as if he were in a different realm. Not only did he feel the Soulmagic flowing within his body, but he also felt connected to the planet beneath his feet. Then darkness hit him. It was pulling at his soul trying to transform it. *You are mine now.* A shrouded figure appeared in the same realm as him, but then as quick as it came it disappeared. *I wonder what that was.*

The blood from his face went back into his body. The Son started to move his head upwards but even with all of his might he could not lift his head. He gave way to gravity, and his head fell backwards hitting the grass. *What was that feeling?* The Son thought to himself. He had never felt that sensation before. It was cold, and he felt shivers down his spine. He then heard what sounded like a young girl and an older woman screaming for their lives. His palms were sweaty, he went for his sword, and as he touched it, he felt his entire soul leave his body and fly towards one of the dark forests on the other side of the planet. *What was there?* The Son was thinking. Then a creature appeared that looked like it was once a man. There was blood on one of his hands, and in the other hand was a black sword. The sword looked like it was bleeding. There were two bodies on the floor, both female. *Who were they? Is this happening now? Is this in the future or the past?* The Son's thoughts couldn't keep up with his brain. This was indeed a glimpse into an alternate future. The Shroud was trying to take control of him by keeping him trapped inside this darkness.

Suddenly, a white light emerged, and what looked to be the spirit of the White Hyrax touched The Son and BOOM.

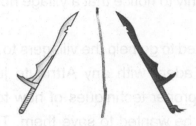

Chapter VIII

A New Day

The Son woke up, his head cradled in the Old Wizard's hands. Next to the Old Wizard stood a White Hyrax, much like the one The Son had just seen in his vision. *Was it even a vision?* The Son did not know.

"This is another one of the Legendary Beasts, much like the White Lion you met years ago," the Old Wizard told The Son. "Before I met you, I was traveling alone on Draefast when I stumbled into what seemed to be an extension of one of the dark forests. This forest felt different. At the center a bright light appeared and seemed to eradicate the darkness surrounding me. That is when the White Lion made its first appearance to me."

The Son was in awe. "I wish I could learn from them, like you."

"Maybe one day you will, I have come to realize that in order to be trained by them they will appear in front of you. They choose the person they will next train," the Old Wizard replied. The Old Wizard and The Son started to smell smoke.

119

They looked up only to notice that a village not so far from them was burning.

The Son wanted to go help the villagers to show his bravery. He was not yet adept with any Attribute just yet, and was still learning the proper techniques of how to wield his sword but nonetheless, he wanted to save them. The Son vowed to himself that he would try his hardest to become the man that the Old Wizard envisioned, but he had so much uncertainty about his life. The Old Wizard knew that until The Son could accept who he truly was meant to be it would be harder for him to unlock his Soullight Attribute. He looked at the Legendary Beast with astonishment. This was now the second one he had ever seen. The Son had become more familiar with them since the Old Wizard had told him, "The Tales of the Legendary Beast are from the time before I had ever met them. These Tales were from when these five Legendary Beasts roamed the universe freely until an unknown evil joined one of the previous Council of Swordmasters. After the tyrant from years ago, took control of Draefast, the Legendary Beasts were forced into hiding. They knew that it was not the time for them to interfere with how Palaleon was being shaped. A particular Legendary Beast stayed on Draefast but instead of taking its original form the Legendary Beast decided to take the form of a human. He knew that one day they will be needed, and that is when they will return. I believe that each of the Legendary Beasts have human forms but it is very rare for someone who knows of their existence to recognize them."

The Son replied, "There was a threat before Hoshek? Wow. At least now we have the Legendary Beasts on our side."

The Old Wizard then said, "Hopefully Hoshek will be the last threat. The Legendary Beasts seem to be on our side, but they will not get involved in any conflict since the tide of the universe will sway in its necessary way for any given time period."

"If they are so powerful, why don't they help us?" The Son questioned the Old Wizard.

"They do not interfere in human altercations. They know that balance will be achieved. They are spectators of our lives, and do not get involved unless it's an absolute necessity. The risk of their direct involvement could shift the balance of Palaleon. Shifting balance defeats the purpose of the unity and equality that we strive for, so we would become seen as the problem instead of the solution. Hoshek's rise in power is our problem since it proves how weak- minded people had become, and now it is time for us to rise up against him." The Old Wizard replied.

The Son then said, "That is very wise. I could never think like that, thank you for this wisdom. I will not fail you, or the people of Palaleon."

The White Hyrax, recognizing The Son's aptitude for heroes, transformed into a bigger version of itself. The Son then jumped on its back and the White Hyrax raced towards the village. As The Son was on the White Hyrax's back, the Legendary Beast got the same sensation that it had when it was around Malikaya. *He seems to have similar traits and qualities to the one I looked after previously*, the White Hyrax thought to itself. The Son then dismounted the White Hyrax and whispered to it, "Go back to the Old Wizard, he might need your help more than I do." He entered the village only to see grunts shooting purple flaming arrows and stealing money.

This village was called Zorgadon. The Son took a piece of

parchment out of his pocket, so he could begin making a map of his adventures. This map includes places he had been, along with areas yet discovered that he yearned to go to. He added Zorgadon to it.

The Son pulled his sword out of its sheath and swung it around himself making a hurricane shape. He slashed each grunt, and watched their black blood splash to the ground. The people of Zorgadon started to get out of hiding. This grunt battalion leader who was assigned by The Dark Warrior, came out of a house, and grabbed an arrow off the ground and shot it at The Son. It hit him in his left shoulder blade. Without hesitation, The Son ran up to the leader of these grunts. With one fluid motion from his sword the grunt was sliced into two pieces. He thought that by killing this grunt he was ready to face the Dark Wizard, since this grunt was in charge of the battalion he just defeated. This grunt battalion leader was caught by surprise that is why he was taken down so easily. He was not aware that the grunt in charge of this operation was not skilled in sword fighting. The Dark Warrior sent him out since he believed that this village would turn over like flies. The Son believed that he had protected this village and made everyone safe since he defeated the immediate foe. He did not realize that Hoshek could feel every ounce of Souldarkness emitting from the planet. He now had a lock on The Son and the village.

The Old Wizard was watching The Son altercation from afar and was disappointed. The Son handled his injury poorly by unleashing his inner Souldarkness Attribute even for a split second the Old Wizard knew that now the two of them were now not hidden from Hoshek. "He should not be using his anger to fuel his attacks, for that shows the pull of the Souldarkness

Attribute in him." The Old Wizard looked at the White Hyrax as he spoke, and watched it disappear.

The Son, now angry at himself, ran back towards the village entry to notice that the White Hyrax had left the Old Wizard's side. The Son bolted out of Zorgadon and into the woods from which he came, leaving a trail of blood behind him.

The people of Zorgadon were thrilled that the grunts would not harm them anymore. However, they did have to rebuild most of the village that later was named New Zorgadon. The "New" in their name symbolized the people wanting a change and fighting for it. The Son's entry had whisked away the Shroud corrupting their minds even if it was for a brief moment they ingrained into their heads a new way of life. The people built a statue of the White Hyrax, which symbolized the Legendary Beast that brought a mysterious sword wielder to their village to free them from the grunts. However, the villagers did not realize that a few days after this affair more grunts returned to destroy any hope they had. Once the grunts arrived they displayed their might by publicly executing a few villagers who tried to fight them upon being Soultaxed. The people who watched knew they did not stand a chance against them the Shroud re-corrupted their minds. The grunts then further taxed the villagers in the name of Hoshek.

Even though Hoshek was able to make an example of New Zorgadon, word of this sword wielder traveled throughout Draefast. The Son and the Old Wizard headed towards the Inbetween. On their journey, the Old Wizard told The Son more about his fight with Hoshek. "I was not strong enough to liberate the people of this world, so I went into hiding. Now I fear that since your venture to Zorgadon, Hoshek is more likely to be aware of your existence. He will now know we are coming for him. We must act swiftly if my plans are to work and we are able to defeat him."

With his head hung in shame, The Son replied, "I am sorry that I lost control. I couldn't help myself it was as if my own inner darkness took control of my body. I guess I am not ready to be the person you want me to be."

The Old Wizard replied, "It is not about who I want you to be, It is about what I know you are capable of and the person I know you will become."

The Son now felt more motivated to do his best in his training to lead the Council of Swordmasters, so that he wouldn't fail the Old Wizard, and so he would finally find out more about himself. The Son craved a family including a father figure who loved him, and that is what the Old Wizard was to him. He was still curious about his past, and was eager to learn where he came from. The Old Wizard could sense this, so he planned to tell him after they defeated Hoshek. *Hoshek and The Son were actually very similar in that they both lost a father figure*, The Old Wizard thought. The Old Wizard knew this but neglected it since he believed that The Son was more pure of soul than the Dark Wizard Hoshek. He knew that by acting as a mentor and as a caring adult figure in The Son's life, he would not turn out to be someone as corrupted and twisted as Hoshek. The Old Wizard was not perfect by any means but he was always there for The Son.

"I thought you should know something. The planet we are on is called Draefast. It is special to you since this is where you were born," the Old Wizard told The Son. On top of having the vision about The Son, the Old Wizard was able to know of those around him who were connected to Soulmagic. He did this by using another Soullight ability he created on his long adventure. Since the hut where The Son was born was not too far away from the castle where the Old Wizard fought Hoshek, he felt the Soulmagic presence on the planet.

The Son was bewildered. "Thank you for telling me. Did you know my parents or anything else that will help me find out about my past?"

The Old Wizard looked at The Son, and then looked down and said "No, I'm sorry." As The Son was about to ask for a more detailed answer, but realized through the tone of voice that the Old Wizard used, he would not elaborate. The Old Wizard's mission was to rid Palaleon of Hoshek's darkness, but more importantly, he wanted to protect everyone including The Son from a future where there was only total darkness. He knew that by training The Son he would become equal to Hoshek if not stronger in the Attributes and in sword dueling. The Old Wizard was also preparing himself by training The Son, since he knew that, if forced, he would lay down his life to ensure that the new Council of Swordmasters had the chance to create a more vibrant future filled with peace, unity, and equality. The Old Wizard knew that Hoshek had been scheming for years. This made him realize he needed to expedite his mission to make a new Council. He wished he had more time to train The Son but that was not the case. He had to select the new Councilmembers before The Son was ready. The Old Wizard thought to himself, *Hopefully when the time comes, the boy will be ready to lead the Council and fight the Dark Wizard. I will continue to train him as much as I can. He is progressing quite quickly. His connection to his soul is far greater than I expected.*

While The Son furthered his training, a new foe was born on the southern side of Draefast. A purple glow emitted from the top of Hoshek's castle as a being arose from the same Counterrock table that the grunts were created on decades prior. It took Hoshek a while to perfect his creation, but he had finally succeeded. For years, the burned body of The Father laid on the table barely clinging to life. Hoshek had scared the body even more so than the burns since he needed to cut into The Father's soul. He read a Tale as a child that a Dranstor can be created by transferring one's Souldarkness to someone else, thus reshaping the recipient's soul, but no one had ever successfully created one.

The Tale was written by a man during the original Council of Swordmasters time period who was rumored to be a simple Souldarkness Attribute fanatic. He was a man experimenting with a magic far greater than he could ever fathom. One day the man was in a cave with a friend on Aestercrat when they heard something rustling outside. Both of them went to check it out and noticed a beast flying above their heads. As the beast flapped its wings, a rock became loose from the mountain side and was heading towards the two men. The beast then flew next to the boulder and touched it with its claw. The boulder was pulverized into bits of sand. The men were astounded and wanted to learn how to perform magic like this. The beast then flew back to the two men and raised its wing and flapped, spreading its Souldarkness Attribute into them, thinking that it would turn this moment into a nightmare for the two men. It did not, they still fully believed everything they saw as if it happened while they were awake. Which it did. The two men went back into the cave. They spent days experimenting with the abilities that the Souldarkness Attribute granted them. They believed they were chosen by this higher being to become its future rival. Both of them yearned for more power than what they were offered. They wanted to become unstoppable. While his friend was sleeping the man picked up a dagger, he imbued with Souldarkness and sliced into his friend's chest trying to reach for the source of his power. He then inhaled his friend's entire soul. This act did not give him the power he sought, but instead, destroyed him as a human. One body cannot store a dead and living soul. The dead soul would accelerate the decaying process of the living one. His greed and lust for something greater ended up severing his connection to his Souldarkness Attribute reverting him back to a simple nobody. He then became referred to as the fanatic in the mountain since every time he entered the village beneath the cave, he would wander around muttering about Souldarkness. The original Council then learned of this man, but as they went to investigate, it was too late. His dead body laid next to the bones of his friend. On the ground nearby was a Tale written in the man's blood. The heading read "Dranstor creation". This is the Tale that Hoshek used to research Dranstor's.

As Hoshek read the Tale he learned everything the man did from experimenting with the Souldarkness Attribute up to consuming his friend's soul and how he did that believing it would turn him into something greater.

Hoshek began pondering on his next steps as he thought to himself, *I am grateful that my Purple Lightning and Purple Fire did not kill this man since then I would be experimenting on a dead body and that did not work years ago so I doubt it would work now.* Then Nahvel's voice whispered to him from inside his head. "When I was young, I also wanted to create a being that rivaled the Legendary Beasts in soul strength. Unlike you, I never found the Tale with the recipe on how to do so. I had only heard about it when my mentor told me that the Legendary Beasts had no rival. I asked a simple question, 'How is that possible?' And he replied in a mysterious manner, 'It is inhumane to experiment with soulless beings.' After that day I never thought about Dranstors again as they were an impossible concept. I never realized that he had actually told me the key to how to create it." Now with Nahvel's newfound guidance, Hoshek found a way to create the one to rival any Legendary Beast. All he had to do was keep The Father's body alive while fusing him with a new soul. Before Hoshek acted on this he went to the top of his castle where he pointed his sword at the Shroud above his head. The Shroud then released a sphere of tangible Souldarkness that rested on Hoshek's sword. Hoshek ran back to where The Father's body lay. Standing over The Father's body, Hoshek raised his sword. It glowed midnight purple as he slashed The Father across the chest leaving a scar far greater than one from the Purple Fire. Hoshek cut through The Father's soul and quickly removed half in order to replace it with the tangible Souldarkness granted to him by the Shroud. The Father's body started to morph. His soul became twisted, physically turning him into a new being. He was neither soulless, nor was he human.

The Dark Warrior was born. He was The Father no more. In his place stood a creature filled with rage. He was now able to use the Souldarkness Attribute and master all of its abilities. Hoshek was not the only one burdened by this darkness anymore. The Dark Warrior was dressed in all black. On top of the left side of his head was a single dark pointed horn that grew from the abundance of the Souldarkness Attribute flowing through his body. He was wearing a dark purple cloak. The scars along his face, chest, and arms were purple as if purple lightning coursed through his veins. He was now a Dranstor, with no sense of any self.

"Here is a sword for you," Hoshek said as he handed over the dark blade. Hoshek had spent years manipulating the black shard into a sword befitting the Dark Warrior. It was not the same one The Father stole years ago; this new sword had a Souldarkness aura around it. It would be the primary weapon in assisting in the atrocities that the being that wielded it will create. "I will train you how to use it, but all you must do is really focus on your lust for destruction and thirst for blood. The man you once were is no more. I am the only family you have. I am your master. Now pick up your sword and attack me."

The Dark Warrior did as the voice commanded. He jumped up and swung his sword down, but Hoshek was able to counter his attack with ease. "Learn to fight using more power in each swing and your opponents will not stand a chance."

The Dark Warrior nodded and ran at his master swinging his sword in sweeping motions, from the upper left down to the lower right, and back up the right side and down to the lower left, crisscrossing in front of his body. Hoshek was reading all of his moves. It was as if he saw them before the Dark Warrior made them. *Block left, then block right* Hoshek thought to himself. Hoshek then quickly raised his leg and kicked the Dark Warrior in the chest. His body could not withstand the power in the kick; it almost broke him. The Dark Warrior was fueled with rage, and because of that he mustered his Souldarkness. His sword glowed purple, and he ran back at Hoshek this time with the intent to kill. He was like a rabid beast attacking at every opportunity.

"Much better. But you still lack focus," Hoshek taunted. As Hoshek made this remark the Dark Warrior put all of his Souldarkness into one downward strike clashing with his master's sword throwing him on the staircase leading to his throne. "Good. That is all the training you shall require. By now you must have acquainted yourself with your new, more powerful body. Your appearance will strike fear in your foes, stunning them, making your targets easier to obtain or kill. Just do not forget who you serve." Hoshek arose and The Dark Warrior knelt. "Go to Droth, demonstrate your soul energy to this planet. Make your grand display. Do not disappoint me. You are my second in command, the leader of my grunt army. Now go, and bring grunts with you as well." As Hoshek walked back to his throne he thought to himself, *I put up a good fight there but I feel out of breath. My body seem to old and weak to fight. I will leave all of my battles to the Dark Warrior.* He then walked back down to teach the Dark Warrior one more lesson.

The Dark Warrior, with an angry look on his disheveled face, motioned for the grunts to follow him and leave the castle. As he turned his back, the Dark Warrior felt a sharp pain in his leg. He looked down and saw his master's sword sticking through it, Souldarkness poison dripping from the tip. "Never turn your back on anyone. You will die if you make that mistake again. The poison won't kill you. It will just hurt you enough so you never defy me and so you fully understand my true power. Overcome the poison and you will be the strongest in this universe. Maybe one day stronger than me. If you can't fight it, you will eventually die."

The Dark Warrior focused all of his Souldarkness to withstand the pain as if his leg did not have a sword sticking through it. He pulled the sword out and threw it back at his master, landing right next to Hoshek's arm. He continued to walk out covering his body in a dark purple shawl. He felt the poison moving through his body, but stayed enraged to keep it in his lower left quadrant. He could not let the Souldarkness poison affect him, he proceeded to act as if it was not there. The grunts looked at him with fear in their eyes, and they were made to not fear anything. Underneath the Shroud they marched out of the city and headed towards Droth. While entering one of the dark forests surrounding the city, the silhouette of what was formerly a man slowly traversed through the dark forest and the trees around him started to decay. He heard a noise coming from the distance and turned his head. His left eye was glistening purple while his right remained black. Across his back rested a sword, dark as the night, thirsting for a bloody feast.

It took a few days, but the Dark Warrior and his grunts had finally arrived at Droth. The screaming commenced. A villager noticed the Dranstor and said, "What is tha..." Before he could finish his sentence, the Dark Warrior threw his sword with enough force to create a hole in the villager's chest. A grunt went to retrieve it. As the grunt handed the Dark Warrior his sword, the Dark Warrior exhaled, focusing all of his Souldarkness Attribute into his sword. He hurled it. It spun slashing through villager's homes, leaving behind Purple Fire. Shrills and screams followed as the villagers would be burned to a crisp. The Dark Warrior motioned to his grunts to loot the homes, showing that he did not care if they burned as well. His sword landed perfectly in the middle of the village. He walked over his shawl flying back from the wind, picked it up and turned around. He motioned to his grunts to follow him back to his master's castle. As he was exiting the village Droth, Purple Fire danced furiously across the village. Bodies laid on the ground. The arm he used to create Souldarkness for his sword was heavily scarred. He learned how to use his Souldarkness Attribute from the fight with Hoshek, believing that if his master could imbue poison in a sword than if the Dark Warrior focused enough, he could inflict carnage upon an entire village with his own Souldarkness. He conjured one of the many skills of a Souldarkness Attribute wielder that being Purple Flames, and he did this with ease.

As the Dark Warrior returned to his master, Hoshek stood from his throne giving a gracious applause. He did not know at first if the Dark Warrior had it in him, but after feeling the Souldarkness Attribute emitting from the Dranstor's sword and arm he knew he had created the perfect being. Hoshek had seen the Dark Warrior's display of Purple Fire from the top of his castle and was very impressed that he had learned that skill on his own. The Dark Warrior was the first successful creation known as a Dranstor, capable of contending against a Legendary Beast in a battle of raw soul energy.

The Dark Warrior knelt before Hoshek. Hoshek opened his mouth and said, "You are my pet and that's all you will ever be. If you want to be a part of my rule over Palaleon and never suffer again, you will do as I say." Since the Dark Warrior did not have a pure soul inside his body, he lost the will and ability to speak. All he became was a mindless tool for his master's every whim. His mission was to destroy villages that did not obey his master. He was also tasked with training Hoshek's army, so that Hoshek could spend his time the way he saw fit and not have to worry about his underlings. His final job was to hunt down and kill anyone who displayed Soulmagic Attribute abilities such as this famed sword wielder. Like stories of the sword wielder that had spread all around Draefast, there were also stories of the slave of Hoshek, otherwise known as the Dark Warrior. The stories always ended in bloodshed and darkness.

The Dark Warrior was born from the Purple Flame. Before that it was nothing, it remembers nothing, and has no one in its life but its master, Hoshek. The Dark Warrior uses anger and fear from others to fuel his own Souldarkness Attribute. Every time he destroys a village, he steals souls from villagers. By doing this, the Dark Warrior's Souldarkness Attribute becomes stronger and so does his ability to control it, weakening the poison that still latched onto his body. As he felt his abilities increasing, he began swinging his sword uncontrollably even going on to kill a few grunts leaving behind bodies cut in half scorched with Purple Flames.

Across the planet in the northern region, Ohr was standing up with one hand tapping on The Son's sword which he was borrowing. He was preparing to relax and had struck the sword into the ground to do so. The one who was unknown to Hoshek and who had escaped his grasp, was laying on the grass breathing in and out. They had no idea what was coming for them. The Son closed his eyelids shut and a vivid image of the Dark Warrior appeared, killing villagers, and destroying villages. "Mentor, I..." The Son said as he shot up from the grass.

"So, he finally was able to do it. Hmm," the Old Wizard replied.

"Do what? So, you saw the vision too?" The Son asked.

"I saw no vision. I just heard the screams of villagers throughout the planet and the laughter of the Dark Wizard. Hoshek has finally created a being to rival that of the Legendary Beasts. I must train you more now more than ever," the Old Wizard anxiously stated.

"But how were you able to hear the screams and visualize the villages. I mean I saw a figure and Purple Fire behind it, but I heard nothing," The Son replied with a puzzled look on his face.

"It just so happened that I was striking your sword into the ground when these monstrous acts occurred. The slaughter of the villagers sent tremors into the ground which I was able to sense through the blade of the sword. As their shrills grew louder, another presence appeared to me. It was that of Hoshek and his contented grimace. Even though my connection to Soulmagic has diminished, I felt it, nonetheless. It is not a difficult trick here, try it."

"It's almost like a tracking ability. Cool. Let me try." The Son then got up and clasped the hilt of his sword. Upon taking it out of the ground and pushing it back in, he heard the screams and visualized the monster causing them even more so. He let go. "I must become strong enough in the Attributes and Soulmagic to prevent that being from reaching other planets or even other villages here. My true training begins now." The Son nodded towards the Old Wizard.

There is a clear connection between The Son and this villainous monster. The Son was able to see him with his eyes closed before touching the sword. I must ensure that this connection is only visual. Maybe we can use it to our advantage, the Old Wizard thought.

Chapter IX

The Mother and
The Daughter

During the time that the Old Wizard was training The Son, The Mother and The Daughter were on their own adventure. They had found a flight manual on the ship and through reading and studying it, learned how to fly. They were living in space on the Old Wizard's ship. After time had passed, they began their travels to each of the other planets. These would be the same planets that the Old Wizard and The Son would visit in due time.

They flew to the planets where each original swords that formed the Planetary Sword was forged. The swords that made up the Planetary Sword had been passed down by the original Council all the way down to Gathran's Council and would become the Attribute Swords that Hoshek took after his massacre.

The Mother and The Daughter traveled to the three planets - Vastrilio, Aestercrat, and Crateolios - before they eventually landed the ship for the last time back on their homeworld Draefast. The Old Wizard had erased their memories of The Father and The Son, along with everything that happened the day of the Purple Lightning. The Mother and The Daughter had the memory of one another, but it was altered so that they remembered living on Draefast in a hut alone in the dark forest. Through their ventures throughout Palaleon, they learned that there were humanoids similar to those residing on Draefast, and that they spoke the same dialect as most people on each planet. At first their goal was to never be seen by grunts or any opposing force, and to live out the rest of their lives peacefully traveling among these new worlds, never staying on one for too long.

One day while further exploring the ship, The Daughter found a metallic object with a green button in the middle. She was intrigued by this object so she pressed the button. A voice emanated from the object.

"*Hoshek tyrant the defeat me helping to key* the are they know will you worthy deem you someone find you if but are Soulmagic or Attributes what know not might you sword a with along Soulmagic though abilities attribute possessed they planets those to connected were and planets different three on living were people three these Swordmasters of Council the of rest the finding help your need I message this hearing are you if Swordmasters of Council original the of descendant a am I Ohr is name my"

The Daughter replayed the message while writing the words on a piece of parchment she found in one of the ship's drawers. The message seemed cryptic. *Is there a way to rearrange the words,* she thought. *Maybe the words are out of order and are meant to be flipped. Ok let me try something.* She rearranged the words by drawing little arrows to the words that made sense in a sentence format and added punctuation. She read the new message out loud.

"My name is Ohr. I am a descendant of the original Council of Swordmasters. If you are hearing this message, I need your help finding the rest of the Council of Swordmasters. These three people are living on three different planets, and are connected to those planets in a special way. They possess Attribute abilities through Soulmagic, along with a sword. You might not know what Attributes or Soulmagic are, but if you find someone you deem worthy, you will know. They are the key to helping me defeat the tyrant Hoshek."

The Daughter ran over to The Mother who was steering the ship into Crateolios' gelid atmosphere. "Mother, I found this device, and it had a message from a man. I think it was the man who owned this ship." The Daughter read the message she wrote on the parchment to The Mother, while showing her the communication device. The Mother wanted nothing to do with this man's goal, so she told The Daughter, "Put that device back where you found it."

The Daughter replied, "But I'm bored of just living on this ship, and this man seems to really need our help."

"Please just do as I ask," The Mother stated.

"Ok," The Daughter replied.

As they arrived at Crateolios, their ship's engines started to freeze upon entering the atmosphere. "Mom, something's wrong with the ship. The engine's flame keeps flickering. I think we are about to have a rough landing." The Daughter peeked out of the side of the ship and noticed an ice patch they could land on but it was surrounded by rough water. "Try landing over there," The Daughter said as she pointed towards the ice.

"I will do my best, but the engine is freezing so I am getting a lot of drag on these controls," The Mother replied as she tried to forcefully maneuver the ship towards where The Daughter had pointed. The Mother was using all of her might to fight the engine that was freezing over. The steering mechanism was turned all the way to the left as they braced for their landing. The glass on The Daughter's window cracked, then shattered into tiny pieces.

"Ahh" The Daughter was holding on for dear life. She had forgotten to strap in after she was up pointing at the landing area they were going towards. The Mother turned her head to notice The Daughter being sucked out of the window by the harsh freezing winds of Crateolios.

"No!" The Mother shouted. She then pushed the steering mechanism down and to the left to try to have The Daughter grab onto the side of the ship but The Daughter was falling faster than the ship. The Daughter plummeted into the harsh waters, as The Mother landed the ship in the water and dove in after her daughter. She spotted her limp body sinking. The Mother tried to swim to her daughter but was fighting the currents, and the freezing cold water temperatures. All of a sudden, a teenage boy dove into the water from the ice floe. He seemed to be unscathed by the freezing cold. He swam to The Daughter first and brought her atop their ship. Then he dove back into the water and got The Mother. As they were warming back up in the control room using heavy blankets they found in the main cabin, they looked at the teenager.

"Thank you so much for saving my daughter." The Mother said.

"It was no problem. I saw that the two of you were in danger and my first instinct was to help out in any way I could. I have to warn you though; raiders have entered our planet and are tearing our villages to shreds. They might have noticed you and your ship, so I would get out of here as soon as possible," the teenager replied.

After he spoke, The Mother and The Daughter looked at one another, as they were unsure as to whether or not he was going to be able to understand and speak in the same dialect as them, but he did. The Mother thought to herself, *I guess all humans on all planets understand basic dialect.*

Looking at the teenager, The Daughter then spoke, "Thank you for the insight. We were sent away from our homeworld and told to travel to other planets. We did not mean to cause such a commotion here or danger you."

"I'm surprised you both are able to speak and move around after dealing with our rough waters. I could tell you were not from around here, and the ship only furthers my suspicion, but I did not know about other planets up in the sky. By the way, you can call me Im."

"Nice to meet you, Im." The Mother and The Daughter said in unison.

"Please be careful and do not just help any random strangers in the future. I think it best if we start to leave since we do not want to make ourselves known to these raiders." The Mother said.

"I enjoy helping people. I believe it is my calling. Let me help you one more time." As Im said this, he left the control room of the ship and dove back into the water. He had a spear made of ice tied to his back.

"OOOOO". A noise came from the depths of the water and all of a sudden, The Daughter looked out of the window to see Im riding a White Manta Ray that created a wave big enough to knock the ship in the air. As the ship gained altitude, The Mother pressed the ignition button. The engine was still frozen.

"We need to heat up the engine," The Mother said.

"I have an idea," The Daughter replied. The Daughter, carefully this time, got out of her seat and made her way to the back of the ship which was not enclosed by metal like the front. She picked up a dry wooden stick that was whittled from a fallen tree branch on Draefast and using the thin air outside rubbed it along the metal railing on the outside of the ship and it sparked. A flame consumed the stick as The Daughter threw it towards the engine thus defrosting it. The Mother then punched the engine button again and it lit. They were able to fight the wind of the atmosphere and make it back into space. Water from the atmosphere spread across where the side window in the bridge used to be and froze over due to the intense cold creating a new thicker window. It became so cold and sturdy that not even the heat from traveling at such speeds, or engine residue could melt it. As The Daughter turned around before breaching the atmosphere, she saw Im smiling at them and she smiled back.

The Daughter then returned to the front of the ship and said to her mother, "Im could be someone this Ohr guy is looking for. He was brave and resourceful. And he helped out complete strangers showing his kindness and care towards others."

The Mother replied, "Maybe. I am grateful to Im for saving

you but I do not ever want to go to the ice-heap of a planet again. Our journey is our own and should not be dictated by a man's voice on a communicator."

They traveled through space for what seemed to them to be a couple days. Through the bridge window, The Mother and The Daughter saw a planet emitting a red glow as if the planet were on fire. The Daughter looked at The Mother and said. "Let's get our supplies from this planet."

When the two of them arrived in Vastrilio they wanted to acquaint themselves with the planet and its people.

The Mother said to The Daughter. "Do not pull any of that nonsense about finding these so called Councilmembers here. I mean it!"

"But mom, they could be the ones to help us fight the tyrant back on our homeworld."

The Mother was tired of sitting in her chair on the bridge so she got up and headed towards their sleeping quarters. While packing a bag with supplies for their journey, she reached to grab a canteen from a shelf high above her bed. As she pulled it down, a rolled-up piece of parchment fell. She unraveled the parchment and realized that it was a map of each of the planets in Palaleon. Around the circumference of the planets were each of their names. The Mother brought the bag along with the map to the bridge and showed it to The Daughter.

"The planet we're about to land on is called Vastrilio." The Mother said as they made their descent from space. They entered the atmosphere of the glowing yet charred planet. The planet had cities with skyscrapers reaching towards the clouds. The clouds were filled with heavy pollution that was generated from the factories outsides the various cities. The planet was once green but that was around the time of the first Soulfire Attribute Councilmember.

"This looks like a place rich in the supplies we need, and parts to repair the ship. Let's land outside the city, speak to locals, and get supplies," The Daughter said.

As she was looking out the window of the ship staring at the well-dressed people entering the city, The Mother replied, "That sounds like a good plan."

The two covered themselves in robes then exited the ship. Upon entering the city, they noticed that all eyes were upon them. The Daughter even saw someone point at them and mouth to their partner. "Those two over there do not look like they belong here."

The Daughter turned to The Mother who said, "Don't worry about them, we will just get the supplies we need and go."

The Daughter replied, "Can't we at least search villages nearby for someone worthy of Ohr's attention?"

The Mother continued to look at her daughter as they entered a metal shop. "Stop thinking of what that man on the communicator wants and start thinking about what we need. Did you bring the currency from the ship?"

The Daughter took her hand out of her shall and showed The Mother five pieces of Zagrad. They walked over to the metal-welder, who was more refined than an average blacksmith. He looked up and said. "We do not sell what you are looking for here. Try the purple smoke lounge in the village over."

Not wanting to be dismissed so quickly, The Mother replied, "We are actually looking for an engine part. Can you help us?"

The welder replied. "Sorry I pegged you for two junkies

looking for spare parts to trade for currency. What engine part are you looking for?"

The Daughter looked up at him and said, "We are looking for a T75c metal ring to fit around our engine to ensure it does not blow out from freeze damage."

The welder looked at her and said, "You have a T series ship that's an oldie. I can make the part but it will cost you 100 Forgen."

"We have twenty five Zagrad," The Daughter replied.

The welder looked down at The Daughter's palm. "I do not know what kind of currency that is and I cannot accept it. Find your business elsewhere."

The Mother and The Daughter exited his forge, and hustled back towards their ship. "I do not think we can buy anything here, The Mother said, "Let's head to another planet and see if they accept our currency."

"Ok that's fine. These people keep giving us weird looks as if we are crazy. I do not like it here. Let's leave."

They made it to their ship but saw two men at the front putting tickets on it. They overheard one say to another. "This is an illegal ship parked in an illegal bay. We will have to tell the Official about this and the grunts will raid it."

The other man replied, "Let's go contact the Official now. There is no way this ship will be taking off with the exterior damaged the way it is." The two men walked away, and The Mother and The Daughter saw a grunt patrol walking to them.

"Now's our only chance. Run!" The Mother said to The Daughter. They ran to the ship. The grunts turned around, saw them, and started chasing them while swinging their swords in the air. One grunt stayed back and grabbed an arrow from his back and was getting ready to fire. The Mother and The Daughter made it onboard. "Punch the engine button now, I will steer us out of here." The Mother said. Without hesitation The Daughter did what she was asked and they took off. The ship was rattling upon ascent but they made it out of the planet's atmosphere in one piece. "Time to go to Aestercrat to see if they have what we need," The Mother said, spinning her chair around looking at her daughter.

On Aestercrat, they landed their ship in between two large boulders so it would not be seen.

"Mom, I see a village over towards the right. Let's go there to get food, other necessities and meet people."

Taking in the events that both of them had been dealing with over the past couple of days, The Mother decided to be more cheery and replied, "Ok, I think that would be a lovely idea, and maybe we can find parts for our ship in the village. The ship still flies but it does not seem like it will for long."

Upon entering the village, they found two long branches on the ground. Picking them up, The Daughter announced, "Look at all these people."

"Yes, but look at their facial expressions. They look terrified of something." The Mother and Daughter were holding the branches, as they walked around the village looking at each shop.

"Mom can we get this?"

"What is it?"

"Well, it looks like leaves, but as we were walking around, I saw people eating them, so I wanted to try some."

"Ok we will use a little bit of our money."

The Mother picked up some of the leafy food and walked over to the counter where the store clerk stood.

"How much for all of this?" Asked The Mother.

"12 Counters." The Mother looked at The Daughter. They had forgotten that they do not have the same currency as the people on this planet.

"Do you accept Zagrad?"

"Hey lady, I don't know who you are but if you do not have the currency, I am asking for, then you can't buy my Leafy Greens," the clerk said curtly.

The Mother was about to put down the food when another woman walked into the shop. She saw that The Mother and The Daughter looked starved and offered to pay for their food. "Hey can't you see how hungry they look? They offered you a different currency, which no one has seen before. Doesn't that fascinate you? Clearly they are not from around here."

The Mother looked at the women and mouthed "thank you" as they left the shop. The woman then bought her food, and as she exited the shop, she noticed the two figures again and ran up to them.

"So where are you from?" The woman asked.

"We are from another world," The Mother replied.

"Another world? There are other worlds besides this one?" The woman said astonished by The Mother's answer.

The Daughter then chimed in, "Yes, there are a total of four planets in our universe that my daughter and I have been fortunate to explore. Would you happen to know if there was anyone in your village skilled in Soulmagic?"

"Sorry, I don't know what Soulmagic is," the woman said.

The Daughter replied, "That's ok. Thanks anyways."

The Mother then asked, "Do you know if there is a place where we can find fresh water?"

"I can tell you about it, but first it looks like you two need new clothes. And why are you carrying those branches? Follow me to my house and I will explain to you how to get to the water, and give you some new clothes."

The Daughter seemed thrilled and asked The Mother if they could go. The Mother replied, "Sure. She seems trustworthy and friendly." As they entered the woman's home, they finished the food she had bought them.

"This was so good!" exclaimed The Daughter.

"I am glad you enjoyed it. Leafy Greens are a specialty of my village. We try not to eat meat here so we focus on the other foods we can have."

The woman went into another room, grabbed a few articles of clothing, and handed them to The Mother.

"I do not need these anymore, and it looks like you could wear them, so here you go," the woman stated.

"Again, thank you so much," The Mother said.

The Mother was thrilled that they could change out of the clothes they had on Draefast. As The Mother and The Daughter were sitting around the woman's table, she came back with a little map of the village and its outskirts. "So here is where we are, and here is where the well is. You should watch out for these evil looking things since a man arrived here years ago, claiming to help our world, but in turn took it over."

"That sounds like the problem in our homeworld. We will handle it, don't worry," The Mother replied.

The Mother and The Daughter then got up and walked to the door of the woman's home. "Hopefully we will see you again," the woman said. Then The Mother and The Daughter smiled at her and closed the door behind them. They walked back out of the village and towards their ship. The moon had risen over Aestercrat, so The Mother and The Daughter were preparing to go to bed once they got on the ship.

"Goodnight." The Mother said to her daughter as she laid a blanket over her.

"Goodnight mom," replied The Daughter.

The next morning, The Mother was going through the ship's inventory when her foot tapped the communicator and the Old Wizard's voice came on. "There are two forms for training with weaponry. Attack and defense. If you want to defend yourself with a staff or sword, the movements go like this. First you step forward then you strike. When defending, always step backwards and use your opponent's forward momentum against them. If you are bigger than your foe, then engage them upfront, parrying each strike. Remember to breathe. A slow and deep inhalation followed by a quick exhalation will help to center you so you can properly attack and defend. This is all I can say for now. Be careful against the grunts. Hopefully I can come back one day and train the rest of the villagers." The message ended.

"Clearly that message was not for me, but he makes a good point that if we want to be able to defend ourselves, we should follow his steps." She then found a little knife in a drawer on the ship and started to carve her branch into a staff. She then gave the knife to The Daughter so she could do the same. "I will train you everything I know." The Mother said to The Daughter. She was going to use the Old Wizard's lectures to train her. They needed these staffs if they were going to get to the water source without running into too much grunt trouble. They had run out of water they had gotten from Crateolios yesterday morning.

While studying the map given to them by the woman, The Mother and The Daughter located a raised plateau. They decided to set out for this area as it might prove to be the perfect place to train. They sparred with one another for many hours, learning how to wield their new weapons. They practiced attack stances and thrusts, and strikes, along with defense stances, blocks, and parries. "Remember the key is to breathe," The Mother said to The Daughter.

The Daughter nodded in agreement, "I understand."

On their way back from a long day of training, and after they collected water in buckets, they noticed grunts lingering around their ship. The Mother and The Daughter looked at one another and simultaneously agreed, "We got this." They drank some water then put the bucket down and ran towards the grunts surprising them, while swinging their staffs around their bodies to make it harder for one of the grunts to land a blow with their sword. One of the grunts turned away from the fight and chanted, in a tongue only other grunts understood. More grunts appeared out of the village and started running toward The Mother and The Daughter's ship. Once they saw that there were more and more grunts on Aestercrat similar to the ones they heard about on the other planets they got scared and decided to head on their ship instead of continuing to fight. They knew they did not stand a chance against this deluge of grunts so getting airborne was their best and only option.

The Mother looked at The Daughter who had taken the helm of the ship and said, "I think that if we are to fight off grunts now it is best if we do it on a terrain we know. I say we head back home."

"I agree mom," answered The Daughter.

"It seems like on these other worlds most people never saw outsiders until the grunts, so maybe they did not believe there was life beyond their own worlds until meeting us." The Mother said.

"I did not that these grunts truly were everywhere. That means the tyrant's truly has absolute control over the universe."

"Yes darling, it is quite unsettling the growth of the tyrants command."

"It is time for us to return home, right?" The Daughter looked at The Mother with concern.

"I believe that we are safer back on our homeworld, so yes that is where we shall stay. As much as I enjoyed our ventures, not knowing the terrain made it difficult to stay on each planet for very long."

"I agree," The Daughter said as she spotted her homeworld through the ship's window. As the ship entered Draefast's atmosphere, The Mother steered it towards a dock on the outskirts of Hoshek City.

While they were docking their ship in a place they thought would not be noticeable to the grunts, The Mother and the Daughter were spotted by a platoon of Hoshek's grunts. These grunts vastly outnumbered the two. As The Mother and The Daughter put up a fight, their trained techniques had effects on some of the grunts. They had put up a good fight but due to the numbers were beaten down destroying their will to fight.

"Unhand me!" The Daughter exclaimed as two grunts grabbed her arms making her unable to fight.

"Get away from her!" The Mother shouted. But the grunts ignored her and forcefully walked with them to their master. The grunts then brought The Mother and The Daughter to the Dark Warrior. He gazed upon them and without a word grabbed them and started walking to his master's castle. Since the Old Wizard had erased their memories of The Father, they did not recognize him. Even so, it was more difficult to notice a familiarity since his body had undergone a transfiguration when he turned into a Dranstor. They tried to fight their way out of the Dark Warrior's grasp, and used the moves they had taught themselves on Aestercrat, but nothing worked. He was unfazed, displaying how powerful he truly was. For a brief moment, The Daughter felt the embrace of a father, something that she had no recollection of ever feeling. Yet just as fleeting as this sensation was, it suddenly vanished. What was left was the shell of what once looked to be a man and a cold dark feeling.

The Mother looked at the Dark Warrior, puzzlingly. *Do I know him from somewhere? This is odd. I feel like I do, but I can't remember.* The Mother thought. Her memory was on the tip of her tongue but just as the night drew closer her memory flew farther away from her grasp.

The Mother then stepped on the Dark Warrior's boot, and as he looked down without thinking he loosened his grip in his right hand. The Mother took this brief moment to escape the Dark Warrior's clutches, but that same result was not bestowed upon The Daughter. The Dark Warriors left hand still firmly gripped The Daughter's arm so she could not escape. The Mother ran past the grunts and was finally able to slow down to catch her breath. *What have I done?* The

Mother came to terms that she had just left her daughter to certain peril. In that moment, fragments of her memory came back to her. She visualized a baby boy being held in her arms, but then shivers went down her spine as she pictured her hut being burned down and only her and The Daughter survived. The Mother recalled the message from the Old Wizard, and vowed to find these people - not for the Old Wizard's sake, but for The Daughter's. Due to her memory slowly coming back The Mother did not fully trust the Old Wizard but envied how much The Daughter looked up to someone they had forgotten that they met. The Mother was now angry. She believed the Old Wizard was not everything he was meant to be. Instead of succumbing to her anger and giving up, The Mother felt it was necessary to preserve in order to reunite with The Daughter someday.

These people could help the Old Wizard save my daughter, if it's not already too late for her, The Mother thought. Since she had already been to the planets to scout them out this task would be even easier now. Since she was able to evade Hoshek's grasp, she knew that she was well versed in being stealthy. The Mother made a promise to herself that once she completely found all of the people the Old Wizard asked her to, she would then look for her daughter. For now, she was all alone.

The Mother stayed in the main city on Draefast, and stole a new set of clothes. She knew grunts would be looking for her, so she had to find a way off Draefast quickly. As she looked around she noticed a man in white cloths, walking, playing the lute, and singing:

I come out here daily
Dusk till dawn
To reiterate about our past
Now that it's gone
From times old that which I sing
The Council of Swordmasters will survive again
To reteach us the ways of peace
Unity we had until the Dark Wizard came to be
We had a time like this before
But I doubt you would remember
Since above us there is a Shroud
Corrupting your mind
No doubt
He isn't perfect
He isn't great
Your mind is already his
Wake up
You must wake up

Walking down a side street of the third tier of the city, she passed by a house with an extension connected to it. *Perhaps there is a ship that I can use to escape.* All The Mother had to do was find her way inside. She snuck around the house, finding an open window that she jumped up to open. She then crawled inside the house. She was scurrying past every corner to avoid being detected. She noticed swords hanging all around the house. *He must have become wealthy by making swords for Hoshek's grunts,* she thought as she looked around the room recognizing the designs for the swords. She had seen them before as she fought grunts on Aestercrat. She walked by the kitchen and noticed some fruit on the counter. The Mother hadn't tasted fruit in a long time. The kitchen was massive, and held so many different tools for cooking. The Mother noticed a photo of the man and what seemed to be his wife. She presumed that the wife made money and gained prestige as well throughout Hoshek City due to how the kitchen looked. *She must work for Hoshek.*

The Mother continued to eye the fruit on the counter. She then ran over, picked up a piece, and just as she was about to bite into it, she was spotted by the owner of the house. He began chasing her around the house. "You filthy worthless slime, get out of my house," he yelled. He started throwing every object he saw at her. She finally made it to the extension of the house which was a storage area. There she saw the ship. *I guess Hoshek gave this man access to fly to other worlds. This man must be very important to him.* It was made out of the nicest material The Mother had ever seen. It was evident that the man was not thinking clearly at the time since he left his key to his ship in the slot. She had guessed he had just gotten home from work. The Mother took a second to pray that this ship would be able to fly past Draefast's atmosphere, since Hoshek usually put a locking mechanism on ships so only order his direct order could they leave his planet. The Mother locked the doors so he could not get in. She then figured out a way to disarm the locking mechanism. Maybe in another life she was meant to be a mechanic instead of just a thief. She took off, right as the grunts had reached the man's house. Hoshek, looking out his castle window saw the ship break the atmosphere. He became furious.

The Mother had made it out of his clutches yet again. Now it was time for her to complete what the Old Wizard said. She sent a transmission to the Old Wizard, through the communicator on her ship telling him that she was on her way to find new Councilmembers. She did not know if the signal was jammed since he was still on Draefast, or if he had received it.

While this was occurring, The Daughter was brought to Hoshek's castle. It was there that she learned from Hoshek that The Dark Warrior used to be the man once known as her father.

"What did you do to him?" She screamed at Hoshek as he was walking from his throne to see his prize.

"My child, this is a Dranstor, he is not your beloved father anymore. He only hears my orders, and acts upon them without any thought."

The Daughter started to cry. "How could you do this to him?"

As Hoshek got closer to her, she reached out her hand to try to hit him. He let it happen. He wanted to fuel her anger to potentially see if she could gain control of her inner darkness. The Daughter noticed a gourd around his belt and a canister made from what looked to be Vastrilio steel next to his throne. Little did she know but the contents inside the canister were souls of people who once walked the planet with her. The souls he captured fueled his body with more Souldarkness, making him believe that he was closer to becoming the ultimate Council leader who would be able to successfully traverse and affect time. He was still searching for the perfect souls and or specimens to be a part of his Council of Swordmasters. He even came up with the thought of allowing the Old Wizard to find and train people strong in an Attribute and then he would swoop in and corrupt them turning them into his Council, since he had already used his old friends' bodies to create the leaders of his army.

While exploring the Soul Realm Hoshek captured dark

souls and began manipulating them. He would enter the Soul Realm travel for three minutes then exit, then he would enter again. It was a monotonous cycle, but it needed to be done. There were dark and pure souls everywhere in the Soul Realm, even near the portal, since they were always moving, so he would always have plenty to capture. Hoshek was able to stay the same old age and build from when he exited the time loop due to experimenting with the dark souls, stealing their pure Souldarkness and fusing it into his own body. His grandfather gave him the idea to absorb this pure Souldarkness to keep him from aging more or growing weaker. He even went on to release some of his Souldarkness Attribute into The Daughter turning her soul from pure to dark. He kept The Daughter barely alive, in a cell above the ruin which held the portal for the Soul Realm and tortured her. He did experiments on her soul to see how much raw soul energy she could produce even with the newly adapted Souldarkness Attribute within her. Eventually her body gave way. Before she closed her eyes believing it was the end of her path, Hoshek stabbed her in the gut. Her eyes widened. She was exhaling her final breath when all of the sudden her conscience moved from her mind into her soul which then left her body. As this happened she heard the screams and cries from above where the canister next to Hoshek's throne lay. It was tainted with too much Soulessence. He could not even use it anymore for rejuvenating his life, it was too damaged. Hoshek placed her soul into a gourd and walked through the hallway and down the ramp to the ruin. He entered the ruin and stood in front of the portal. As he opened it he exiled her dark soul to the Soul Realm deeming it useless, but also sparing it from being destroyed for some strange reason. The gourd then broke, and he knew he would either have to find another one or craft a new one. When Hoshek returned from the ruin where the Soul Realm portal was, the Dark Warrior was still standing over The Daughter's body. Hoshek tapped the body with his sword burning it with his Purple Fire so nobody would come looking for her again.

Prior to The Daughter children all around Palaleon had been disappearing. They were being brought to Hoshek by the Dark Warrior to have their souls captured. These souls were the key for Hoshek to not only remain alive but to also further his eventual goal.

Hoshek would keep the bodies of the souls he captured underneath his castle. If he ever needed to create a stronger grunt army he knew what to use to create them.

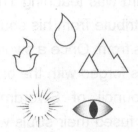

Chapter X

Learning The Attributes

The Old Wizard and The Son were getting tired from traveling long distances, so they stopped by a secluded body of water which was not too far away from their next destination. "We can resume your training here by this freshwater tarn," the Old Wizard said as he dropped his bag on the ground and motioned to come next to him. This water source was usually guarded by grunts, so while they were training, The Son and the Old Wizard had kept their eyes and ears peeled in case grunts were in the area. The grunts typically guarded this water source and brought its clean water back to Hoshek, while the villagers in the surrounding area were left to drink and use polluted water from Hoshek City. Since no grunts were in sight that day, The Old Wizard and The Son could rehydrate using this tarn and store water from here in canteens for future use.

The Old Wizard had formulated an idea as to who the Dark Warrior was now but since he was still unsure, he did not believe it was the right time or place to tell The Son. Nor did he feel it necessary to reveal to The Son details about his family. The Old Wizard was teaching The Son how to unlock his inner Soullight Attribute from his soul. That is where all of the Soulmagic comes from. Once a sword is crafted, a portion of the wielder's soul is forged with the blade.

"The original Council of Swordmasters had created Attributes when they fused their souls with their swords. The way to control an Attribute is through your sword. Since I am training you to become the leader of the Council and the Soullight Attribute Wielder, you must also learn how to control the other Attributes," the Old Wizard said.

As The Son was practicing his control over water with his sword he replied to the Old Wizard, "This is really difficult. I have to be 100 percent focused all the time since if I lose focus, then I ..." His voice trailed off. Then the water he was controlling with his sword turned to ice which almost impaled him.

Seeing The Son in distress, the Old Wizard replied, "I felt that the Soulwater will be the easiest Attribute for you to learn, since I have taught you how to meditate and be at peace with your mind. I believe in you; you just have to believe in yourself."

The Son regained his composure, and continued practicing the movements that the Old Wizard had taught him. After some time, he had partially learned how to control the flow of water, and how to generate orbs of water from his sword to shoot at targets. The Son was keeping an eye on his sword as he was controlling water, and realized that he had been traveling and training with Ohr for around five years now. Ohr was teaching him the best he could since his knowledge of each Attribute was far superior to anyone else's. He taught The Son various sword movements that would ease his mind almost like a dance connecting himself to the flow of the water. The Son practiced lifting his sword vertically above his head then quickly swinging it down and around, behind his back while twirling his wrist in a circular motion. Both of his feet were facing forward planted in the ground, with his left foot a little before his right. His torso twisted towards his left side. As The Son progressed by stepping forward following through with each swing of his sword keeping it semi-close to his body to protect his blind and weak spots, he rotated the sword spinning his wrist in front of him so fast that it created a water mirage of multiple swords. He then pulled his left arm back, creasing at his elbow, holding his sword upwards on his left side, with his right leg bent in front of his left. As The Son swung his sword in an upward diagonal motion from left to right, it looked as if multiple swords were moving in the same direction. He went through these motions advancing in speed and accuracy of his swing every day. The Son made sure he could not hurt himself from his sword by keeping it pointed away from his body unless he was practicing defensive movements behind his back. He needed to guard every part of his body and be swift about it in order to stand up against his imaginary foe. Not only did the Old Wizard show The Son all of his stances, motions and moves, but he tossed freshly cut tree logs at the boy in order to see how precise The Son could cut through the logs, leaving no splinters, and trying to infuse the Water Attribute with his sword.

The Son was not the best at conjuring water from his sword, but he would keep practicing the motions in order to do so. Maybe it just wasn't in his soul. He also learned how to encase his sword with flowing water which made the blade sharp enough to cut through Counterrock with one swing. Counterrock was stone that could only be cut with the strongest Water Attribute Soulmagic from a sword.

He wasn't able to fully control it but he learned new abilities that would help him in the future. The water eased his aggressive temper, making him think more clearly and become more focused. The Son meditated for hours in the stream. While meditating one day, he felt a presence in the water. It was a fish. He quickly rotated his hands then clasped them together. He had caught the fish. He brought it to the Old Wizard who was pleased to see that The Son's reflexes were enhanced. He then created a fire to cook the fish on. This was their dinner for the night. The Old Wizard was happy that The Son was honing his skills.

The Son asked his mentor, "I believe I am ready to learn one of the defensive Attributes, since in order for me to fight Hoshek and win I must learn how to defend myself. Will you teach me this now?"

"I too believe you are ready. At this stage of your training, learning how to defend yourself is more important than learning how to attack. The three defensive Attributes are Soulwater, Soullight and Soulrock. Since we have already started your Soulwater Attribute training let us continue with that one."

"Don't I need to learn the Soullight Attribute in order to be the Leader of the Council?"

"I will teach you that one in due time. It might be more difficult for you since it takes more concentration than even the Soulwater Attribute, and you have to be completely at one with yourself in order to unlock the Soullight Attribute. You displayed your rash thinking and behavior by running into the village before so first we must try and break this habit. You are too important to be injured or killed before our main fight has even begun. I do believe that your soul has the ability to unlock the Soullight Attribute; it will just take more training."

"I understand. I will try my best to control my feelings."

"Very well," answered the Old Wizard. "Through mastering the Soulwater Attribute, you will obtain defensive moves using water and ice to break an enemy's guard while still being able to protect yourself leaving no openings for your opponent to take advantage of. One of the many defensive qualities of the Soulwater Attribute is the ability to create the mirages like you did. If you continue practicing that skill you will be able to turn those mirages into swords that can guard your body against a group of enemies while you are focused on one enemy. Your Attribute abilities are an extension of your soul and your soul wants to protect you so the water will act as a shield of swords while you strike. The stances and movements you learn while mastering this Attribute is another reason why it is considered one of the defensive Attributes. You flow like water, so whilst in a fight or battle your opponent will have a tough time landing any sort of blow against you since you will be able to dodge most of their moves as if you're moving with the flow of water. Ice is also sturdy so if you are able to focus your Soulwater Attribute through your sword coating it with ice, your foe will have a tougher time disarming you or breaking your sword."

As the Old Wizard was speaking to The Son, The Son became antsy and wanted to test the abilities his mentor was telling him about. The Son took a deep breath focusing intensely on his soul and jumped towards the water. His sword was sheathed on the right side of his belt. The Son opened his eyes and noticed that he landed perfectly on two mossy rocks. He almost slipped. The Old Wizard watched as this was happening but continued his lesson. The Son caught himself and remained balanced. He then unsheathed his sword and began running through the defensive motions, with the more difficult task of not falling in the water. His sword movements were controlled. He was making two sets of mirages as he spun his sword around the front of his body and then his back side. He believed he could do the motions even quicker, but as he tried, he lost his balance and fell in the water. It was much colder on his skin than he expected. While clinging to his sword, he swiftly swam over to the bank of the tarn, where the Old Wizard was standing. He climbed out of the water, and removed his outer garments so they could dry atop a nearby boulder. The Old Wizard opened up his bag, pulled out a thinly woven blanket and gave it to The Son so he could warm his body.

"The next Soulmagic Attribute I will try and teach you is the Soulfire Attribute. Soulfire Attribute sword movements are focused on quick precise strikes, encasing your sword with fire and zapping enemies with lighting from it. The powerful strikes and slashes you can achieve using the Soulfire Attribute come from focused aggression. Using the Soulfire Attribute will heighten your offensive fighting abilities. This Attribute increases in power the more enraged you get. You want to be able to control the flame with your sword and shoot fire from the tip, along with encasing your sword in fire. If you are able to focus your anger and pinpoint it to specific people then your connection to this Attribute will increase making it easier to control," the Old Wizard then continued his lesson. "There are a total of five Soulmagic Attributes that each include

Sub-Attributes. For instance, The Soulwater Attribute includes the Sub-Attribute Soulice. The Soulfire Attribute includes the Sub-Attribute Soullightning. The Soulrock Attribute includes the Sub-Attributes Soulwood and Soulmetal. Then there is the Souldarkness Attribute which includes the Sub-Attributes Purple Flames and Purple Lightning. Finally, the last and most powerful Attribute is the Soullight Attribute which includes the Sub-Attribute of Soulwind."

The Old Wizard knew he just threw a lot of information at The Son, but The Son seemed very engaged so he went on to say "The Soullight and Soulwater Attributes were the only two with healing abilities, and the Souldarkness Attribute was the only one that was a poison to the wielder and the victim of the blade. Only the most powerful Souldarkness Attribute wielder could handle the poison without being affected." This poison can be seen affecting Hoshek, making him weaker in his age. It also affected Nahvel when he had a body.

The Son digested all of this information and said, "I am in awe of how you know so much about each Attribute, and their unique abilities. Thank you for teaching me about them, and for making me your student. I will do my best to learn each of the Attributes and their Sub-Attributes in order to become the Swordmaster you think and believe I will become."

The Son then thought to himself, *I want to make the Old Wizard happy, but is this truly my path. I guess I will push myself to my limit and then some to see if I am truly the Swordmaster he was seeking.* Thoughts like these could hold The Son back from what the Old Wizard believed was his potentially or even change his path entirely. It was not the first time The Son felt and thought this way.

The Old Wizard showed The Son the motions of how to control the Soullight Attribute through his sword and the Sub-Attribute Soulwind since those were the most important for him to learn, while also being the most difficult. The Son practiced the stances and sword techniques, but continued to get frustrated at himself because he was not able to generate beams of light around his sword or any bursts of wind from it.

"I know in my soul that in due time you will be able to use the Soullight Attribute. We will focus on it along with the other Attributes since Palaleon's time is running out. The universe could become fully consumed by the Shroud any day now and any hope of defeating Hoshek will be gone. I fear that with each passing day his army of grunts along with his Souldarkness Attribute grow in strength. While trying to learn the Soullight Attribute, clear your mind of any dark and evil thoughts. Be at one with your sword. Forget about who you are on the smaller scale and focus on who you will become through this energy." As the Old Wizard spoke he saw the anger in The Son's face. *Did I say something wrong. I am giving him the same advice my father and mother gave me as a child,* the Old Wizard thought.

The Son dropped to his knees. "Mentor, how can I become something greater if I don't know who I am or my purpose?"

The Old Wizard replied, "I understand your self-doubt, and confusion. I want you to know that our souls were drawn to one another. I was meant to be your mentor and you my student. I believe in you and what you will become. If you get lost in your way just know that I will always be here for you. When this is all over I promise I will help you find your memories any way I can."

"Thank you. Your belief in me gives me the strength to be something greater," The Son replied.

The Old Wizard was teaching The Son about each Attribute to further his suspicion that he was indeed the one from the Tales.

The Old Wizard went on to tell The Son about a Tale he read years ago, he had taken it from The Son's hut years ago, in order to show him the scroll now. As The Old Wizard unraveled the Tale, The Son peeked over with interest. The Old Wizard then said. "This Tale states that a person, who lost everything, will be able to defeat darkness and create a new Council of Swordmasters to create a more peaceful age for Palaleon."

Now more confident than ever The Son replied, "I can do my best learning all the Attributes you can teach me, since I learned a bit of the Soullwater Attribute. I am starting to believe I can be the person in this Tale."

The Old Wizard knew that even as The Son spoke he was still doubting himself and that he was hiding something from him much like how the Old Wizard was hiding something from The Son. While they stayed near the tarn, during the nights that The Son believed the Old Wizard to be asleep, he would try and practice controlling the Soullight Attribute. The Son could not get the hang of the Soullight Attribute or Soulwind Sub-Attribute; it was like he had a mental block when it came to those. As he was thinking of his next questions to ask his mentor in the morning, he thought, *maybe it's because I do not know who I am? I feel more connected to the darkness in my thoughts.* The Son then sat down under a tree propping his back against it and fell asleep. In the morning The Son asked his question to the Old Wizard. "Were all Souldarkness Attribute Swordmasters bad people?"

The Old Wizard replied. "No, the original one, Hosra, was not tempted by anything. He just craved knowledge, so he studied a lot. He invented abilities using his Souldarkness Attribute that some could only dream of. Some were torturous indeed but others were of no harm to anyone it was used against."

"That's amazing. I would love to learn them someday," The Son replied.

"Maybe when you are ready; your soul is still in a very malleable phase. I do not want to tempt you with what the Souldarkness Attribute has to offer. I myself do not know everything about it yet, and I can't afford to lose you." As the Old Wizard finished his sentence he saw The Son nodding in agreement.

The Old Wizard continued, "The Tale also had a dark path where the one true heir to the leader of the Council of Swordmasters will turn to darkness and secure his vision of Palaleon." The Old Wizard paid no mind to this Tale, and told The Son to do the same. "I believe that this part of the Tale was fulfilled by Hoshek."

After devouring their fish, The Son and the Old Wizard started to hear grunts enclosing on their position so they quickly grabbed all of their belongings. The Son gave the Old Wizard back his blanket and got dressed in his clothes that had not completely dried. He put his sword in his sheath on his belt and grabbed his bag and canteen and was ready to move with the Old Wizard.

They continued towards the Inbetween. While they traveled the Old Wizard thought it was best to share more stories of the olden days with The Son to prepare him for what might come in the future. He told The Son, "Like most people say, history does indeed repeat itself, and that is the purest fact." The Old Wizard was growing more and more fond of The Son, treating him as if he were his own blood. They traveled for many days farther north through different dark forests, eventually leading to a desert. "This is the entrance to the Inbetween. We must travel through this desert quickly so we do not lose sight of our goal. If we get lost we could be in the desert for years. Luckily I have been here before and have obtained a map for the area." The Old Wizard reached into his bag and pulled out his map of the northern region of Draefast including a detailed path through the desert. "Do not forget to drink the water we got from the tarn; you are looking a little dehydrated. Once we exit the desert we will reach the base of Lightning Hills." The Old Wizard pointed at the map showing The Son where they were and where they were going. "We will not be able to stop for long in the village we are headed towards."

The Old Wizard suddenly stopped in his tracks, looked over at The Son and stated in a serious tone, "You should know that the Inbetween is a beautiful, yet terrifying place."

Chapter XI
The Journey Onward

Situated in the northwest region of Draefast, the Inbetween is comprised of various areas including an expansive desert, a number of villages including a sulfuric hot spring, Lightning Hills, and a crater leading to the center of the planet.

When the first generation of humans appeared, they separated into groups migrating to several different locations of the planet. Some groups traveled southeast through the region home to the dark forests. Others traveled southwest and built villages close to water sources, but still residing either in or adjacent to one of the many forests. Another few groups traveled northeast and made villages in the forest close to water sources. The remaining groups traveled northwest to the tarn, then entered the desert marking the entrance of what would later become referred to as the Inbetween. The people traveled as a pack through the desert marking down which areas were prone to sandstorms and coyote attacks, so they knew which areas to avoid in the future. Many didn't make it. The only source of food available were the ferrets that would pop up from holes underneath the sand. Someone would have to be quick enough to catch one and kill it, but one was not enough to feed the many travelers.

In order to save resources, the people splintered into three smaller groups. One group continued for weeks east and the other two traveled northeast. These three groups set up a trade system that passed down to their children and their children's children. The two groups that traveled northeast created maps for their descendants to use as they sojourned back and forth through the desert. Settling around a hot spring, each of the two groups founded their own village. The third group made it with some casualties to the base of Lightning Hills and formed a village around the planet's natural heat source crater. People who resided in each of these villages rarely traveled south since the journey back north could take a long time. The settlers had created a home for themselves surrounded by fertile land allowing for an agrarian society. Trees were cut, and the timber was used to build houses and other small buildings. The land was cultivated, and within a short amount of time, crops were sown and harvested. The people knew that this is where they wanted to build their lives and start families, since as they exited the desert, all they could see until Lightning Hills was green grass, and luscious trees. Their eyes widened as they had just gone through a lot to make it here and they finally made it to their own paradise.

Adventurers believed there to be hidden treasures through the desert so they traveled from their villages all the way back west towards the tarn. Each adventurer returned back to their villages empty handed, but had created very detailed maps of the desert that they started to sell as more people from the south and east began traveling to their region. Inhabitants of the two villages on the outskirts of the desert, were not only known for being keepers of the hot spring, but also their maps that guided travelers through their lands. The children of the first generation dug wells in the village making it easier for them to collect water instead of having to travel great distances. Throughout the next couple of decades people from other regions heard of the Inbetween and all of its mysteries so they began traveling north. When some of those people made it to the villages successfully, they began trading with the villagers for food, water, and maps, trading materials that one could not obtain by living near a desert.

As time went on villagers from each of the three villages came to the realization that even the stars could not guide someone through the desert, so the cartography business thrived. Nahvel was fascinated by these maps from the time of his youth in the southern region. As he aged into his role of being the Souldarkness Attribute wielder he collected these maps, realizing they held the power for people of the south to escape his clutches. He could not have that if he were to become their ruler. During his last trip north before he declared himself ruler, he brought one of the adventurers from each village to the village center and murdered them in front of everyone. He then declared that all maps be burned, or more people will fall to his hand. The villagers became terrified by his power and ruthlessness so they did as he commanded. Only a few brave souls secretly kept maps hidden underneath the floorboards of their homes.

At this current moment, only a few accurate maps of the desert existed. People who had forgotten about the northern region due to Nahvel's rule, lost trade routes cutting off the northern villages access to different materials. When villagers from the south felt it was best for them to try and escape Nahvel, they traveled and a few of them made it to the hot spring. Villagers from the two villages surrounding the hot spring opened their arms to these new folk as they had not seen outsiders in years. They were offered goods to trade so that these people could spend time at the hot spring relaxing, almost forgetting about the tyranny happening around the planet slowly reaching the north. Nahvel had kept maps but Malikaya had destroyed them when she ventured north eventually meeting Gathran.

The nights on Draefast were getting colder underneath the Shroud of darkness. Under Hoshek's rule, the hot spring had frozen over since the Shroud appeared making it non-viable for the villagers to use it as a source of income or for their own benefits. The lightning atop Lightning Hills, which used to strike in beautiful iridescent colors illuminating the sky, now appears black. In the center of the village at the bottom of Lighting Hills there is a crater leading to the planet's core. Waves of heat had spewed out of this fissure warming up the rest of the world. The villagers did their best protecting this heat source from Hoshek but once the Shroud seeped into the village it traveled down into the planet's core, cutting off heat from reaching the surface. The Old Wizard and The Son's main destination in the Inbetween was Lightning Hills. Lightning Hills was the only place on Draefast that was constantly bombarded by bolts of lightning. This vast region was the second place the Old Wizard saw lightning strike in years.

As the Old Wizard and The Son arrived at the village at the

bottom of Lightning Hills, The Son noticed a sign with the name of the village and repeated it to the Old Wizard. "The sign says we are entering Choliot."

"I have not been here in a great many decades. It is looking more somber than I remember," the Old Wizard replied as they walked through the streets. "Through Tales, I have learned that generations of Swordmasters have trained and studied Attributes atop Lighting Hills; it is a sacred place to any Councilmember. I am glad it has been untouched by Hoshek."

They went through the village to get food, and some other supplies they needed to continue on with their adventure. "The people here look different than in other villages in the southern region," The Son remarked to the Old Wizard as he glanced at other villagers going about their days. The Son had wrapped his shawl around him extra tightly since he was getting colder the closer they got to the center square of Choliot. He noticed that people around him had orange color hair and their skin was a tad darker than his. All of the villagers surrounding him did not seem affected by the cold; they were in shorts, skirts, and t-shirts. Their bodies had become strained due to their journey through the desert. The Son and the Old Wizard met the Merchant in the village. The Son heard him singing and was intrigued by this and ran up to the Merchant to ask him about the time before. The Old Wizard thought that camping for the night with the Merchant might not be such a bad idea since nighttime was about to fall upon them. The Merchant posed no threat to The Son and the Old Wizard. He seemed kind and trustworthy; this was why the Old Wizard was able to make such a quick decision without even knowing the man.

After all they were all travelers of this world searching for their true purpose.

The Old Wizard took cups out of his bag while the Merchant got tea. "I'm sorry it is not hot. It also might be bitter but it is the best I can offer as I do not earn that much money," the Merchant told them as he poured them each a cupful.

The Old Wizard and The Son were grateful for his hospitality and the fact that he was able to share even if he did not have much. The Son watched as the Old Wizard and the Merchant began to exchange stories over their tea. They were bonding. Then the Merchant looked over at The Son really analyzing his face.

"Hey I recognize you; you are that boy I saw entering the main city with what looked to be your father many years ago. And by the looks of it you got what you came for." The Merchant's eyes gazed at the sword. He had his own special connection to it. The Old Wizard stared at the Merchant who still seemed infatuated by the sword. As he took a deep breath in to center himself, he figured out who the Merchant was and why he was staring at The Son's sword. He thought to himself, *That is why we were able to bond so quickly. Our pasts are connected. He knew my ancestor. He is connected to my lineage. He is and will be a great friend to have one day but for now I must shut this down.* Without letting on to his realization, for his safety, The Son's, and the Merchant's, the Old Wizard remained quiet.

"I do not remember you. Are you sure you are talking about me?" The Son replied to the Merchant looking confused. "The only family I have is this old man here. He is my mentor," Before the Merchant could say another word, the Old Wizard gazed at him as if he were telepathically telling him to change the subject. The Merchant complied.

"Sorry, I have been traveling for so long, you must be reminding me of someone else I met on my life's escapades." The Merchant had to resist interfering with what was going on more than he had already done. He decided to get back to his song.

> *I come out here daily*
> *Dusk till dawn*
> *To reiterate about our past*
> *Now that it's gone*
> *From times old that which I sing*
> *The Council of Swordmasters will survive again*
> *To reteach us the ways of peace*
> *Unity we had until the Dark Wizard came to be*
> *We had a time like this before*
> *But I doubt you would remember*
> *Since above us there is a Shroud*
> *Corrupting your brains*
> *No doubt*
> *He isn't perfect*
> *He isn't great*
> *But you can't think that our gone will be*
> *Your mind is his already*
> *Wake up*
> *You must wake up*

The next morning, The Son and the Old Wizard said their goodbyes to the Merchant and traveled up Lightning Hills. "Would you have any idea about what the Merchant was talking about yesterday. He said something about me looking like someone he knew and an older figure with me?" The Son asked.

"I'm sorry, but when I met you and pulled you out of the fire you were alone. I did not know you before that day so I cannot speak to that time," the Old Wizard replied as they continued their climb to the top of Lightning Hills. The trip took days. As they continued upwards they had to be wary of the black lightning and avoided being struck. They bundled up their clothing as the misty air turned to sleet the higher they climbed. The Son and the Old Wizard had found outcroppings in the mountain where they rested before continuing the climb. When they finally made it to the top of Lightning Hills, The Son looked out across Draefast the view was breathtaking. "Look mentor, in the distance, there is the tarn," The Son excitedly said as he pointed west.

"Yes and look at the three villages. From this height, you can see each perfectly," the Old Wizard replied. Even with the Shroud above their heads and surrounding them, they could not unsee the beauty of not only the Inbetween but most of the planet from where they stood. They were standing on the highest point in all of Draefast.

As they set up camp since they knew they would be staying up here for a while, the Old Wizard started to tell The Son a story. "Long ago, the first the Council of Swordmasters unlocked their Attributes, through possessing and harnessing their Soulmagic. They passed down this ability to future Swordmasters, who continued to study the knowledge of each Attribute and Soulmagic as a whole. This knowledge was passed down by and to each generation much like how I am passing it down to you. Everybody had the same question you have been thinking since the day we met which is: why me? The answer, confusing yet simple is Palaleon made it so. It might not be the answer you are looking for, but only the founders of the Attributes had a true reason and that is because they had a part of the soul of a Legendary Beast inside of them. I am related to two of the original Councilmembers so I was born into this role already having a connection to my Soulmagic from a young age. You are like the others who were not related to anyone by blood, you are gifted in your own way the universe knows it and so do the Legendary Beasts."

It was the Old Wizard's goal to have The Son eventually become very powerful in the Attributes, but the Old Wizard did not know if he would be around to see that happen. In light of this, he wanted to complete The Son's training to perfection in the speediest way possible. The Son and the Old Wizard trained for months atop Lightning Hills. It was the perfect place for training since lightning could strike at any time, always keeping The Son on his guard. He was able to enhance his reflexes through meditation strengthening his bond with his Soulmagic and the Attributes he had learned thus far. Using The Son's sword, The Old Wizard continued to show him sword techniques and stances, in hopes that The Son could mimic the movements in order to further his connection with both the Soulfire and Soulwater Attribute's. The Old Wizard borrowed The Son's sword to show him how to control his swings with both aggression and while being calm. The Old Wizard thought to himself, *To be able to master the Soullight Attribute he needs to understand the techniques from the other Attributes as they will make him a more advanced sword wielder and more connected to his Soulmagic.* The Old Wizard then returned The Son's sword back to him and said, "Now it is your turn." He watched as The Son displayed each of the moves the Old

Wizard had shown him. "Do not forget to breathe. Show me that you are in control of your sword and its path."

The Son then took a deep breath, as he thought to himself. *My mentor is relying on me to lead. I must not fail him. No. I will not fail him.* He swung his sword horizontally as he exhaled and for a brief second the Old Wizard saw wind rush off the blade. "You're close. Try it again, but this time, focus more on your slash and the purpose of it. What is your goal? See it not only with your eyes, but with your mind and your heart."

The Son then thought to himself, *My goal?* He then shouted, "My goal is to rid this universe of evil and restore it to a peaceful age." As he shouted he led with his right foot forward gripping his sword in both of his hands and extended it, flicking his wrists while rotating his hips. His eyes were wide open now as he saw the wind protrude from his sword cutting into the side of one of the other hills to the west. He was amazed at his own abilities.

"Rest now. You have earned it. You were able to tap into the Soullight Attribute by commanding the Soulwind Sub-Attribute. You are close to reaching your full potential," the Old Wizard said as he was still in awe of what had just occurred.

The Son walked over to the Old Wizard and sat next to him looking exhausted. It was almost nighttime and that meant dinner. The Old Wizard reached into his bag and pulled out two pieces of bread with cheese and jam spread on it. "I am sorry, but this is all I could obtain food-wise at the village. Hope it is enough." The Old Wizard handed him one of the pieces.

"Thank you mentor, this is more than enough. Not just for the food, but for your teachings, and giving me a purpose," The Son replied.

"I should be thanking you. You trusted me; this old man

you really do not even know. Not only that, but you have taken my teachings seriously and have proven to be an even greater Swordmaster than I was in my prime. You will make all the people of this universe proud. We all stand behind you. Don't you forget it," the Old Wizard said as he started to lay down tossing a blanket over himself. "Get a good night's rest. Tomorrow we will continue your training. We have no time to waste," the Old Wizard said.

"Understood," The Son replied.

The following day, The Son woke up early to shadow-spar working on offensive and defensive sword movements. After a brief meditation, The Son got up again to practice swinging his sword diagonally creating an X shape in front of his body. He was concentrating on thinly slicing the air and through his intense focus was able to shoot water from his sword. Then all of a sudden, lightning struck down his blade and traveled through his body. He was falling to the ground as the Old Wizard finished his tea and rushed over. The Son briefly lost consciousness. The Old Wizard grabbed The Son's sword, tapped it on the boy's chest where the lightning was flowing to his heart, and began pulling the lightning out of him.

The Son woke up, and started remembering small parts of his past, like the exact location on Draefast where he had grown up and lived in a hut. He then had a vision of a man who laid next to him. He started to sweat. The Son's body was overheating; it was as if he was being surrounded by fire in his vision. He could not make out what he looked like or why he was there. The Son was trying harder and harder to visualize what the man looked like, but as he strained his concentration, all he saw was a sheet of darkness. The Son asked the Old

Wizard, "I just had a vision. It was very hot, my body felt as if it was on fire, and there was a man next to me. Do you have any idea who the man is?"

The Old Wizard replied, "I am sorry, I do not know who he was in relation to you, or where we can find this mystery man now. I did not see this vision so I truly have no clue as to who that can be, and if they are still alive or not." The Old Wizard suspected that the man in The Son's vision was The Father. He told The Son the partial truth as he did not know what had become of The Father after the Dark Wizard took him.

The Son tried to stand, but was unable. The Old Wizard conjured a little water from the frozen air by swinging The Son's sword and made The Son drink. He was only able to do this since for a brief moment more of the Old Wizard's Soulmagic became unlocked. It was as if The Son being struck by lightning awakened more Soulmagic in the Old Wizard. He feared losing The Son, and did not want to have that happen so he was able to muster enough soul strength to control Soulwater through the sword. The Son now had half of a star-like shape scar on the left side of his chest. It was similar to the scars on his palms from being struck by Purple Lightning years ago. The Son lifted up his hand and pointed towards his sword in The Old Wizard's hand which now had sparks emanating from and surrounding it. The Old Wizard gasped, dropped the sword, and The Son fainted once again.

Chapter XII

Baraka

As The Son's consciousness traveled closer and closer to the center of his soul, he was trying to unlock doors to his past. His feet landed on what seemed to be solid ground. He was still getting his bearings as multiple doors floated around him. As he opened one of the doorways a Shroud-like figure appeared. "If you let me take control of your mind and body I will give you back all of your memories," the figure said. The figure was in The Son's soul leeching onto his inner darkness and amplifying it. It came from a piece of the Shroud. The Son was intrigued by this offer but thought to himself, *If I stick with my mentor I will be able to unlock my memories on my own without making any deals.* The Son then turned around and walked to another doorway. The figure followed him. The Son started to run. He was all alone and felt a wave of cold wash over his skin. He was speaking to his inner darkness. Finally he made it to another doorknob and as he touched it he got zapped by something more controlled and powerful than regular lightning. The Shroud-like figure disappeared as the

Soullightning Sub-Attribute entered The Son's body. He was baffled. *How could this happen?* He thought to himself as he entered a new place. Where the doorway once was, now stood a glowing figure made out of lightning behind him. She then introduced herself to The Son.

In a booming voice she stated, "My name is Baraka. Who are you? An old friend of mine told me one day I would meet someone worthy enough to train. Is that person you?"

Confused, The Son replied, "I do not know my name. Where is the Old Wizard?"

"Who is this Old Wizard you speak of? There are only two people in your living world I know to possess Attributes and Soulmagic. Judging by the name 'Old Wizard' I believe you are talking about Ohr, since Hoshek could never take on a name like that. He is filled with too much pride to refer to himself as old," Baraka replied.

Recollecting a story he had once heard, The Son asked Baraka, "Ohr? Hoshek's brother Ohr? But he was defeated by Hoshek and just barely escaped with his life. How could my mentor be the same man?"

Not wanting to answer his question, Baraka continued, "I am the soul of a previous student of the Council of Swordmasters. I studied under the Councilmember who controlled the Soulfire Attribute. Now since I am just a soul with no body, I can control my Attribute and Soulmagic without the necessary use of a sword. I can teach you the ways of lightning, but I must warn you - to perfect it, you must not rush our training."

"Wait, hold on a second," The Son interrupted, "Ohr and my mentor. Are they the same person? You did not answer me."

Baraka replied, "Yes, but there is more to that than anyone

realizes. It is hard to fight a family member especially when one has the intent to kill the other. Ohr just wanted to help his brother, but Hoshek was so far gone into the darkness that it was too late."

The Son questioned, "How do you know so much?"

"I used to be friends with Hoshek and Ohr, until Hoshek turned on us in the middle of the night. He killed me, my friends, and our mentors. Now I am trapped in the Attribute of Soulfire as a soul. Anyone who is able to unlock this Attribute will meet me. To my knowledge, I was the only one to escape Hoshek's wrath and was able to transport my soul before he destroyed my body. Even though I live inside the Attribute of Soulfire itself, I still heard the screams of my fellow Swordmasters as their souls and bodies were morphed into leaders of Hoshek's army."

"How can you be trapped in an Attribute? Isn't it part of Soulmagic?" The Son asked.

"Since my soul could never return back to my body, it needed to connect with something that resembled a soul. The closest outlet to a soul that there was when I died, was my sword, which was my extension of the Attribute of Soulfire that lived inside of me. Through my sword I was able to survive. It just so happened that when you obtained the half star scar on your chest, the sword that lay in Hoshek's castle - *my* sword - shattered into pieces, allowing my soul to be free. I was drawn to your soul energy. I felt your fire and was drawn to it."

Baraka moved closer to The Son, and continued, "Thank you for freeing me. I know what I must do when I am done training you. I will find the next Soulfire Attribute wielder and latch onto their soul to train them. After that, perhaps my soul can rest in a place I heard about when I still lived in the material world. The Soul Realm. I heard that provided one's soul is not fully depleted of energy, it can be transported into the..."

Before Baraka could finish speaking, The Son's sword fell from what seemed to be a door above his head and landed blade down on the ground. Lightning was radiating in all directions from the sword. As Baraka opened up her palm and raised it vertically, the hilt of The Son's sword flew into her hand. Lightning was now flowing through and around her body as she prepared to engage The Son. She started to charge towards him. His training had begun. She thought to herself, *Ohr can teach him the essence of the Soulfire Attribute and how to control it. I will focus on the Sub-Attribute.* This was the first time in decades Baraka used a sword. Though out of practice, she displayed immense power and connection to the Sub-Attribute Soullightning.

"Unless what?" The Son asked while blocking Baraka's attacks.

"Ohr's mother once told a bedtime story to me and the other children learning to be the next Swordmasters about this being that was able to create an alternate timeline. Maybe if that was real I could have my own body, mind, and soul again," Baraka replied.

"The Old Wizard told me time is linear. There is no way for me to go back in time and figure out who I was. I doubt there is a way for a separate timeline to coexist next to ours. If there were such a thing I would hope the people there would never have to deal with a tyrant that we have here. But you have just displayed Soulmagic without the use of a sword so I truly still do not know everything and I have a lot to learn." The Son said.

"Don't focus on what is or what can be, focus on what is

in front of you. I am in front of you. I am your adversary; thus I should be your only focus," Baraka commanded The Son.

Baraka wanted to test The Son's willpower, evasiveness, and sword techniques along with his Attribute and Soulmagic abilities, so she posed herself as a threat to him. Her intentions were to teach, not harm him, but she had to give it her all. She knew that for him to face his destiny, he had to be ready.

I am not in the material world so maybe I can try this, The Son thought as he lifted his hands up in a supine position. He then splayed his hands away from one another and a blade made of ice appeared in his palms. The Son was able to produce the Soulwater Attribute of Soulmagic outside his sword believing that this technique could only be achieved where he was now. The Son then announced, "Now I can fight you."

"Ah, so you have learned to harness the Soulwater Attribute. And you're a quick learner. Even with my advanced experience I would not have thought to create my own sword using my soul. I applaud you for this but your technique will only get you so far in this fight as your sword falls short in comparison to mine. Didn't Ohr ever teach you that water is a conductor for lightning? The lightning that radiates from my sword will travel through yours upon impact and shock you, causing immeasurable pain. Can't you make a sword out of the Soulfire Attribute, or even the Soullight Attribute?" Baraka taunted The Son.

"As if your puny lightning will hurt me in comparison to what I have already experienced in the real world." The Son snarkily retorted.

Baraka was fed up with giving The Son accolades and proceeded to engage him in a sword fight to truly test his abilities. They clashed, but it was evident that The Son could not manifest enough Soulmagic to maintain his ice sword for long. Mid-block, his sword snapped. The Son then jumped back to gain some distance and rethink his strategy. After all, he knew she was trying to teach him and not hurt him. That being said he still needed to give this fight his all.

The Son then asked Baraka, "I am ready to learn. What must I do first?"

"First you must take your sword from my hands." As The Son ran towards her and tried to grab his sword it was as if his body got stunned and he lost control and suddenly flew backwards. Baraka disappeared.

The Son shouted, "Where did you go?"

Baraka replied, "I am behind you." The Son turned around. He felt little trickles of lightning as the sword was swung at him. He jumped back.

"You can teleport?" The Son asked Baraka.

She replied, "Not teleportation, but I am as swift as the lightning coursing through my veins."

The Son continued to dodge Baraka's attacks as if he could predict each strike she would make before it happened. As he became cocky and let his guard down, all it took was a second for Baraka to strike The Son in the stomach by the hilt of his own original sword. Baraka then alerted him, "You thought I was predictable and I used that to my advantage."

The Son got angry and rushed towards Baraka. He was running quicker and quicker as if the lightning bolt that struck him earlier in his chest had moved to his legs. With ease, Baraka knocked him back again. "Anger and aggression is the way of the Soulfire and Souldarkness Attributes. One must be able to simultaneously control their anger while being calm in order to control the Soullightning Sub-Attribute through their body and sword. Think of the meditative and peaceful training Ohr put you through to learn to use the Soulwater Attribute. Now if you add a little edge to that form of training you will be able to control the Soullightning Sub-Attribute," Baraka revealed.

The Son took a deep breath. Baraka was now blasting bolts of lightning towards him through the sword in her hand. He was able to successfully dodge the storm of lightning cast in his direction with ease. He moved so quickly evading each bolt that he suddenly appeared behind her. The Son went for his blade, this time thrusting his hand through the lightning-encased hilt. He touched his sword and pulled it from Baraka's hand. Baraka put her left hand on his shoulder and shocked him with lightning. As he flew backwards, his hand was still firmly holding onto his sword, reclaiming what was once his.

Baraka was preparing for her next phase of attack. She was now facing The Son who was several paces away standing tall ready to defend himself. She pulled her hands apart from one another and a blade appeared which was as white as the moon above Draefast. "Shall we continue?"

The Son had not realized it but even throughout this fight his body was becoming more accustomed to handling different Attributes. His soul was adjusting to his body and his mind. He was not as skilled wielding the Soullightning Sub-Attribute yet like Baraka, but she was noticing improvement in his fighting. As they were preparing for their next clash The Son's body started to twinge. He then looked down at his sword and noticed little bolts of lightning were bouncing off of it and his body. He was controlling his breathing, while mentally and physically preparing for what was to come.

The Son made the first move and began sprinting towards Baraka. Each time their swords clashed; a thunderous roar echoed throughout the metaphysical plane that was The Son's soul. The Son was a quick learner, but he could not yet conjure lightning bolts from his sword. He also knew he could not use the Water Attribute through his sword since that would just work in Baraka's favor.

Even though The Son's speed had increased he was still no match for Baraka. She was pushing him to his limits in this fight seeing if he could break them. He was getting sloppy, slowing down, and becoming more and more predictable after each encounter. As their swords met above their heads, Baraka quietly swung her leg around and kicked behind The Son's knee, causing him to collapse. The lightning that was surrounding Baraka's body disappeared as she pointed her blade at The Son. "Never fall on your back! You are at your weakest on your back," she exclaimed. With a quick jab of his foot to her ankle, she too had fallen to the ground. The Son then grabbed his blade and jumped up. While in the air, he felt a power floating around him, but also inside him. His eyes turned alabaster, and his scar glowed as lightning began to generate from his sword.

Baraka was thrilled, but also scared. The Son had finally unlocked the power of the Soullightning Sub-Attribute, but now needed to learn how to control it. While hovering in the air, The Son flung himself towards Baraka with his sword extended from his chest. His body began spinning as sparks erupted from his soul encasing him in a ball of the lightning. Baraka shot a lightning bolt at The Son, but he absorbed it. He then swung his sword at her. She met his attack with her own blade which then snapped in half like a twig off a tree.

She began to move away and in doing so was shocked by residual lightning from her broken sword, which in turn only increased her speed. The Son continued to swing his lightning sword and blast bolts in her direction to slow her down, but Baraka was still able to dodge his onslaught of attacks. She then stopped moving and by touching her palms together she replicated herself. The phantoms went on the offensive, thrusting their arms made of lightning at The Son. All the while, Baraka took this time to gain even more distance from him. The distraction allowed her to focus inward as she began to meditate by touching her thumbs and pinky fingers together.

After The Son dispatched Baraka's duplicates, he bolted towards her. As his right foot touched the ground for the third time in his stride, he noticed that the lightning surrounding his sword slowly began dissipating. With her eyes still shut, Baraka appeared in front of him grabbing his sword by the blade with her index and middle finger of her right hand as if it weighed nothing. Her body then became surrounded by more and more lightning since she pulled it out of The Son's sword. With her other hand Baraka touched his scar, taking the lightning out of his body. He was now calm. She then opened her eyes revealing their new shade of alabaster. By absorbing all of The Son's Soullightning Sub-Attribute his eyes reverted back to their original hue.

"As you leave this place remember that the sword you wield and all Attributes of Soulmagic are an extension of your soul," Baraka relayed to The Son. "Let the lightning become wild through the blade, but once it is met with your hands, you need to control it. With practice you will master this technique." Baraka then sat him down and they meditated. The Son rested his sword by his feet, and now without touching it he felt connected with his sword more than ever. The Attributes he had learned were flowing through his soul while his sword almost verbally called out to him. HIs bond with his sword was complete. From being its creator to wielder, he hoped it would stay sheathed to his side for as long as he needed.

The only thing in his mind was the question - What was his true purpose? The Son then arose in the material world as if all that just occurred was a dream. He knew everything that had just happened was real, at least to him it was.

Chapter XIII

The Old Wizard

The Old Wizard stayed by The Son's side for all of the three days that the young man laid unconscious. He could not leave The Son alone atop Lightning Hills since he could get struck again by lightning and that would be disastrous. For the first two days the Old Wizard meditated, only to break his focus when he was hungry. The fruit in his satchel was all the nourishment he needed. He wanted to save the chickens they bought from the village for The Son's eventual return to his body.

The night before The Son awoke, the Old Wizard found himself to be fidgeting with the communication device that he had the blacksmith, Azure, make for him decades earlier. Suddenly it chimed. There was an incoming message. The Mother's voice was heard reciting a list of the names of three people who resided on three different planets who he should meet since they displayed connections to what he had told her were Attributes. She believed these three people were worthy of becoming the next Swordmasters, the people who would aid in repairing Palaleon to a more prosperous time. Content with

191

this news, the Old Wizard thought to himself, *we have the next phase of our mission laid out for us now.* He then closed his eyes to get some rest.

The next morning the Old Wizard woke up early only to find that The Son was still not conscious. Then the Old Wizard went for a walk around the top of Lightning Hill's to stretch and exercise his body as he exercised his mind and soul the night prior. Suddenly the Old Wizard heard a noise coming from where they had set up camp. "That has to be The Son. He is finally back." The Old Wizard ran over. "You must be hungry. Stay still, let me make some food for us before you readjust to being in your body. You have been gone for three days." The Old Wizard quickly built a fire in order to cook the chickens.

The Old Wizard and The Son began to eat. The Son was ravenous. As The Son started to stand, the Old Wizard assisted him while asking him, "Are you ok? Where did you go? What did you see?"

The Son replied, "I met Baraka."

The Old Wizard gasped, "Baraka, the Student of Soulfire. I thought she was dead. I was led to believe Hoshek had killed everyone but me that day. I remember she was in control of the Soullightning Attribute the last time I saw her."

The Son replied, "Yes well it could have been a dream but wherever I was she seemed very much alive. We dueled and I was able to touch her skin, so I think it was real. She taught me how to conjure and control the Soullightning Attribute. Through focusing on my soul I was able to emit lightning from my sword."

"That is amazing. All this time I really believed I was the last one left. Now to hear that she survived through her soul gives me an extra ounce of hope. Leave it to Baraka to find a way to escape death. I do believe it was truly her, at least I am not putting it past her to achieve a new ability in such a short amount of ti..." As the Old Wizard was about to finish speaking The Son cut him off.

"She told me who you really were, and who your brother is. How come you never told me you were Ohr?" The Old Wizard heard anger and disappointment in The Son's voice.

The Old Wizard admitted, "Yes, my name is Ohr, the descendant of the original Soullight Attribute Wielder, Ohtav, and one of the members-in-training of the Council of Swordmasters before your time. The person we are destined to defeat, the one who caused all this," Ohr then pointed to the Shroud above their heads. "I am ashamed to say, but Hoshek is my brother. In fact I am ashamed that he and I are the only two that know that we are related not only to Ohtav, but also the first Souldarkness Attribute wielder, Hosra. I didn't want to burden you with this knowledge of my past. I did not believe that it would benefit your growth as I am training you to pave a new way of life for the people of this universe. A better one. You are my first pupil but you will not be my last. If needed I will assist in training the next generation of Swordmasters. For now, I promise you I will complete your training and create a Council of Swordmasters strong enough to defeat my brother. Where I have failed, you will not." Through training and bonding with The Son, Ohr was slowly gaining the Soulmagic he had lost decades earlier from fighting his brother.

The Son understood. "It is not my place to get angry about your past and for not being able to stop your brother when you had the chance. However, I am still upset that you could not stop this Shroud from happening and effecting so many people,

193

but if you had then I do not know where or what I would be. Surely I would not have been chosen to be the next leader of the Council of Swordmasters. All I know is that the past cannot be changed. I must focus on the future and my battles ahead, as together we have a chance to end this tyranny." The Son couldn't stay angry at someone who had always been there for him and protected him.

"I appreciate what you have said. We will win. I have faith now more than ever that it is possible. Thank you for showing me such kindness even when I did not tell you my true identity," Ohr responded.

The Son continued, "Baraka told me that after she trained me she would be looking for the next Soulfire Attribute Sword wielder to teach. She informed me that she had latched onto my soul when I was struck by lightning so let's hope that as I regained my consciousness, she was able to amplify her soul's energy to search for our future ally."

"I hope she will be able to train this person since then we will be closer to our goal. Plus we do not have that much time left before Hoshek is able to enact his plan and for the Shroud to fully corrupt the universe, severing everyone's connection to their soul," Ohr replied.

"Then we better get moving, but first let's rest for the night so I can fully regain my strength," The Son stated.

"That is a great idea," Ohr responded.

Both Ohr and The Son then set up their tents and settled for the night. Sleep came easily for both of them. At the crack of dawn of the first sun, The Son awoke, stretched his body, and began to meditate. He had learned how to bring peace to his mind and inner thoughts by watching Ohr sit cross-legged on the ground, closing his eyes and breathing in and out deeply. The Son had witnessed Ohr do this while he was training, learning new sword techniques. Ohr woke up when the second of the three sun's rose. He left his tent to find food, and saw that The Son was outside meditating. There was a newfound silence on top of Lightning Hills. The Son opened up his eyes and lifted his sword to the sky. All of a sudden, lightning crashed down and struck The Son's sword. The Son's sword glistened white and blue. Ohr was amazed.

He was able to summon lightning from above to encase his sword. He truly has progressed. I am very proud of him, Ohr thought to himself.

The Son stood up and looked at Ohr who brought back breakfast. They would now begin their next adventure down Lightning Hills, back to the village and into what once was the heat source crater for Draefast. A new chill was in the air as if something or someone was approaching them.

"We must go quickly into the crater," Ohr instructed. "Since the Shroud froze over the top our best chance is to go further down."

The Son nodded his head. They continued to walk alongside the crater that extended deep into the planet's core to see if there was a weak point they could break into. On the side of the cylindrical crater closest to him, The Son jumped in the air unsheathing his sword and thrust it down trying to create an opening for the two of them to slip into. It did not crack. "Let me try again," The Son said to Ohr as villagers started watching them with confused looks on their faces. The Son then jumped up and again thrust his sword this time channeling the Soullightning Sub-Attribute. There was now a hole in the crater big enough for the two men to go into. Souldarkness started spewing from the heat source escaping back into the Shroud above them.

"We must go now. I am afraid we just endangered the villagers," Ohr said as he grabbed The Son. Both of them then jumped into the crater. They were falling. "Was this really a good idea, mentor? We could fall to the center of Draefast, which I bet is still hot. We could die!" The Son shouted looking over at Ohr as they continued falling, almost separating themselves from one another.

"Over there. There is a ledge we can land on. Try moving your body closer towards me and I can fling you to the ledge." The Son did as Ohr commanded. He landed on the ledge protruding from this never ending crater. Ohr was closer to him now but still falling down with great speed. Acting quickly, The Son dove to the edge of the ledge, and was able to grab Ohr by the arm pulling him up.

"It is not as warm as I expected it to be," The Son said looking at Ohr.

"Even though we broke through a layer, the Shroud has overcome the heat source for over a decade. I believe that it will remain cold until Hoshek is defeated, since only then the Shroud will be eliminated, bringing warmth back to Draefast. In the meantime, let us continue your Soulfire Attribute training, as we are as close to the core of the planet as we can get. We will use what little embers are left down here to help ignite the Soulfire Attribute within your soul by controlling it with your sword," Ohr replied. As Ohr finished speaking, the two of them started to hear the screams from villagers. Ohr turned to The Son, and said, "Grunts have arrived. We must remain hidden.

I know you want to help the villagers and that their suffering is our fault, but if you get captured we are all doomed." Ohr knew that what he said disappointed The Son, but he hoped The Son understood.

The Son's soul had become enraged yet focused. He was about to command the Soulfire Attribute through his sword. He began sparring with Ohr keeping in mind that they only had so much room since the ledge they were on was not that big. He moved his right foot then his left to continue to remain balanced as he gave all his might into each swing of his sword at Ohr. "Don't hold back. Use your raw soul potential, for that is how the fire on your sword will remain lit and active," Ohr stated.

When Ohr was atop Lightning Hills waiting for The Son to regain consciousness, he whittled a stick he found underneath one of the only trees at the top of the hill. He used his knife from his satchel turning it into a staff. He had begun carrying it with him and was now using it as a defensive weapon against The Son. He used it to block one of The Son's sword swings and was able to push him backwards. Ohr felt his hands start to get hot and dropped the staff. As it touched the ground it incinerated. Somehow The Son had conjured the Soulfire Attribute from his sword using just the slightest amount to decimate Ohr's staff. The Son was focusing on regaining balance looking at his feet, so he didn't realize his sword, which still had embers emitting from it now, was too close to his face until it was too late. The Son had burned the left side of his face in a horizontal line. He remained calm as he summoned the Soulwater Attribute through his sword to cool the burn, but a scar remained.

"Are you all right?" Ohr asked as he ran over to The Son.

"Yes, do not worry. It was not your fault, it was mine. I need to remain focused and balanced at all times even when my enemy poses an even greater threat than I originally anticipated." The Son still needed to master his control of the Attributes, but the two of them knew he was running out of time. Time meant everything now and they seemed to be running out of it.

"I think the grunts have stopped attacking for now. Let's quickly get out of here and head to the eastern forests where we will begin your Soulrock Attribute training," Ohr told The Son as they started packing up their belongings. They then climbed up the side of the crater. Grabbing onto cold and hot rocks their journey was quick. Neither of them dared look down as it was endless. The Son stuck his sword into the side of the crater and used his other hand to grab onto protruding pieces of the crater. He then pulled himself upwards using his sword as a foot holder. When he inched his foot up to another piece of the crater that was sticking outwards, Ohr would do the same following The Son's way of climbing. Since The Son did not want Ohr handling the weight of his satchel on the intense climb upwards, he had both satchels strapped around the right side of his chest. As they reached the surface, The Son peeked out and saw two grunts attacking a shop owner. The Son inched up, but Ohr grabbed his shoulder and shook his head. "We do not know who else could be with the grunts. We must play it safe and leave. If the grunts are here looking for us and we leave then the villagers will be safer since they have no information to offer," Ohr said as The Son lifted himself up out of the crater. He then grabbed Ohr's hand helping his mentor up. They ran, hiding behind houses and shops as grunts searched throughout the village. A boy was outside picking fruit in his family garden and saw The Son and Ohr run out of the village.

The boy smiled and nodded at The Son reaffirming to him that they will be ok. As the two entered the eastern forest a new darkness swept into the village. The Dark Warrior followed by more grunts had made their appearance.

When Baraka's sword broke in Hoshek's castle, Hoshek had a vision. A vision as clear as day of lightning striking a man. The man looked like a younger version of The Father before his transformation. He also seemed to be connected to Soulmagic. It was as if Hoshek was inside the mind of this young man as he was fading away. Before his mouth closed he whispered "mentor." Hoshek became scared. *There must have been someone else in that hut before I arrived. It all makes sense now. That's why two swords were stolen. I must find this young man and his mentor. They most likely have Soulmagic strong enough for me to absorb. Then I can go back in time and change the past, fulfilling my goal. If he is who I need, I will also mind corrupt him to be on my Council of Swordmasters. His mentor might also prove to be useful. This mentor figure must be the same person from the hut who came looking for the man*, Hoshek thought to himself. He then gave the order to the Dark Warrior and a grunt battalion to search the north since that is the only place lightning strikes. "You are searching for two men; one will look young and the other will look old. Both possess Soulmagic and most likely a connection to an Attribute. Capture them., but under no circumstances shall you kill them."

As Ohr was about to begin teaching The Son about the Soulrock Attribute they saw a Purple Fire erupt from the village they had just left. "My brother has finally caught up to me. I believed he was the only one who could create Purple Fire unless he finally ..." Ohr dropped to his knees. "No he couldn't have. Could he?"

Bewildered, The Son asked, "Could he what? What did he create?"

Ohr replied, "When we were young, my brother was fascinated by the Legendary Beasts. I remember he used to talk about wanting to meet these strong beings that were connected to our universe as a whole. Then one day I remember he found a Tale written by a nobody. Someone who was not on any council, who was not connected to any Attribute or have Soulmagic of his own. He found it as we played in a cave in Aestercrat. It was written in blood. It showed the ability to create something as powerful as a Legendary Beast, yet this creation would obey your every command. I never thought Hoshek could stoop to this new low but he did. Not only did he kill everyone I loved, but he also used his Souldarkness Attribute to create a mindless being. We must avoid this new foe at all costs since neither of us are ready to fight him."

The Son arrogantly replied to Ohr. If I was destined to be as great as you say, then I should be able to defeat the Dark Warrior. The Son then focused a minimum amount of Soullightning Sub-Attribute from holding his sword transferring it to his feet giving him blazing speed. *Baraka was able to do it so I should be able to as well*, The Son thought. He had achieved an ability nobody had been able to do in the material world. The Son then started to run. Ohr was astonished.

Maybe I can mimic his Soulmagic technique, but in my own way, Ohr thought to himself.

Ohr then mustered enough strength in his soul to create a new sword made out of wood by tapping on a nearby tree. He proceeded to move the sword by twirling his wrist. This caused the trees to sway aggressively in front of The Son, preventing him from going any further. The Son turned around in disbelief. Ohr was the first person The Son had seen using an Attribute without a sword outside of the realm where he and Baraka met.

"I thought you told me that one can only use Soulmagic and an Attribute with the use of a sword. Was that a lie, to? What power are you trying to hide from me?" The Son screamed in anger. This ability was one that Ohr had come across through his studies of the Soulrock Attribute, it was never actually done before so he did not believe it would truly work.

Ohr then screamed back at The Son "You are not ready to face them, boy!"

Furious by the fact that he has been called a boy, his emotions took over. He was fed up with being treated like a child and being lied to. The Son said, "Ok, old man, let's see what you can do." The Son was fully enraged. The Son then thought to himself, *There were abilities that Ohr had yet to teach me and I did not understand why. If I was supposed to be the Leader of the next Council, I need to be trusted.* The Son's inner darkness was creeping closer and closer to his soul preparing to take over. The fact that it seemed that Ohr did not trust him only fueled The Son's anger even more. A man who supposedly taught him everything, who promised not to lie anymore, lied again.

The Dark Warrior who was miles away felt a sudden wave of darkness within his body. Intrigued by this feeling, he told his grunts to go back to Hoshek immediately and that he was going to see what this feeling was. Little did the Dark Warrior know, but Hoshek felt the odd feeling as well. He recalled one of the first conversations he had with his master when Hoshek told him, "I need you to go around Draefast collecting more souls with this gourd." The Dark Warrior was clutching onto the gourd filled with more souls for his master as he was thinking. His destiny was painted for him by his master.

The Son and Ohr clashed. Swing by swing they were parrying one another, but Ohr noticed that The Son was relying too much on his emotions. Ohr used The Son's aggression to his advantage. Knowing more about each Attribute made Ohr a more well-rounded and skilled fighter compared to The Son. Even though Ohr was older and weaker, he had been training with a sword since before The Son was born. He did not land any strikes on The Son. The Son encased his sword with Lighting using the Soullighting Sub-Attribute but that was not enough to defeat his mentor. By using the momentum of The Son's following strike Ohr was able to disarm him. Ohr then knocked The Son to the ground, thus winning the fight. While on the ground, The Son inhaled deeply to recenter himself and his thoughts. His inner darkness became dormant once again. Ohr then sheathed his new sword and reached out to The Son with his hand. The Son grabbed his arm and got up. Ohr apologized. "I am sorry I called you boy, and that you believe I have not taught you all you must know. To be honest I did not think my wooden sword trick would work. I believed that swords were the only extension of our soul but now I might be wrong. After we defeat Hoshek we should flesh out this newfound ability. I am trying my best to protect and train you. Your biggest lesson now is to be able to control your emotions.

That will make you a better fighter and Councilmember." The Son accepted his apology.

"It's ok Ohr. I need to learn to get better at controlling my emotions so that we have a chance of creating a new council."

Ohr replied, "You are progressing in your skills though. Keep up the good work along with training and clearing your mind, and you will be an even better sword wielder and Attribute master than myself." He needed The Son's emotions in check especially if he were to lead the Council and defeat Hoshek. Another slip up could lead to an entirely different outcome.

They continued to walk down to the village, being aware of every step they took. For now their bond was growing even closer than before.

"How do I unlock the Soulrock Attribute?" The Son asked Ohr.

"The Soulrock Attribute is a defensive Attribute. The way to unlock it in a fight is by focusing solely on protecting yourself and others, while tiring your foe. When your soul connects to your defensive reflexes and your compassion. Your sword will become covered in Counterrock, and you will be able to create boulders and launch them from your sword," Ohr said, satisfied that he was able to impart his knowledge of the Attributes to The Son.

During this time, the Dark Warrior used an ability he perfected with his Souldarkness Attribute. He was able to transport his body in the direction in which he threw his sword. This was an ability only the truest Souldarkness Attribute wielders could obtain. From afar, he watched The Son and Ohr duel, but decided not to intervene since he did not believe he could defeat both of the men, even if they were exhausted from fighting one another. The Dark Warrior then remembered another mission given to him by Hoshek. He needed to find and capture a Legendary Beast. For now the two men in the forest can wait, he knew he would be seeing them eventually and have another chance, a better chance at defeating them. He then threw his sword back to the village and then again to the desert where he had more grunts waiting his command. He would wait for The Son and Ohr to leave before making his next move.

The Dark Warrior's grunts were about to get on their ship with more of the goods from the town they just pillaged. The Dark Warrior had rigorously trained a group of three grunts to become his main followers. These were the strongest grunts in Hoshek's forces, and would be known as grunt leaders. These grunt leaders were created, around the same time as the Dark Warrior, from more than just a piece of dead tissue from Hoshek's old council friends. Hoshek removed their faces and created a new grunt body for them. He embedded them with his own Souldarkness Attribute which was not as pure as the Shroud but was still powerful. These grunt leaders had somehow retained the knowledge of their former sword fighting style, but since they had no pure soul their connection to Soulmagic or an Attribute was no more. It was replaced with Souldarkness. Hoshek was one step closer to creating his perfect council. He just needed one more mind and body to control. That is why he wanted to capture The Son. Only Baraka's soul was able to escape into a different realm before Hoshek could get to it. Since her soul was not inside her body, Hoshek could not create a fourth grunt Leader. Enraged, Hoshek burned her body using Purple Fire. This made it so Baraka's soul could never be at peace and find rest in her body. The three leaders would go on to train grunts on how to fight. Their purpose was to find the other destined Councilmembers on the other planets and defeat them in a sword fight, capture them and bring them to Hoshek so his Shroud can corrupt their minds. They were no match for Ohr's Soulmagic even though he was still weak. With a few swings of his sword while emitting small beams of light, the grunt leaders realized they were out classed and retreated back to the Dark Warrior. They knew that they had another mission that thy were needed for. As Ohr started up the ship, The Son returned the stolen goods back to the villagers.

Chapter XIV

The Hunt for a Legendary Beast

Ash drifted across the Dark Wizard's boot from the village surrounding the heat source burning behind him. As he continued walking, he motioned to the newly arrived grunts to follow him. He left his original battalion behind in the north as he began traveling east with these new grunts. His black cloak floated around his body, as he sheathed his sword. While he was on the quest of finding The Son and Ohr, he sent grunts to hunt down a Legendary Beast both he and his master had heard resided on Draefast. Since the Dark Warrior failed in capturing Ohr, he now needed to prove his worth to his master by hunting down, extracting the soul of a Legendary Beast, and then killing it.

As they neared a village surrounded by a forest, the Dark Warrior motioned for his grunts to ransack the village. The grunts destroyed it, burning it much like that last one. Two grunts then brought a barely surviving villager to the Dark

Warrior. Gasping for air the villager looked terrified at the Dark Warrior. The Dark Warrior quickly unsheathed his sword and pressed it up against the villager's throat. "What do you seek? Knowledge? I will tell you everything I know. Please don't kill me." The Dark Warrior kept a blank stare on the man. "If you are looking for an older man who has been traveling around villages suspiciously, my cousins told me they first met him in Hoshek City. I just met him a few days ago. He told me he was traveling south. He did not seem like the rest of us. He moved around unburdened. He had no home."

The Dark Warrior lowered his sword. He had gotten all the information he needed. This man the villager spoke of sounded like someone who Hoshek needed to see. Just as the Dark Warrior was about to walk away, he turned around, and with one swift stroke, he sliced the villager horizontally in half. The grunts snickered in amusement. The Dark Warrior and his accompanying grunts then headed through the forest to the next village south of here. They marched all day and all night until they made it to their next destination.

The Merchant had stopped in this village to rest and relay his song's message to everyone when he felt a dark presence. He had been traveling with his lute tied behind his back. He knew he could not run anymore, but he also knew he could not get involved. He needed to be captured. The Dark Warrior signaled for the grunts to surround the Merchant in the village square. He was outnumbered and had no weapon. "You look like a reasonable being, looking for accolades. Why don't you bring me to your master and extract my soul in front of him, you do want to make him proud isn't that why you are here in the first place. After all what's the difference from extracting my soul now versus in front of him?" The Dark Warrior had one hand on his gourd. He grasped his sword with the other, and from it came chains made from his Souldarkness Attribute. The chains tightly wrapped around the Merchant's body, immobilizing him. "You have caught me now, spare this village," the Merchant said.

The Dark Warrior looked at his grunts and with one nod chaos erupted. It was a massacre. The Dark Warrior wanted to make an example of the village that was hiding this man from him. Blood filled the streets of the village as the Dark Warrior dragged the Merchant and headed towards the city. He decided that he was going to bring the Merchant chained up to his master instead of in a gourd. This would prove his strength and worthiness. The Dark Warrior trudged through the forest for days until they came by a water source being guarded by grunts. The grunts let them pass. The Dark Warrior did not need food or water but the Merchant did in order to survive. They had a long journey ahead of them since the Dark Warrior could not teleport the two of them to the city. After drinking water and spending the night near the water source they were back on their way. "Hey do you ever talk. This journey would go a lot quicker if you did. Plus I am hungry and won't survive without some food." The Dark Warrior stopped and looked at the Merchant menacingly. "Well I guess you don't talk. Maybe you're too powerful to talk. Ha, imagine that." The Merchant continued to taunt the Dark Warrior. The Dark Warrior who was fed up with his voice used the chain of Souldarkness emitting from his sword to tie the Merchant to a tree. Every time the Merchant tried to move around; he became burned by little embers of Purple Fire from the chains.

The Dark Warrior now needed to go kill an animal with his bare hands so the Merchant could eat. When the Dark Warrior returned with food, the Merchant was gone, and the tree he was tied to was burned in half still lit by the Purple Fire. The Dark Warrior believed that the Merchant's strength would only amount to the same as a Swordmaster, and since the Dark Warrior had trained against phantoms of Swordmasters created by Hoshek, he thought that this would be enough. In anger, the Dark Warrior retracted the chains turning his sword back to normal and swung it in a circle around himself cutting down each tree. Then the Merchant appeared.

"Oh wow, you thought I left you didn't you? And you did all this deforestation for me, thank you very much." The Merchant continued to take jabs at the Dark Warrior who was furious. "All I had to do was use the bathroom and I did not want to go on myself, so I loosened the chains a bit, but trust me I know better than to run away from you." The Dark Warrior sat down and created a fire to start cooking the food. He was puzzled. To him this man could either be useless or useful. A trickster of an old man or a Legendary Beast. It did not matter soon he would be able to showcase his strength in front of his master by killing this man. The Merchant ate. "Thank you for the food. We can continue walking now. In fact, I know a shortcut to the city that will cut our travel time in half." The Dark Warrior let the Merchant lead but kept his sword to his back. The Merchant was right; they made it to the city gates three days earlier than expected. They walked towards the castle. Upon entering they went straight to Hoshek's chambers. Hoshek's chambers had many windows and took up a majority of the fourth story of the castle.

"You brought him to me, not what I originally expected but still excellent work," Hoshek said to the Dark Warrior. Turning to the Merchant, he continued, "Change into your true form you foul beast."

"I can try but what if you have the wrong guy," the Merchant replied toying with Hoshek. Hoshek looked up at the Dark Warrior in frustration. The Merchant took this opportunity to escape. He ran towards the window. Hoshek noticed and threw his sword, but the Merchant tilted his head dodging the fatal strike. The Merchant then kicked the glass in the window, shattering it, and jumped out. The Dark Warrior flung his sword as his body turned into a shroud that moved swiftly to where his sword landed. The Dark Warrior was on the south side of the castle on the first tier of the city close to the forest. He had teleported to where he thought the Merchant would have fallen but no one was there. Hoshek screamed. "We had him! Why didn't you kill him when you had the chance, or better yet why did you not entrap him in the gourd like you were originally told. You are supposed to be the most powerful being in Palaleon but you got tricked by a mere jester, someone who might not have been a Legendary Beast after all." The Dark Warrior returned to his master's castle, only to be met by grunts. He heard Hoshek's voice from above. "Attack him." The Dark Warrior prepared himself for the grunts attack. They all came at him at once. He inhaled clenching his sword in both of his palms using his Souldarkness Attribute to create phantom versions of himself to fight of most of the grunts while he took on a few. With ease the Dark Warrior slashed, struck, and burned through the grunts directly in front of him showing Hoshek that he was truly powerful. As his master walked down the stairs to see his creation, the Dark Warrior bowed. Behind him were grunt bodies lit on Purple Fire. The phantom versions of the Dark Warrior disappeared. Hoshek looked at him and spoke, "Failure like this will never happen again. I see you are able to put your sword and Souldarkness Attribute to good use. Next time you see a foe, kill it instead of bringing it to me."

Chapter XV
The Mission

After their run-in with the grunts, Ohr realized that The Son's training was nearly complete. They now had to move on to the next part of his plan which was to recruit members for the new Council of Swordmasters. This Council would be devoted to peace and justice. Beyond training The Son, Ohr needed to meet people who had become one with their Attributes. This was important because it would allow him to see if they were capable of defeating Hoshek in order to bring back peace to Draefast and ultimately Palaleon as a whole.

The Son and Ohr used the stolen ship they had absconded from the Dark Warrior's grunts. This ship permitted them to escape the planet undetected, so they could travel safely to the three other planets. Typically, the only way a ship would be able to leave Draefast was if it did not have a Souldarkness lock on it, which was placed on each ship that was manufactured according to Hoshek's design. The other way would be by breaking the lock. This could only be done by those strong enough with the Soulfire Attribute. The Son poured Soulmagic into his sword unleashing a little bit of the Soulfire Attribute, then swung his sword and broke the lock with ease. They were then able to leave Draefast's atmosphere.

Ohr had three people in mind for the new Council, but wanted to make sure The Son felt the same way about them. Each person had dealt with a tragedy in their life, but had the drive to overcome it and live on. This fortitude unlocked their Soulmagic Attribute.

"Your mother helped me find the names of the people we are looking for," Ohr said to The Son.

"You knew my mother? How come you never told me this, either?" The Son replied.

"I met her the same day I found you. She seemed lost, thinking that you were dead, so I sent her on my ship to assist with my plan. Much like saving you, I saved her by giving her a purpose. I believe that someday you will meet her and that will be a grand reunion, one not forced by my doing. I never told you since I did not want the knowledge of your family holding you back from your potential. I also have had problems with my family and I did not want to burden you with the same dealings."

The Son looked at Ohr. He was not angry at him for not telling him about his mother. He understood that he had a mission to complete, but now he had hope that he would meet her one day.

When The Mother and The Daughter were captured, The Daughter gave the communicating device to The Mother. She was then able to give Ohr the three names: Ehven, Lehavah, and May.

Ehven was the first person Ohr and The Son met. He was born on Aestercrat, a planet that, to its core, he felt a very strong connection on a soulful level. He was a tall, strong masculine figure with curly brown hair. His wardrobe consisted of brown tank tops and brown shorts. All of his shorts passed his kneecaps. He wore longer shorts, since he did not like to wear pants especially since he spent most of his time training by lifting rocks in the hot sun, and meditating while sitting on the dirt filled planet surface. His clothes represented who he was, and how he was connected to his Attribute. Ehven was strong enough in his Soulmagic, and therefore was able to connect with the Soulrock Attribute through his sword. He had crafted a single edged sword out of a piece of a rare metallic tree called Rathra. The hilt of the blade was made from Counterrock, which only he could hold since he was connected to this form of rock due to being the Soulrock Attribute Swordmaster. The Soulrock Attribute insignia was carved into the center of the hilt. He trained from Tales his mother had left behind from the previous Swordmaster who controlled the Soulrock Attribute. From a young age he trained himself in sword combat and went on to study the Soulrock Attribute so he was as prepared as he could be when the grunts started arriving. He had heard stories about the Swordmasters and how they met on his homeworld but since they, along with their headquarters, disappeared, the people on Aestercrat stopped believing that they were true protectors. This made Ehven almost doubt them as well, until he heard stories of a man who helped fight off grunts on his homeworld before his birth. This mystery man also helped train villagers to defend themselves. The man in those stories was Ohr, and he inspired Ehven even from a young age to train in his Soulmagic and Attribute and help defend his homeworld.

Ehven was the only one on Aestercrat who was able to

master the Soulrock Attribute along with its Sub-Attributes Soulwood, and Soulmetal. He was able to manipulate wood and metal to do anything he imagined through his sword. He could coat the blade in Counterrock, rock, metal, and wood. He learned how to manipulate each material coated on his blade, whether he wanted to shoot wooden spikes from his sword, or break an object using Counterrock his options were, to him, endless. He was as tough as the rocks around him, and was so connected with them that he could throw them while moving his sword around in his palm. One day, when Ehven was outside training, he saw what looked to be a meteor falling from the sky. This was actually The Mother, who was trying to brace for a safe landing on the planet's surface.

The Mother exited her ship which got stuck between two larger boulders near Mt. Calasmic. Since Ehven was close by he saw that she needed help. By moving his sword in a downward motion, he was able to flatten the boulders which dislodged the ship. The Mother saw this and knew he was strong in his Soulmagic and therefore his Attribute. She then went over to him and said, "Thank you so much for helping me get my ship out of that mess.' I can be such a clumsy flyer sometimes."

Ehven replied, "Ma'am, are you ok? I have never seen a ship come from the sky before."

"Oh yes, where I come from planetary travel is forbidden as well. I take it that the Dark Wizard has High Ranking Officials on this planet." During her time in captivity, The Mother learned that Hoshek sent High Ranking Officials to other planets throughout Palaleon to wreak havoc and take control. This was something The Mother reflected upon during her conversation with Ehven.

"I do not know anything about a Dark Wizard, but yes, there are some cruel people who have come here with an army of these unhuman beings to try and take over my planet," Ehven said.

The Mother continued, "Do you mind if I ask you some questions? I am searching for worthy people who are willing and qualified to stop Hoshek's reign and power on all planets in Palaleon."

Ehven proceeded to answer her questions. "What is Palaleon?"

The Mother replied, "Palaleon is the name of the universe in which four planets reside, including your homeworld. Not many people have the gifts that you have. These abilities are called Soulmagic, and since you are so connected to yours, you were able to unlock your very own Soulrock Attribute, and its Sub Attributes." The Mother continued by telling him the story that Ohr had told her about the origins of the Council of Swordmasters.

"That's incredible! I never knew that I was this special. I was just trying my best to help out the villages, since I knew that people were being treated unfairly."

"Your display of humbleness is another reason why I believe you are to be one of the five Councilmembers."

The Mother proceeded to ask him for a demonstration of his abilities. He was confused since he still had no idea who she was, but he did what she asked. He had also been saving villages from Hoshek's grunts his entire life. "Thank you for showing me your swordsman skills. Remember to continue to train. My friend will be here ready to meet you and when that time comes you must be prepared for anything, since that will mean the fight for this universe will commence." The Mother, realizing she had just referred to Ohr as her friend for the first time, smiled and went to her ship. As she entered the cockpit she signaled Ohr on their communication device. Ohr's voice came over the device, and he sounded very grateful for all The Mother is doing to help now. Before she left the planet to travel to her next destination she stumbled across Tales in a compartment next to her sleeping quarters on the ship that she had never thought to open. They were Tales written by each of the original Council of Swordmasters members explaining what Soulmagic was along with the different Attribute. The Mother could not access any of these abilities personally but through her reading learned how to train someone who has this potential. She now had the knowledge to be a vital part in training Swordmasters for years to come.

This conversation between The Mother and Ehven occurred several years earlier. Before Ehven met Ohr or The Son, he told stories to fellow villagers of how there were people standing up for what they believed in and helping their homeworld fight back against the evil that had taken over. This started the chain reaction of townspeople on Aestercrat knowing of life on other worlds outside their own.

Ehven was the first person that The Mother told Ohr about, which is why The Son and the Old Wizard went to Aestercrat first. They searched multiple villages before finding Ehven. The people seemed joyous and free. They were no longer under any tyrannical threat. The ground was scorched though, as if an all-out planetary fight had occurred days prior. Ohr and The Son walked by multiple farms exiting the village watching the smiles on the people's faces shine brighter than the sun above them. The Shroud was still present but had diminished quite a bit.

The Son finally noticed a man meditating outside one of the villages This man heard the presence of the two outsiders, opened his eyes, and stood up. The village they were near was next to a cave that was filled with Counterrock. The Son looked over to Ohr and said, "I bet he was in that cave before."

Ohr replied, "He seems to be very connected to that cave and the ground on this planet."

Ehven finally introduced himself. "You two do not look like you're from here. I had met a woman a while back telling me that two men would come and find me. I presume that she was talking about you."

"Yes my name is Ohr and this is my student and friend."

"Do you have a name?" Ehven asked, looking at The Son.

"Of course I do, but I don't remember. These past few years I have been focusing solely on training to be one of the five Council of Swordmasters members, and we want you to join." Ehven finally signaled them to follow him into his cave. The Son went in right after Ehven, followed by Ohr. The Son looked around, the cave was plain, there were a couple torches for light, what looked to be a bed made out of rock, a fire pit, and a shelf made from Counterrock which had food, clothes, and one photo of a young boy and two adults. There were various Tales spread about the cave. He put his sword upright leaning on where he was about to sit.

Ehven sat on a piece of Counterrock that was flat and vertically sticking out of the ground. He then motioned for them to take a seat on his bed. They sat down. "I have to ask why are you sleeping on a rock? Do you find comfort in this?"

"I find comfort in my surroundings. I am able to let my mind be at ease due to the amount of meditation I have done, so sleeping on that is not bad. Besides, it is a somewhat smooth rock." The Son proceeded to feel it and understood what he was talking about. Getting back to their original conversation Ehven said, "Well I have always wanted to visit other planets, I do like my home, but I feel like there is more to offer me out there." Although they were huddled in the cave, Ehven raised up his arm, extending his fingers, as if pointing to the sky.

The Son and Ohr went on to tell Ehven of their mission.

"Hoshek, the Dark Wizard, is gathering his forces to prepare to create his own Council and protect the world in his eyes, but that will only bring chaos to Palaleon."

"That sounds horrible. I want to do my part and protect everyone including people on other planets," Ehven replied.

The Son found Ehven trustworthy and enjoyed his company, so he opened up about the others they were looking for. Both Ohr and The Son looked at each other in agreement. He was indeed the next member of the new Council of Swordmasters. Ehven was very powerful in his Attribute and Soulmagic, and had a drive to protect those around him. All of these things made him a perfect candidate. The Son looked at Ehven as he was finally settling into their ship and said, "Before we head back to Draefast there are two more people we need to recruit."

From a young age, Lehavah always heard a voice in her head. The voice was calling out to Lehavah as she did not know it yet but she would become the next Soulfire Attribute Council of Swordmasters member. This voice happened to be someone The Son had already met. It was Baraka.

Years past and she tried dissociating herself from the voice, but it would not leave her alone. She went on to tell her parents about it but they never believed her. Finally she was fed up.

One night, Lehavah left her city apartment on Vastrilio, after getting into an argument with her parents. She ran through the city eventually making it to the edge and noticed ash flying in the air. This was not new but instead of a typical greyish ash it was blueish. Lehavah then saw rocks on fire and started going closer to them. She had long red hair, and was in a red dress with a blue symbol of fire in the middle. The fire symbol was designed with two small flames joining each other at an angle. Lehavah tripped and fell over one of these rocks and landed in a pool of fire. She felt her skin should be burning away but it was not. She started screaming and yelling for someone to come help her, but nobody in the village heard. She took a deep breath and submerged herself in the fire. Moving her hands around in a flowing motion, like how the fire was dancing around her body, she felt a zap and fainted.

Lehavah opened her eyes to see the same thing that The Son would see years later. It was Baraka. She extended her arm to help Lehavah up while asking, "How did you get here girl? What do you want?"

"I want to go home. My family must be worried about me. Wait a second. Your voice. It's the same one I hear in my head." Lehavah quickly became intrigued by this figure who was made out of lightning.

"You are the one I was calling out to. You are destined to learn about the Soulfire Attribute and be its next wielder, and I am destined to teach you," Baraka replied.

In the outside world, Lehavah's parents searched their city

221

for her, and ended up on the outskirts where they noticed a girl seemingly stuck in a fire. Upon closer examination, they realized that this young girl was their daughter. They tried in vain to rescue her from the flames, but each time they reached in to grab her, they, too, were burned. They were confused as to how their daughters' body had not been consumed in the flames. The citizens would pray to Baraka, who was the previous Soulfire Attribute sword wielder from the village that was once where the city lay now, for Lehavah's safe return. Baraka never returned home when the Shroud appeared. People believed her to be dead since she could not come and save them now.

Baraka trained Lehavah, teaching her everything that she knew. Lehavah became the hot-headed Soulfire and Soullightning Attribute Swordmaster.

Baraka knew that one day soon Ohr would be looking for new Councilmembers, so right before Lehavah was ready to join the real world, Baraka gave her a sword she had crafted using lighting and fire. Lehavah was now able to pour her Soulmagic into the sword and conjure her Soulfire Attribute and Soullightning Sub-Attribute through it, thus being able to shoot fire blasts and bursts of lightning from it.

Lehavah felt connected to this sword, and through that connection she was able to craft it and bring it back into the physical world when her mind returned back into her body as she stepped out of the fire. The sword was single edged and the Soulfire Attribute insignia was carved in the center of the hilt. As Lehavah exited she turned and waved at her mentor, who was waving back. "You will always be with me and I will pass down your teachings when the time is right. Thank you, and I will do my best in finding your body so you can return home," Lehavah said.

Baraka replied, "Don't you forget I will always be here to guide you. I believe that now that you are connected to your inner fire all you have to do to see me again is to meditate." Then Lehavah vanished.

She went back to her home where her parents were astonished to see that she had survived a year in the fire. To her it felt like a week. They were so happy to have her home and she was so happy to be home. When she displayed her new abilities to her parents they became scared and thought that she was not the same girl that left their home a year ago. Lehavah knew that she was still the hot-headed girl they had raised, but clearly her parents did not accept her. Realizing that she had scared her parents, she thought it would be best if she left the city and went to live on the outskirts of the food factories. She had packed a bag with essentials, such as a canteen for water, food, a blanket, and tools to start a fire. She was wearing her long red dress and packed multiple other versions of the outfit. She wore brown boots up to her kneecaps. All of her necessities were in a brown satchel she carried over her shoulder. She looked over the city for many years, fighting many grunts. This continued until The Mother found her and told her that she will soon be meeting Ohr, but until that day, she needed to continue her training in order to be ready for what's to come.

The Son and Ohr traveled to Vastrilio after meeting Ehven on Aestercrat. The new Councilmember Ehven was thrilled to have new friends and help find new members to fight the darkness that was spreading to other planets. Each member of the new Council was bonded by the fact that they lost family members or friends to the tyrant causing the Souldarkness Shroud surrounding them, and had to defend their home from Hoshek's grunts. Each member met Lehavah and through their initial interaction decided that she was qualified to be the newest Swordmaster, particularly since she had been trained by Baraka. Ehven went up to Lehavah and said, "Hey, I'm also new here, but these guys seem really nice and are fighting for a good cause so I believe it's worth it. My name is Ehven."

"Hey Ehven, I am glad to meet new people and you seem really nice and relaxed. I am ready to fight and defeat all the grunts to restore Palaleon." Ehven and Lehavah hit it off, and become very close, fairly quickly.

Hoshek had to travel quickly off Draefast since his Souldarkness Attribute teleportation ability would not last long. Due to his age, the poison from overusing Souldarkness Attribute was slowing him down. His body had morphed into this older more decrepit state, one far too ugly to be seen by average Draefast citizens. He would find people with strong souls and steal them, bring them back to Draefast to siphon their souls, and turn them into grunts and grunt sub-leaders.

Originally he used dark and pure souls to further his lifespan but his Souldarkness Attribute overpowered souls incinerating them withing his body, so it had no effect. Even if he absorbed fifty souls nothing in his appearance changed. His body had already taken on the full effects of his power, it was like lighting an already lit match, he was decaying.

Then he tasked the sub-leaders and mindless grunts to go to the other planets to start stealing more people so he could absorb their souls like what they were doing for him on Draefast. He also commanded then to mine for resources useful to his plan. He believed his goal of creating the perfect Council was getting closer and closer. *Soon I will bring Palaleon back to harmony,* Hoshek thought in his own twisted way. He only communicated with his grandfather about these mini adventures. He did not even tell the Dark Warrior. He wanted to keep full control over him and not give him the ability to leave and travel to the other planets. Going to other planets could give the Dark Warrior a sense of curiosity and Hoshek could not have that if he wanted the Dark Warrior to remain under his control.

Inevitably, traveling off world slowed by himself slowed his plans. Hoshek had to come up with a better idea, so he went into the Soul Realm for four minutes and let his darkness take over so that he could create a blast strong enough to break Draefast's atmosphere and travel into the universe. Once the blast was produced Nahvel helped his grandson regain control over his darkness and left the Soul Realm. This blast kept the Soul Realm portal open so that it could send the High Ranking Officials to all the planets in Palaleon, but it also weakened Hoshek's control over the Shroud of Souldarkness making it so people started regaining control of their minds. Hoshek also made a point to send grunts and sub-leader grunts to reinforce his rule through his High Ranking Officials, and try to make it impossible for strong Attribute wielders to unlock their Soulmagic, and if they did they were to be captured and brought to Hoshek. This helped prevent people from stopping Hoshek's plan. Once the High Ranking Officials and their grunts landed on the planets the blast disappeared and the Soul Realm portal closed.

Hoshek knew he had to leave his planet in order to fulfill his and his grandfather's goal, but he had also come to the conclusion having to leave Draefast so frequently could lead to his downfall. The Dark Warrior did notice that grunts and sub-leaders were missing, but he did not know why. So he just ignored it.

Crateolios was a planet with air as thin as a butterfly's wing, and as cold as a frozen tundra. The Mother had difficulty finding someone to be the next Soulwater Attribute Councilmember. She never learned how to swim on Draefast, and most of the villages on Crateolios were covered by a thin sheet of ice. The Mother reported to Ohr of a boy who saved her and The Daughter when they had first arrived at Crateolios, after The Daughter's capture. The Mother did not return to Crateolios since the planet reminded her of her daughter and the grief she felt for leaving her. After hearing about the conditions of the planet Ohr trained The Son how to survive in harsh weather conditions, including freezing cold water. Im was the name of the man who they were looking for.

Im grew up surrounded by water. His only close reactive was sister, May. Im and May didn't know of any members of their extended family, and both their mother and father were dead. Their mother died while they were both very young, and their father died of an unknown disease shortly after. Im had taken care of May since they were young, she looked up to him as a father figure since she could not remember her father. Im had told May that she looked like their mother from when she was very young, and they had a drawing of their family that Im kept with him at all times in his pocket to prove it. They were four years apart. Their parents had left them with a home, books to study from and currency after they passed. Their father was a teacher at the school in the village, and their mother was an ice architect.

Unlike Ehven and Lehavah, May was a very shy girl who kept to herself most of the time. Her hair was long and wavy, and was as blue as the water beneath her feet. As for clothes, she wore a blue coat and black pants. Her coat was always zipped up, over her shirt, to her chin and she never took it off in front of anyone but her brother. Im taught his sister how to control the Soulwater Attribute since he was a known hero in their village, always collecting the biggest food for the village to survive on. He would also fight off grunts who would try to steal the village's various supplies and water currency. May felt like she was living in Im's shadow, but she respected every lesson in life that her brother taught her.

One night, as she was finishing up her studies, she heard a blast and looked outside to see hooded figures holding her brother's body and running away. May lost the only family member she had known, and this pain changed her. She vowed to learn everything she could about the Soulwater Attribute which also included its healing ability and the Sub-Attribute of Soulice, along with her inner Soulmagic.

She wanted to find the beings who kidnapped her brother and make them pay for their deeds. May spent years honing her skills of the Soulwater Attribute and Soulice Sub-Attribute. Im had learned how to control water through his sword from a young age. He was self-taught in his inner Soulmagic, just like how May was teaching herself when he was kidnapped. May crafted her sword out of ice and stored flowing water in the center, so that if the ice ever broke she would be able to control the water, which was indeed sharper than the ice. The sword was single edged and the Soulwater Attribute insignia was carved into the hilt. She eventually found her brother's kidnappers, who happened to be a few of Hoshek's grunts. They were ordered by Hoshek's High Ranking Official, who was placed on Crateolios, to kill anyone who posed a threat to their rule over the planet. She was just in time to watch as they disposed of her brother's body over an ice cliff into water rapids. Calmly but aggressively, May began to shoot ice spikes from her sword. Each landed a fatal blow. After killing each grunt and their sub-leader, May dove into the rapids to get to her brother. She grabbed his body and carried him while swimming to an ice floe. May climbed atop the ice, then pulled Im onto it. He laid there on his back, motionless. May thought that since she had trained using Soulwater Attribute to heal that she could go even further and bring him back to life. She came to the conclusion that all she was doing was healing his outside wounds. He still lay dead in her lap. May began to cry over her brother's body. Her tears fell upon Im's left pocket. She put her hand in his pocket, and found the picture of their family. She glanced at it while moving to sit closer to the water. She noticed that the water was reflecting writing from the back of the drawing of her family, so she turned it over. It read, "Hey May, if you are getting this, then either I am gone, or I have given it to you so you can have something to hold onto from our past. I just want you to know how proud I am of you, and all your accomplishments. By the rate you are going with your studies, you will be far more skilled than I in the Soulwater Attribute. Just remember to not take life for granted, and only do what you deem is right. Protect our village however you can. They along with our planet need someone like you. I love you. - Im."

Looking back at her brother's dead body, she knew she had to make her own path, while still going by her brother's words and teachings. May then jumped to another ice sheet, and with a stroke of her sword created a wave to push the floe her brother's body was on far away, sending him off in the best way she knew how. As May walked back towards her village she promised to never use ice shatter spikes from her sword until she had fully mastered how to heal. She spent most of her days practicing the healing ability on animals and people in her village who were hurt by the grunts. May looked up from healing an animal as her eyes caught something swimming against the harsh current. The creature sped quickly just under the surface, and then shot through to the air and glided above the waves. A moment later, it returned to the water and hurried away. The White Manta Ray had made its first appearance to the young woman. This encounter symbolized the change May's soul was going through as she was ready for the next chapter of her life. Arguably, the most important one yet for the sake of Palaleon.

She also began to practice her aim of the ice spikes to become more controlled. May thrust her sword into the ice next to her and cut out rectangular sheets that she could write on. Since her sword was coated with her Soulwater Attribute these tablets were so cold that not even the light generating crevasse on Draefast could melt them. As her training progressed, she carved notes into several Ice Tablets, describing her new-found skills.

Ohr, The Son, Ehven, and Lehavah traveled to Crateolios as their final destination to find May. They searched many villages, and each village leader told them the same thing. "We have not seen her in weeks. Last time we saw her she left our village and headed toward Rippling Wave." Rippling Wave was a group of waves only heard of in Tales, but it was on the other side of Crateolios. The new Council found May there. She was in between two waves on a sheet of thin ice feeding native animals.

Ohr told the others, "Stay on the ship I will go talk to our new friend." After a long hour of waiting, both Ohr and May climbed aboard the ship. She was enthused to meet new people. She finally had a new family, one that would help her grow in her Attribute. She was the final member of their new Council of Swordmasters. "Hi everyone my name is May."

The Son replied, "Those looked like some intense waves."

May smiled. "Water and ice are my specialty, so I knew I was going to be fine." Both The Son and May clicked upon their first conversation.

The sub-leader grunts and grunts had stolen souls around Palaleon but would never find and obtain Ehven, Lehavah, or May's souls. They were always destined to be on the Council of Swordmasters, they just needed to prove that they were ready, which each one of them had done.

Chapter XVI

Knowledge: Back to Draefast

Ehven sighed. Along with the others, he had finally saved their homeworlds. Now it was time for them to rid the universe of the tyrant who brought devastation to their people. "Did any of you also have a leader of your homeworld, with an army that would make people disappear?" May and Lehavah nodded.

"It's interesting you ask that. I actually freed my planet from our leader a day before you, Ohr, and The Son showed up," Lehavah said, as she pointed towards the three of them.

"I also fought the leader of my world the day before." May stated.

Ohr then spun around from his captain's chair and opened his mouth, "Those must have been Hoshek's High Ranking Officials. How were you able to defeat them with minimal training?"

"I was finally able to help my people stand up against his

rule," Ehven began telling his story that occurred a few days before Ohr and The Son arrived on Aestercrat.

"I feel like today is the day to end this tyrant's rule. I have been training for this for years. Now it's time for the people to rise up. I went into a village near my home cave. I walked through noticing that something was different. People were outside crying. I walked over to a young girl. 'What's wrong?' I asked. 'She is gone. They took my mother.' I was angry. I had not felt this way in years. For my entire life I watched as the people around me acted mindless. 'Who took your mother?' I asked the young girl. 'It was as if a shadow did. I could not make out who did it.' I then replied. 'Don't worry I will try to get her back.' I then jumped on top of a house and shouted to the people. 'My name is Ehven. I do not know if all of you have heard about me, but I am the one who has been fighting against our tyrannical ruler for years. Now it is our turn to strike back. I have tried to train some of you before, as I know a man once visited here to do the same. When that man came here you were all too scared to fight back. Well now this has gone on for too long. Are your lives really yours anymore? Or are you just puppets on a string?"

"The people looked around. They were becoming rallied as one group. 'What should we do, Ehven?' The young girl asked.

'I need you to go to other villages, cities and towns,' I said, 'Inform the people of what has happened here. Tell them that I am finally taking the fight to the castle. If we have enough people fighting instead of remaining complacent then we will win and everyone will be free.' The people cheered, as they grabbed racks resembling an angry mob and traveled in different directions to different villages. As I ran towards the castle I recalled to the day I had heard stories about when everything changed. The day a beam of Souldarkness struck my planet acting as a teleportation mechanism bringing sub-leader grunts, grunt battalions, loyalists, and the High Ranking Official to rule. This evil wretched man that no one knew what to call, had already corrupted the minds of the people with the Shroud looming over them, now he also had an interim ruler for the world along with an army to keep that person in rule. He sent his loyalists to people's homes to ensure that they would remain complacent under the rulers care before grunts became involved. I knew it was up to me to free my world but I could not do it alone. As I ran, my sword sheathed on my back, I was smiling. I broke through to the people, it had taken years but something about this day was different than the rest."

It was as if Hoshek's control over the Shroud had dimmed. As Ehven's connection to his Soulmagic and Attribute abilities grew, Hoshek's control over the world faded.

The High Ranking Official stood proudly atop his castle. He took in a deep breath. From the corner of his eye, he noticed a grunt walking up to him. A voice then emerged from this grunt. The High Ranking Official was confused. He had believed that grunts could not speak. "He is coming today, rallying the people behind him. How could you let this happen? Defend your castle at all costs. Keep the people around and inside your castle entranced by the loyalists you brought with you. Remain in power or you will fall." The grunt then disintegrated into a shadowy black orb.

The High Ranking Official was not scared of this one man since he believed he still held onto the minds of the people.

He was in charge of the planet for decades and no one ever dared to defy him much like the other High Ranking Officials and their worlds. *This one man is no match for my grunts,* The High Ranking Official thought to himself.

He continued to think, *That voice sounded like Master Hoshek's. I do not want to lose my power.* "GRUNTS!" the High Ranking Official bellowed to all of his forces, "Defend this castle, kill anyone who stands in your way!" The ground started to shake as his words flew from his lips. A plume of dust arose from the ground all the way to the sky where the wall once was. As the dust settled behind the fallen wall, a man appeared. From the sword that he plunged into the ground, Ehven had created a seismic disturbance on the planet's surface, focusing his Soulmagic towards just the wall. by just striking his sword down in one fluid motion. Behind him stood hundreds of citizens. The people residing in the common ground between the wall and the castle were scared. They had been directly under the High Ranking Officials thumb for so long. They began to scream and panic. 'We are going to die. The Insurgents are here. Run, hide, if you fight them you will die.'

Ehven heard these words coming from the High Ranking Official to his followers, the people who still resided around the castle. Ehven continued with his story. "I then jumped onto the roof of a building and shouted, 'To all the people who believe we are here to hurt you. You are mistaken. We are here to take back our home. For too long this man,' I pointed my sword at the castle, 'has been governing you on no basis of being an actual leader. He along with his loyalists do not care about you. I do. You do not need to join me. But if you do not want to get hurt, leave this city as I cannot protect you while I am saving our world.' People started running towards the gate towards the mountain side. Others stayed and joined me. I continued onward as the people began overpowering the grunts. At the foot of the castle, I swiftly unsheathed my sword slicing open my own entrance. I ran through the castle, swinging my sword and hurling metal shards from it which killed the grunts with ease. 'I am doing this for the people, and for my world. The man I was told about,' Ehven gestured towards Ohr, 'should be proud.' This was the only thought running through my head. I made it to the top of the castle. I locked eyes with the High Ranking Official, but all a sudden a mysterious foe lunged at me. I parried. It was the sub-leader grunt. His sword was coated with Souldarkness. As I engaged in a sword fight with this sub-leader grunt I noticed that the High Ranking Official tried to escape to his ship. He ran around me and tried making it to the stairs. I saw this, and quickly dug my sword into the ground and swung from my right side to my left shoulder. Multiple rocks emerged from the ground blocking the High Ranking Official's way out. They also acted as a defense since the sub-leader grunt was about to land a fatal blow against me. I had captured the sub-leader grunt in between two spiked rock formations. With ease, I stabbed it in the chest, but as this happened the High Ranking Official started coughing. I ran over to him placing my sword back in my sheath as I thought the fight was over. 'I'm dying,' he said. 'How could this be.' A billow of black gas emerged from the High Ranking Official's body. As the life was about to leave his body, I said to him, 'I guess you were supposed to keep a closer eye on me. I out-witted your strongest grunt, and when I defeated him, your own master felt that he needed to silence you. To him we are all just pawns in his game.' I knelt down towards the High Ranking Official showing that I had respect for him, as he realized that he was just as blind as the people were. The High Ranking Official suddenly sent his arm upwards towards my head. He was holding a knife. 'If I die so will you. Long live Hoshek's reign.' I swiftly unsheathed my sword, cutting the arm of the High Ranking Official off with one fluid motion. The High Ranking Official's body then went limp as his eyes glossed over in a greyish color. I stood up, and re-sheathed my sword. At that moment, the rock formation guarding the exit sunk back into the ground. I guess they were really no threat after all. All I needed was the people to back me up." Ehven was done recalling his story to his friends.

The Son then said to Ehven. "I think that the sub-leader grunt lost, due to the High Ranking Official's haste in wanting to leave so badly. If he had not left, then you would not have been able to trap the sub-leader grunt so easily." Ehven nodded in agreement.

"I am just happy my world is safe. Along with the people who reside there," Ehven said. Ohr nodded in agreement.

"Ehven, your story sounds similar to mine." Lehavah said.

"Several days ago, I was traveling through to Vastrilio's city to confront the High Ranking Official and his loyalists who were ruling over my world," Lehavah continued.

"For too long I had watched my family, friends, and fellow citizens succumb to this 'normalcy', but it was not normal. I watched people in the city act as if the children were not being stolen from them. I was fed up. Not a single parent cried for their child, they just let it happen. My own parents refused to recognize who I was, especially when I decided to stand up against our leader. Most people then began guarding the castle entrance as if they all heard what I had said privately to my parents. Infront of the people stood the loyalists. To avoid all of the people, I jumped on a rooftop and landed in front of grunts. I needed to make a scene for the people to see that this was not a normal living situation. I was working in the shadows fighting grunts for too long. As I landed I conjured fire from my sword swinging it around my body. Grunts started burning up in a wall of fire. The people turned around and saw this, and it was like clockwork, the people's minds started coming back to them. With no training at all the people charged the grunts with flaming torches. Blood was spilled. Grunts were consumed by the flames, but people were dropping like flies. I saw this before I entered the depths of the castle. I turned back towards the fight outside, and ran up the stairs. Word traveled quickly of the fiery tempered girl starting an insurgency against the leader of Vastrilio. I saw my parents through a window, they were now in the back of the people's riot. They seemed disappointed to see me start this fight. The two of them turned away and walked back towards their home. I remember yelling. 'Why. Why don't you trust me? This is not right.' I pointed her sword at the grunts fighting the people and took a deep breath. Flames emerged from her sword; all the grunts burned."

"I heard Baraka's voice in my head. 'Remember aggression will only get you so far. Be sure to stay calm as well.' Then I turned back facing the inside of the castle, and made my way up to the High Ranking Official. Burning grunts left and right from the edges of my sword I had no one in my way. Then a figure dropped from the ceiling above."

"The sub-leader grunt swung its sword at me. I ducked. I did not have time to waste with this grunt, I needed to fix my world. We fought. He tried hiding in the shadowy areas of the castle. I made it to the stairs. The sub-leader grunt chased me. Its body was covered in scratches, I could see it as its cloak flew as he ran toward me. The entire castle felt cold. The sub-leader spun his sword and tried to stab me. I was able to conjure the Soullighting Sub-Attribute splitting his sword in half, going as far to cut him in half. The two halves of the sub-leader's grunt sword fell. I could feel wind bouncing off the pieces of the sword. They almost hit my feet. I continued upwards to the High Ranking Official's chambers. I opened the door, there he stood on the windowsill. 'What are you doing, you coward.' I asked him. He replied, 'If I die like this then you will look like the villain to everyone on this planet including your family. You would become the girl who freed her people at the cost of a life.' He jumped. Instincts kicked in, I was not a bad person and I felt that I knew what I was doing was not just for me but for my planet. I jumped out the window after him. I was falling trying to gain speed to catch up to him. Then I heard Baraka's voice again, 'You can do this. I believe you will figure this out." I started spinning my body to gain more speed. I caught up to the High Ranking Official, and was able to stab his cloak into the side of the castle. We hung there as lightning emanated from my sword. "Tell them the truth now!' I told him angrily. 'I will never speak ill of Hoshek.' The High Ranking Official replied. 'Fine, but once you die I hope you know I will free these people. Completely.' I gave him one last chance before kicking off the side of the castle. The High Ranking Official fell to his death and as all the people gathered around him I fell. I pointed my sword upward closed my eyes and took a deep breath in. 'This is the end for me.' I thought to myself. Suddenly, I opened my eyes and I was on the other side of the planet holding my sword which was producing lightning out of it. That is when I met you guys. I think I freed my people but I am not entirely sure. I hope I did."

"Wow. All of our stories are sounding the same." May stated.

The Councilmembers ship was closing in on Draefast's atmosphere.

May continued to speak. "After I lost my brother Im to the sub-leader grunt, I fully immersed myself in learning how to control the Soulwater Attribute. Before I met you guys I had figured out how to use my emotions to fuel my Attribute. Like Ehven, I had no teacher. I was alone. But like Lehavah, I did not have the support of my fellow people to stand up against the High Ranking Official. They all thought I was crazy. A few of them watched me kill the sub-leader grunt but due to their clouded minds mistook that for me killing Im. They believed I was the villain who could not control my actions. But let me assure you, I did not kill my own brother. I used the remainder of the days prior to when you all showed up to hunt down the High Ranking Official. I believe he inferred that something was wrong when the sub-leader never returned. He kept fleeing his various homes, always on the move, but I was after him. I did not want what happened to my brother to happen to anyone else. I was finally able to swim in the cold depths of Crateolios with no harm. I was able to catch up to him. He never saw me coming, as I swam underneath the ice, cutting a hole. He fell in. I stabbed him in the chest, and used my Soulice Sub-Attribute to freeze his body which then sunk to the lowest part of our ocean. A place he will never be found. A place he could never possibly escape. I then got out of the water, only to be seen by the High Ranking Officials family and loyalists. I told them that he feel in the water and I tried to save him but couldn't get there in time. They believed me. The Shroud's effect was already starting to wear off on them. Hopefully they told the rest of the planet that everything will be good now, and that everyone and their children will be safe. When I return home, I hope they do not believe I am crazy."

The Son replied, "I doubt they will. The universe is about to change, it will soon be better than it has been."

Fighting the High Ranking Officials and their sub-leader grunts took most of the strength possessed by each young Swordmaster. The timing could not have been more perfect as The Son and Ohr would travel to each planet right after these victories occurred.

The grunts on Draefast had an even harder time then on the other planets since they were tasked with capturing Ohr and The Son, with help from the Dark Warrior but had never succeeded. Hoshek created swords out of souls he captured using his Souldarkness Attribute. He gave each grunt a sword, and grunt leaders got two swords. Hoshek had the grunt leaders stay on Draefast as extra protection for himself. He gave the grunt leaders the swords from the council that he and Baraka trained to be on as kids.

Sending High Ranking Officials, sub-leader grunts, and grunts, was part of Hoshek's plan dictated by Nahvel for a more ordered universe through the jurisdiction of a new council. One with no dissent. Hoshek needed the Swordmasters from other worlds in order to create his council. When he realized his forces could not capture them, he had to think of something new. That is when he had decided to create the grunt leaders. As his grandfather whispered into his ear, Hoshek thought to himself, *instead of taking these Swordmasters, I have created my own. I have full control now and have created my version of my Council through Souldarkness.* These Dark Councilmembers included Hoshek, the Dark Warrior, and the newly perfected grunt leaders.

Ohr and the others arrived on Draefast to see the whole planet in ruin. The ground was battle torn. Villagers finally had the will to stand up against Hoshek's grunt army. Their ship prepared for the landing sequence, but The Son wanted a closer look, so without any hesitation he said, "I will see you all on the ground." He then proceeded to leave the bridge, sword sheathed to his belt and jumped off the side of the ship. He landed to see dead grunts, and the bodies of villagers strewn about him. Over his right shoulder, The Son noticed more grunts approaching. The rest of the Swordmasters exited the ship. "We need to make sure they don't get to the ship," Ohr commanded. All the Swordmasters replied in unison, "Understood." More and more grunts started to surround them.

"We need to get to the castle as soon as possible. We can't focus on this if we want to stop Hoshek," The Son said. They engaged the grunts. Swords clashed. Grunts fell, but more kept coming. Ehven saw that Lehavah was fighting three at once so he threw his sword at one of the grunts, piercing its body. With his bare fists, he proceeded to bash the head of another grunt in his vicinity. Lehavah stuck her sword in one of the two remaining grunts, burning its body to a crisp. She left her sword in its body as she picked up Ehven's sword to clash with the final grunt in her way. She had carved a path for them to escape.

Ehven ran over and picked up her sword, and as Lehavah defeated the last grunt in her sight the two of them ran into the forest. The others followed, leaving their ship behind. Grunts decided to stop chasing the Swordmaster, and instead they made a line touching each other's shoulders transferring what little Souldarkness Attribute they had to the one in front, who with one swing of his sword summoned Purple Fire destroying their ship but also disintegrated the other grunts. The last grunt then started his journey back to the castle to warn Hoshek that the Swordmasters had arrived. Hoshek already knew.

Members of the Council of Swordmasters were able to wield each other's swords, due to the strong connection they all shared. Ohr was the only Swordmaster who could wield more than one of the swords at the same time channeling his Attribute and Soulmagic if needed through both. He had the knowledge of each Attribute and the focus to go along with it. They all stopped in the forest to regain their bearings as they had a bigger fight ahead. The Son took this time to relax his mind and meditate for he had a lot of weight riding on his shoulders. Ohr took this time to meditate as well. Now being in a relaxed peaceful state of mind, Ohr unlocked a new aspect of his Soullight Attribute. He visualized that he is able to form the most powerful sword on Palaleon, the Planetary Sword. This would be accomplished by using his Soulmagic to pull each Councilmember's sword to him to merge into one. The Planetary Sword can grant the user access to control time, but Ohr did not know how to unlock this power yet. Each Councilmember had read Tales about the Planetary Sword, and dreamt about what they would do if they had the ability to control the Time Attribute, alas, they did not know how to obtain this ability, so their dreams were just illusory. Even The Son who had no memory had dreams about an unknown past, and how he could go back and relive it. These dreams did fulfill their purpose in keeping their minds active, each member thought about what could have been instead of what is. They continued to ponder about this even as Ohr told them more about the Planetary Sword and the Time Attribute. They were all glad that they did not find a way to act on their dreams, since they felt grateful for where they are now in their lives even if each of them had troubled pasts. In unison The Son, Ehven, Lehavah, and May let out a sigh of relief "ah". As if a mental weight had been lifted off their shoulders. The Council was now heading towards Hoshek's castle. It was time for them to take the fight to him instead of waiting around to be captured.

Penultimate Chapter

The Son vs. The Father

Ehven, Lehavah, and May were stopped in the middle of the ramp between the first tier and second tier of the city adjacent to the castle by the opposing grunt leaders. "Time to do our part without destroying homes or harming the civilians around us," Ehven said.

"You guys go ahead," Lehavah and May said to The Son and Ohr.

The three Swordmasters stood across from their foes. The grunt leaders prepared to strike.

"Teamwork. Let's try it," Ehven called out to the others. Lehavah and May nodded in agreement.

Ehven then thrust his sword into the ground creating a mini fissure. It disrupted the grunt leaders causing them to go into evasive maneuvers. The grunt leaders threw their swords encased in Souldarkness to try to poison the Swordmasters but each of the three dodged them with ease, rotating to the left so their right shoulders pointed towards their foes. The

Souldarkness blasts from the grunt leaders' swords destroyed trees in the forest northeast behind the Council of Swordmasters.

Ehven, Lehavah, and May were training for this exact moment throughout their entire lives. They acted swiftly and as a team. The grunt leaders then noticed that they could not move their legs. In unison, they looked down and noticed water turning into ice crawling up their legs. May snickered, "Let's finish this," as she looked at her peers. Ehven released a Counterrock boulder infused with bits of metal from the fissure by thrusting his sword upwards. He then conducted the boulder over the grunt leaders' heads. More grunts started to appear around them. Ehven released his grip on the boulder by lowering his sword. It fell, and as it did it broke into metallic shards that Lehavah lit on fire by shooting fire blasts from her sword. Each shard impaled the grunt leaders killing them easily. "I thought they were supposed to be difficult," May said. Ehven looked at her then replied, "They would have been if we decided to fight them one on one, but since we worked as a team, they were no match for us. Now let's deal with all of these grunts." All three of them ran towards the castle entrance. They faced outwards touching their backs, ensuring that they would be protected. Grunts started running at them from all different directions swinging their swords. The grunts goal was the kill these Swordmasters then enter the castle and defend Hoshek. Parry. Strike. Attribute. The three Swordmasters continued through the motions protecting one another while defeating their enemies. Everything they had trained for throughout their lives on their homeworlds was coming to fruition. The dust in the air from the charging grunts had cleared, and the three Swordmasters remained standing while the grunts lied on the ground. Some were dead, while others were critically injured. Now all the Swordmasters had to do was guard the front of the castle, preventing the grunts from entering.

As The Son and Ohr ran into the castle, The Son turned his head to see multiple different aspects of Soulmagic being used with each other. He felt bad about leaving his friends but knew it was the best thing to do. May happened to be gazing upon the castle while The Son had turned his head. She thought to herself, *I hope he will complete his mission and return to us safely.*

The Son and Ohr reached the third tier of Hoshek's Castle and were stopped by the Dark Warrior who stood opposite them emitting pure Souldarkness. The Son told Ohr, "Go to Hoshek, I can handle this."

"Are you sure you are ready? We can easily defeat if we band together."

The Son replied, "This is what I have been training for. Just go!" Ohr smiled, for he realized that his training had given The Son the confidence and determination he needed to battle the Dark Warrior. Ohr was able to run past the Dark Warrior and onto the next tier of the castle without any problems, since the Dark Warrior knew that his master wanted to confront Ohr himself.

The Son ran towards the Dark Warrior, shouting, "This is for my home and everyone you have hurt here!" Both The Son and the Dark Warrior were exchanging blows, their swords clanging in engagement, yet the duel was looking more and more like a choreographed battle between light and darkness. Every time the Dark Warrior swung his sword, a shadowy essence followed the blade, while every time The Son countered or went on the offensive, his sword glowed in a white glistening light. This light illuminated the otherwise gloomy ashen chamber. The Son jumped away from the Dark Warrior encasing his blade in ice from his Soulwater Attribute and then shot ice spikes into the air. The ice spikes rained down at intense speed towards the Dark Warrior. The Dark Warrior met this attack by turning his sword into chains made of Purple Fire eradicating each spike before it landed. Mist started to appear around the Dark Warrior impairing his vision so The Son took this as an opportunity to strike. He gripped his sword tightly and inhaled. Upon his exhale, bright red flames surrounded his sword. He was using his Soulfire Attribute now. The Son charged into the mist. He saw the Dark Warrior and lunged at him swinging his sword from above his head to the middle of his chest. The Dark Warrior's sword suddenly turned into a shroud and flowed through The Son's sword. Upon his sword turning back into its physical form again, the Dark Warrior twisted it so the flat edge hit The Son with enough force to propel his body into the air. As the mist cleared, the Dark Warrior lifted his sword up from his right side pointing the blade at The Son. While The Son was in the air, the hilt of his sword pressed against his chest pointing the tip of the sword at the Dark Warrior. The Son then extended his arms away from his chest and lightning began to flow around his sword. The Dark Warrior was preparing to throw it towards The Son to teleport but was not given the opportunity to do so. Using his Soullighting Sub-Attribute, The Son began shooting bolts of lightning at the Dark Warrior as he was falling back to the ground. The Dark Warrior met each bolt with his own Purple Lightning nullifying The Son's attack.

The Dark Warrior began to feel a pain which was debilitating his movements in his leg. He was still fighting the Souldarkness poison coursing through his body from years early and dueling with The Son was weakening his hold over the poison.

Every time I use an Attribute he meets it with his own Souldarkness Attribute techniques. Maybe I need to try running at him and breaking his guard with my sword, The Son thought. The Son was quicker than the Dark Warrior, but the Dark Warrior was far more powerful in his swings. They parried back and forth for what seemed like a fortnight. Eventually, the Dark Warrior used his anger displayed in his Souldarkness Attribute and overpowered The Son. Their swords were being held together only by the might of one another's souls, and their connection to Soulmagic. "Woosh" was the sound that came from the Dark Warrior's sword as he twirled around The Son's hilt, finally disarming him, as he knocked The Son to the castle floor. The Son's sword had spun behind the Dark Warrior landing with its blade pierced into the ground.

"It is time for you to die," the Dark Warrior bellowed. That was the first time anyone heard the Dark Warrior speak.

He had a powerful, deep booming voice. "This is what my master wants, so this is what I must do."

The fact that he could speak made the Dark Warrior accept himself as more than someone's warrior. He thought to himself, *How could this be, words coming out of my mouth? I have never done that before.* He felt connected to his opponent's soul, but he did not know how or why. He had continued to do his master's bidding by fighting to kill The Son, even though he had no clue as to why he was truly fighting. He did not want to disappoint the man who brought life to him and trained him. He wanted to please Hoshek.

The Dark Warrior then thrust his sword towards The Son's heart. With almost no time to react, The Son moved his body slightly so that the Dark Warrior's sword could not land a fatal blow. He still became injured and screamed in pain. The sword was thrust between his left pectoral muscle and shoulder. The sword lodged itself in the same place that Ohr had touched years ago transferring a bit of his soul to The Son. His connection to Soulmagic and all of the Attributes had become tainted, and now unlocked the Souldarkness Attribute within himself. The Son screamed, and Ohr heard it. The poison from the Dark Warrior's Souldarkness Attribute was inside The Son now, causing him great agony. The Son's voice boomed and echoed through the castle fueling Hoshek and grunts with Souldarkness. All of Draefast which was starting to become pure again suddenly shifted into darkness even worse than before. The Shroud was pulsating. The Son took a deep breath and then closed his eyes. His body had flowed like water that quickly moved through a ravine. The Son turned into a Shroud of darkness, only to materialize a moment later releasing the Souldarkness poison from his body. Without hesitation, he then grasped the hilt of the Dark Warrior's sword, preparing for an attack. As the Dark Warrior was leaving the scene to help his master fight Ohr, he felt a pain in his upper torso. He looked down to see his own sword blade protruding from his back through his chest.

When the Dark Warrior's sword pierced his heart, it was like putting a key in a lock. During this moment, most of The Son's memory came back to him. It was as if embracing the Souldarkness Attribute within him freed him from his amnesia which was caused by a previous Souldarkness Attribute ability.

Hoshek hadn't realized it, but with The Son and The Father being struck by Purple Lightning - a Souldarkness Attribute ability - they were also affected by another ability - mind corruption. This resulted in the long-lasting amnesia that just began to subside. Only through his newfound Souldarkness Attribute did The Son finally understand his place in all of this, but now there was a twist. Was he the man he seemed destined to become? The Son was unsure now more than ever. The Souldarkness Attribute that awoke in The Son corrupted his vision of leading the next Council of Swordmasters. His thoughts did not feel like his own anymore. *You will go to the top of the castle, take your newfound sword, kill Hoshek and take his place,* The Son thought to himself. "No!" The Son shouted, shaking his head. He needed to break free, but he did not know how. Ohr never trained him to use the Souldarkness Attribute; he was lost. "Help me!" The Son shouted loud enough that Ohr, Hoshek, and his friends in the lower level heard him.

The Dark Warrior turned as his body hit the floor. He watched The Son hold his wound with one hand and from his other hand Souldarkness emerged. The Son's left hand was glowing black. The last thing the Dark Warrior saw was The Son walking towards him. Then his head had fallen limp backwards onto the ground. The Son had succumbed to one of the Dark Tales he had unlocked with his inner darkness. This act created a shift in Palaleon one that will inevitably change the tide of the grand battle.

The Son removed the sword from the dead man's chest, claiming it as his own. Then The Son's old sword transformed back into the white shard and attached itself to the sword The Son was holding now. The sword began to change size and shape. The hilt had transformed to fit The Sons' sword fighting style, since before it was in the Dark Warriors hand. The Dark Warrior had focused more on heavy strikes, while The Son's style was based around his speed and accuracy. The sword now had a deeper connection to the Souldarkness Attribute since it became connected to The Son's untamed Souldarkness which was more powerful than Hoshek's. Once The Son held onto it, darkness tried to corrupt him leaving his emotions cloudy. He was holding a weapon that, prior to his touch, was created with the most powerful Souldarkness. As the white shard fully merged itself into the dark sword, it began to glow. The shard altered the sword's appearance into a combination of the swords that The Son and Hoshek had crafted forming the outline of a lock from where the two cut-outs were on each of the individual swords. Instead of maintaining a white or black color, the blade changed to grey. As this metamorphosis occurred, The Son's familial memories started to return.

The Son, now remembering parts of his past, left the castle as he carried his father's body on his back. As every memory came back, the Souldarkness Attribute that was corrupting his mind had weakened, even though it still had a hold over him. Instead of falling into this abyss of darkness, The Son was able to see a vision of a young girl that he recognized being sent to the Soul Realm. With perfect sight of this occurring as if he were there in real time, he was seeing a fragment of the sword's history. Everywhere the sword had gone with the Dark Warrior, he was able to see. He had created a more powerful bond with this sword than anyone had ever done before. He then realized that on top of becoming the wielder of the Souldarkness Attribute, he must figure out his place in this universe once more. Ohr was the only one able to detect that The Son left the castle. The Son was carrying his father's body over his shoulder as he wanted to bury it by the hut where The Son was raised.

While The Son was fighting The Father, Ohr was engaging in what he believed was the fight for his life against his brother. They were equally matched in their Soulmagic and Attribute abilities, which made the fight turn into a grand sword battle. They were clashing left and right, swinging their swords looking for an opening to initiate a fatal blow. Hoshek was able to gain the upper hand and hurled a mini wave of pure darkness towards his brother pushing him to the ground. As this occurred, Hoshek sensed the loss of the Dark Warrior, but more importantly the soul bond of The Father and The Son fully diminished. Hoshek knew that The Son had just learned that his father was the Dark Warrior. But as long as the two of them were still alive, or at least in Hoshek's eyes, as long as the Dark Warrior was alive, his plans would come to reality. Ohr felt a pain in his chest as if a piece of his soul were being corrupted. *This could only mean one thing. The Son has unlocked his true nature. A nature I did not expect, and now we might have a bigger problem,* Ohr thought to himself. He had to now put all his effort into restoring the light in Hoshek's soul as Ohr knew that would create balance in Palaleon and the universe would then change for the better. Ohr knew he needed one more member for the Council if The Son turned, and that person would have to be Hoshek. *If I can reason with my brother, he might just become what our father wanted him to be in the first place. He could lead the Council, as the the Souldarkness Attribute wielder, and I can help with the little amount of the Soullight Attribute I have left. Hoshek's goal was clearly to make his own Council and lead the people of the Palaleon to a new age, but due to my potential error of training The Son, Hoshek might join us to defeat him.* Ohr motioned to his brother as he stood up. Their fight was about to continue, but Ohr now had a new purpose. Ohr believed due to the cries he heard moments earlier from The Son that he had shifted from his pure light nature to pure darkness. In Ohr's mind, The Son was now the only threat to the universe. He needed to reason with his brother to turn back to the path of good in order to defeat The Son. Little did Ohr know that upon leaving the castle The Son had chosen to not engage in any more fighting, thus becoming neutral. He was not the greatest threat to Palaleon at this current time. Another threat, even greater, still lurked in the shadows.

The Final Chapter

For The Safety Of Palaleon

Since he had felt The Son's growing agony, Hoshek embraced an emptiness in his chest as if it were his own from decades earlier. His childhood nightmare had come painfully true. He had become the ruler of Palaleon through Souldarkness and by the whispers of a distant family member. He had destroyed the old Council of Swordmasters and was beginning the process to create his own. The only difference between his nightmare and the current status is that his brother Ohr was still alive. The only living being from his past thought to be dead, was beside him. Throughout his life he was chasing a dream, wanting to undo his mistakes as a child, but he finally came to the realization that what's done is done. He might be able to go back in time, but he cannot change anything. Hoshek remembered the night he killed his own father, feeling the same way that he knows The Son does now. He then began reflecting upon his life and came to the realization that his grandfather had been manipulating him since he was a boy and had been fueling him with corruptive notions of domination and supremacy, antithetical to Hoshek's true nature. Ohr was now able to turn his brother back to the light. This disrupted Nahvel's ultimate plan, and he knew he would need to get involved sooner than he anticipated.

"I am so sorry for everything," he said to Ohr as tears were running down his cheek.

Disheartened, Ohr replied to his brother, "I never carried hatred towards you for killing mom and dad, and our friends. I feel more sadness in myself as I was unable to help you when you needed someone. I should have been there for you. I am angry at myself for not seeing your inner turmoil sooner, Hoshek, my dear brother. For if I did, I would have helped you turn back towards us, your family, and friends instead of having you rely on your Souldarkness Attribute and your betraying thoughts. I want you to know that everyone in our shared life loved and cared for you. I know that our father was a tough man - especially to you - but he did what he did because he cared for us. He kept stories about our grandfather to himself since he feared one of us might become like Nahvel."

Hoshek lamented, "Well look at that, dad was not wrong."

Ohr was the only one able to feel through his Soullight Attribute, that his brother's soul was close to turning away from his inner darkness. Then something strange happened. Ohr felt a darkness he had never felt before, more powerful than what The Son was emitting after defeating the Dark Warrior. It stemmed from Nahvel. Until this point, Ohr was unaware of his grandfather's presence in all of this. The true threat to the universe was staring Ohr right in the face, and he knew that now. He could feel the cold stemming from Hoshek's body, as if it were embracing his own soul.

Hoshek revealed, "The Soul Realm contains our ancestor's sword. Use it to create the Planetary Sword, as it was part of the original one." Hoshek then forcefully struck his sword into the ground beneath his feet causing it to crack. He then poured his Souldarkness Attribute through the sword creating streams of Purple Lightning from it but since there were cracks the sword could not handle the Souldarkness thus it broke in half. Hoshek then threw it to the side of the room, as a gesture to assure his brother that he had changed. Hoshek and Ohr walked all the way down the tiers of the castle through secret passageways until they reached the Soul Realm portal. Hoshek was going to open it for his brother, but as he placed his hand on the portal sigil, Nahvel suddenly took control of his body. Hoshek could not fully complete his redemption. The Soul Realm portal then opened as Nahvel used Hoshek's soul to open it.

Ohr watched as who he thought was his brother placed his hand on the sigil. From his perspective everything seemed to be fine until the portal started to emit little bolts of Purple Lightning, destroying the stone tiles around the ruin.

"What's wrong?" Ohr asked as he walked closer to his brother.

Nahvel, who was in full control of Hoshek's body while still placing his hand on the sigil, turned his head over his left shoulder and sneered, "Your brother is no more. I am surprised you could not see that I, Nahvel, your grandfather, will now take his place as the rightful ruler of Palaleon. Your act of redeeming your brother actually worked in my favor. At first I thought my plans would be no more but your gesture of peace with your brother weakened him. Thus, I was able to take over his body."

Now that Nahvel inhabited a vessel, he entered the Soul

Realm and picked up Hosra's Attribute Sword. Nahvel recalled his Obsessor telling him about a vision from decades ago. He then thought to himself, *Hoshek grabbed the sword. That must have activated a hidden Souldarkness Attribute ability that Hosra encased in it. Only his bloodline can wield the sword, and since I do not share his blood until now it could not become the sword, I wanted it to be. Maybe if I manifest enough Souldarkness into the sword I can alter it to become my Planetary Sword.* Nahvel was able to conjure excess Souldarkness from the sword and put it in Hoshek's body, making him appear decades younger which meant that he was now more agile. He did not want to foster the balance that Hoshek or Ohr envisioned. Instead, he wanted to rule Palaleon through the Soul Realm, keeping the portal forever open, corrupting the universe with dark souls. Acting upon this desire would turn the newly created harmony back to the imbalance that previously existed.

Nahvel exited the portal and saw his grandson still standing there frozen in the despair that just took place in front of his eyes. With great fury, he swung his sword at his grandson. Through this motion, Nahvel believed that he had re-obtained a connection back with the long-lost sword. Ohr quickly went on the defensive but was overtaken by the strength of his grandfather's Souldarkness Attribute making it impossible for him to successfully parry the attack. With a powerful roundabout blow, Nahvel's sword clashed with Ohr's sword, shattering it into pieces.

Sensing imminent danger, Ohr fled his brother's castle leaving through the grate on the bottom tier and met up with the other Swordmasters. They had decided to leave the second tier and wait for Ohr outside the city when they noticed that the

Shroud had become thicker. Nahvel let them all flee as it finally gave him more time to enact his own plans. As he walked around Hoshek's chambers eventually moving towards a window and looking out Nahvel thought to himself, *My grandson was able to build upon the structure I created. He made a more grandiose castle and city surrounding it.*

Upon gaining some distance and elevation, Ohr turned his head to glance at the city and the castle. He noticed that rocks protruded out of the ramp between the first and second tier, along with ice spikes stuck in the ground, and flames paving away from the city gate to the castle entrance – remnants of the battles fought by the other Councilmembers. Ohr now had to prepare them for the true final battle against his grandfather. This fight would be the grand battle. All of the remaining members of the new Council of Swordmasters fled further into the forest, miles from the castle and the city. Their ship was destroyed but they needed a way to get off world. Ohr then summoned the White Lion and the Councilmembers got on its back. The White Lion opened a portal to Aestercrat and they all got off. Before the White Lion turned around to leave it spoke to Ohr's soul. *We Legendary Beasts can be summoned by Councilmembers but are not supposed to aid or get involved in your affairs. I know that the White Hyrax is helping The Son and that is why I chose to help you, but now I cannot be summoned by you until after this battle is over.* Ohr nodded as he understood that the Legendary Beasts could not interfere any more than they already have throughout the years, especially now that the fate of Palaleon was resting on either the Council or Nahvel. Ohr turned away as the White Lion left and sat down. He took this time to meditate, and realized that his brother was now fully gone. Previously, he thought there would be a way to bring his brother back, but now he knew that it was impossible.

Deep into his meditation, Ohr was able to unlock a portion of his soul that combined Soulmagic and his Attribute miraculously without the use of a sword to conjure the ability. He dug deep into the portion of his Soulmagic that still remained in his body and awakened it. This technique was said to be written in a Tale prior to Ohr's existence, but he could never find the Tale. Regardless, he was able to connect with his soul and converse with the White Lion. The Legendary Beast helped him start to unlock this ability. Since this experience happened while Ohr was in his soul, to him it felt like it took years to learn and perfect this new ability, but it only took a few days.

Ohr now took what he thought was The Son's place as the leader of the Council of Swordmasters wielding the Soullight Attribute, along with his knowledge and skill in all of the other Attributes through his original sword. He had been training The Son this entire time for the key role in this universal fight, when he was the one who would pick up that mantle.

When Ohr opened his eyes after meditating on this realization, his appearance changed. Half of his white hair turned black and on that same side, the iris in his eye turned from grey to black, signaling his transformation to becoming the true Council leader. He was now at perfect balance with all five Attributes including each of the Sub-Attributes. He had obtained hidden knowledge of each of the Attributes through his meditation, but was still too weak to use them. Ohr's eyes were drawn to his satchel as he glanced at it. He felt the urge to rummage through its contents. At the bottom, he noticed two pieces of parchment. They were shining.

"The Tale of Soulattributes by Malikaya". So, my mom was the one who was able to use Soulmagic without the use of a sword. Maybe that is why I can do it as well. I will teach everyone how to do it after we defeat my grandfather, Ohr thought to himself. The second parchment read "Tale of the Soul Realm portal". It had no name next to it so Ohr did not know who wrote it, but it stated, "Using the Souldarkness Attribute will open the Soul Realm portal for three minutes, before whoever is in the Soul Realm becomes corrupted by their inner darkness and without control releases all of their soul energy. If one uses the Soullight Attribute to open the portal it will turn into Purple Flames, thus burning anyone who enters. The only way to keep the Soul Realm portal open for as long as you wish and be in command of it is if you sacrifice both a limb of a descendant of the original Council and a part of that person's soul."

The Son, still struggling to cope with the fact that he had just killed his father, continued to run away through the vast reaches of his homeworld. By using the Souldarkness Attribute, he was purged of the knowledge and ability to control and use the other Attributes of Soulmagic. He came to terms with his newly repaired memory and found his way to the place where his family hut once stood. He turned his head, and noticed a figure nearby.

"You're my mother, aren't you?" The Son asked as he approached the woman, worn by time and grief, sitting on the dirt. A ship was parked directly behind her. The woman slowly stood up and looked at him. She walked closer and as he started to cry, she embraced him. All of her memories that Ohr had erased the night of the Purple Lightning started flooding back into her head. Not only did the memories from the day that Ohr arrived remain in her head, but her memories of The Father and The Son returned unaltered. She now truly remembered who she was before the night when she lost her son and husband. She remembered her family. *Thank you, Ohr, you brought my boy back home to me*, she thought. She then let go of The Son and proceeded to speak, "My son, we are reunited at last. How are you?" He went on to tell her everything that had happened to him throughout the past nine years, even showing her the sword that was now a combination of his old one and her husband's.

As The Son finished, The Mother said in disbelief, "I had always thought he was dead. I couldn't even recognize him as he brought your sister to Hoshek."

"I saw a vision of a young girl. Was that her? Where is she?"

"Oh yes, my son, she was kind, smart, and very brave, but Hoshek took her away. I am afraid she is now dead."

"No mom, I do not think that she is dead. I can feel her soul through my Souldarkness Attribute. It is faint, but she is not dead."

The Mother's eyes glistened, and then she started crying more and more. First, she was reunited with her son and now she learned that her daughter was alive, somewhere. "I heard that the souls of children were siphoned by Hoshek in order to help keep Palaleon under the Shroud of darkness."

"Then she is somewhere either in Hoshek's castle or around that area. I will find her, and bring her home to you, mom," The Son replied.

The Mother nodded her head, "My son you are destined to save Palaleon, you must complete this task first with Ohr..."

The Son cut her off, "But Ohr lied to me. He only recently told me about you, he never told me about my sister or my father."

The Mother continued to say, "But he protected you all this time, and eventually led you to me. As your mother I can't be more grateful. He also might truly not have known what Hoshek did with your father. Much like how you needed him throughout your life, Ohr needs you now more than ever."

"I understand, mom. I can't be mad at him, he was there for me when nobody else was, and yes he has protected me thus far. Now it's my turn."

The Mother then said, "Do not let this Souldarkness corrupt you, as it did Hoshek. You are destined for something greater and should remember who your father was before all this chaos, instead of who he was turned into. Remember, it was not your father's fault." The Son knew what he had to do, and after pondering about it he came to terms that the day his father died was the day the Purple Lightning struck his hut. Controlling his rage, he knew that the person to blame for his father's death was Hoshek. The Son realized he must go back to the main city on Draefast and rejoin the Council so that they would have a chance of beating the tyrant and his army of grunts.

He summoned the White Hyrax using his blood, and mounted the Legendary Beast. "I will come back, and help you find my sister," The Son said to The Mother. She nodded and replied, "I almost forgot to tell you. Happy birthday."

The Son smiled; his mother had just helped him unlock a new memory. He was born nineteen years ago that very day. As the White Hyrax began to run, The Son felt a joyous relief. His act of selflessness unlocked an inner light within himself that healed the poisoned portion of Ohr's soul that resided within The Son. Since The Son was able to connect with his own inner Souldarkness Attribute for a brief moment

263

without being overcome with rage, he came to the realization that he needed to give Ohr back the piece of soul that had helped him survive decades earlier. He then created sword motions to use to fight properly as the Souldarkness Attribute Swordmaster. These motions helped him stay in control of his inner darkness for short periods of time. The Souldarkness Attribute was all about striking with his emotions intensely heightened. Since The Son was becoming connected to his soul without displaying hate or anger he could better control his fighting ability thus not going overboard and killing his foe but drastically injuring them.

GRAND BATTLE

Ohr recalled a story that his father told him that up until this point seemed to just be a bedtime story. The Council was in dire need to get back to Draefast so it was time to see if this bedtime story were true or if it was just another lie from Gathran. Ohr gathered the others and began to speak. "Much like how we got to Aestercrat, my father once told me that Legendary Beasts could teleport to other locations using their connection to Soulmagic from their souls. I believe that if the Legendary Beasts, who were the creators of Soulmagic, could do this, then it stands to reason that we should be able to do it, as well. My father told me that the first Council could teleport as they were created from a piece of the Legendary Beasts, and I am a descendant of the first Council, but I have never had a teacher to show me how. Since I have not fully restored my Soulmagic, maybe we can find a different way to teleport. We are the Council of Swordmasters after all, it is our destiny to confront this evil as a united front. Wait a second." Ohr paused. Then he continued to speak. "That's it, we are united. If we combine Attributes, maybe we can create a teleportation portal. May, Lehavah, I have an idea." Ohr pointed at May who got up and walked over to him. "Can you create a sheet of ice from the Soulice Sub-Attribute right here." May nodded, pointed her sword at the ground and suddenly the puddle in front of them turned to ice. "Now Lehavah, can you come here and zap this ice with your Soullighting Sub-Attribute."

"Sure," Lehavah said as she got up from sitting next to Ehven and headed over towards Ohr. Lehavah then pointed her sword at the sheet of ice and zapped it.

"Now May, focus on that puddle of water over there. Visualize it in your mind but continue pointing your sword at the ice in front of us." May nodded and tightly closed her eyes and pictured the puddle to their east.

"Ehven, I need you to create a rock from your sword and place it on this sheet of ice." Ehven got up and did what Ohr asked. All of a sudden, the rock went through the ice due to being coated in lightning and popped out of the puddle which had suddenly been frozen over by May. "It worked!" Ohr exclaimed. "Now we must figure out how to do it on a larger scale. May, picture a waterfall, it is flowing the clearest water you have ever seen almost as if it is light itself."

"Ok I am picturing it," May replied.

"That is where we must go," Ohr affirmed.

They tried the same technique again but as Ehven dropped the rock on the sheet the lightning became out of control and decimated the rock.

Months had passed, and Ohr and the new Councilmembers were now ready to go back to Draefast to rid Palaleon of Nahvel. All of them had practice their roles in order to successfully create a teleportation portal. While training they were able to travel around the planet using teleportation.

"We will try again tomorrow. We have a bit more time, until I fear Nahvel will be far too powerful to defeat. Everybody rest, tomorrow will be our travel day," Ohr stated as the Council of Swordmasters began to set up their sleeping arrangements.

As the sun rose over Aestercrat each of the Swordmasters awoke. It was time for them to try this new technique again, and with their bodies well-rested, it should work. "Instead of a rock this time I will stand on the sheet of ice. I believe in all of you and could not have made it this far without each one of you. Let's go save Palaleon," Ohr proclaimed. May and Lehavah began the teleportation, this time remaining super focused. Ohr then dropped through the ice.

"Did we do it?" May looking concerned, turned towards the other two and asked.

"I will go find out." Ehven stepped on the ice, got zapped by the lightning that Lehavah placed there and disappeared.

"Let's go together," Lehavah said as she looked at May. They both stepped on the ice and disappeared.

The Council successfully made it to Draefast, and arrived at the Waterfall of Light.

"Is everyone ok?" Ohr asked as the others exited the Waterfall.

"I am fine," Ehven said as he began tapping his body making sure he did not lose any body parts in the teleportation process.

"I can't believe it worked," May said looking at Lehavah.

"See we can do anything we put our mind to as long as we stick together as a Council," Ohr said.

May reached into her bag and pulled out her Ice Tablets to write down this new way of teleportation. *Now I will always know how to create a portal, in case I will need to do this again,* May thought to herself.

Nahvel had hoped his plan was further along by this point. It was too late for him to dwell on his thoughts. Now that he had Hoshek's body as a vessel, he would use all his Souldarkness Attribute to shape the universe to his desire. He walked over to the portal and put his hand on the sigil. The portal opened but after three minutes it closed again *Why won't it stay open? My soul is made of pure darkness. This body should be emitting my own Souldarkness Attribute, and enough of it to keep the portal open for good,* Nahvel thought to himself as he looked down into his palms. Nahvel then walked back to where a piece of Hoshek's sword was and picked it up. Walking back to the portal he had one idea. He recalled back to a portion of a Tale that he read as a child. *I must unlock the Souldarkness Attribute in this body connected by my soul by damaging it. This body belongs to the descendant of original Councilmembers meaning that his blood is special. I might have taken over his body and destroyed his soul, but I can feel bits of his soul remaining connected to his blood. I must dispose of his soul entirely.* Nahvel raised his left hand holding the part of the blade and sliced his right arm clean off from his elbow. "AHHHHH". Blood splattered all over the ground. Within a minute, a Purple

Fire started forming out of the remaining stub. This Purple Fire cauterized the open wound, and the bleeding stopped. Nahvel walked over to the portal. *I should now be able to control the portal keeping it open for however long I want.* Using his left arm, Nahvel threw his right arm at the portal as he leaned on the sigil. The portal glowed white, Purple Fire emerged, but then as quick as it appeared, it vanished. In its place was the sight of the Soul Realm. *It seems the last ounce of my grandson's soul and his blood opened tampering with the rules on how this portal works.* Nahvel waited. Once the time passed three minutes he knew his plan was soon to be successful. "It worked. It is permanently open. I am in command of this portal now. Dark souls I summon thee. Go take over the people of this universe and become my subjects." During the five months, Nahvel had transferred all the souls from the children Hoshek abducted and stored in the gourd to the Soul Realm. He also began to surround his castle with dark souls from the Soul Realm. He was starting his takeover of Palaleon. His plans were finally starting to come to fruition.

These dark souls began morphing with the people beginning to entrance them in a state of total control. Their souls laid dormant while the dark souls were taking command of the bodies. The people started losing every ounce of free will that they had left along with control over their actions and thoughts. With each dark soul commanding its host body's movements, they charged towards the Councilmembers. Rather than engaging with the dark-soul corrupted people, the Councilmembers ran from the Waterfall of Light towards the castle. Since the journey took days, they slept up in the trees in the dark forest for a couple hours, as the hordes wandered aimlessly wondering where their prey had gone. The Council took this deceitful opportunity to continue their journey, stopping and climbing to eat and occasionally rest. When they had finally made it back to the city, Ohr, Ehven, Lehavah, and May stealthily traversed up the castle to Nahvel's chamber. Nahvel had grunts physically lift the Soul Realm portal out of the center of the ruin and place it in his chambers.

With one swing of his newly acquired sword, Nahvel turned each planet into a place of pure darkness. No warmth and no light. His command over the Shroud was more intense than Hoshek's, but because of that his sword shattered into pieces. Then it disintegrated as if it were touched by Purple Fire. *I guess this sword was not meant to be the weapon to help me rule,* Nahvel thought to himself. The Soul Realm contained more dark souls than pure ones already tipping the balance within. He now had enough power to travel into the Soul Realm and stay in it while continuously transport the dark souls into Palaleon. The Soul Realm's eternal darkness did not corrupt Nahvel's mind instead he embraced it, as if he was the embodiment of the eternal darkness itself. Nahvel felt stronger in the Soul Realm and could control his actions in Palaleon from there but decided that he wanted to be closer to his Shroud. He exited the Soul Realm where he had moved his throne too and instead stood inside his castle. He knew he needed a new sword, so he asked one of his many grunts to go find him one "Hey you, go fetch me a sword from the artifacts room," Nahvel said as he pointed at one of the grunts. The grunt nodded and turned around. As it arrived at the artifacts room the grunt noticed a rusted sword behind the work bench. The grunt grabbed the sword and brought it back to Nahvel. "I have not seen this sword since the day my daughter betrayed me," Nahvel said as he lifted it. Nahvel held onto the sword tightly as he went on a journey through the sword's past. *I see, so my daughter took it after she tried to kill me, and sheathed it around her waist until the day she died. As I am reunited with my once most powerful weapon, I will use this to take control of Palaleon.*

From the window in Nahvel's room, Ohr, Ehven, Lehavah, and May used all of their Soulmagic, to dissipate the Shroud of darkness, but instead of shrinking it only grew larger. Nahvel used the Shroud as a distraction so he could witness his dark souls take over Palaleon. The Council noticed that Nahvel was not paying attention and took this opportunity to stop attacking the Shroud and to instead go after him, but since they did not have their fifth member there was not much they could do. Ohr hoped that The Son would return to the Council since without his help they had no chance of winning. The Council of Swordmasters was incomplete without The Son.

All of a sudden, a mysterious figure entered the chamber.

The Son finally made his grand entrance as he quickly ran to the top tier of the castle where the rest of the Councilmembers and Nahvel were. Nobody saw him coming; it was as if a shadow were melding with Nahvel's, and out of it came The Son. He attempted to push Nahvel into the Soul Realm portal, believing that by holding onto him tightly they would both plummet to their death. Ohr was thinking the same thought at the time only he wanted to activate the portal with his Soullight Attribute as he pushed his grandfather in order to burn them both in the Purple Fire. He saw The Son running and without thinking pushed him out of the way so that he could run at his grandfather. Ohr grasped onto his grandfather's torso with one hand and touched the sigil with the other. Before Ohr could emit Soullight from his hand Nahvel opened his palm which opened the portal, and the two of them entered the portal. Nahvel did not even attempt to unsheathe his sword, it was as if he wanted the two of them to enter the Soul Realm. *My plan failed. Why? He must be...* Ohr thought as the two of them were falling Ohr noticed Nahvel clenching his left fist. Then Ohr turned his head to look at the portal which suddenly closed. *He seemed to be in full command of when the portal opened and closed. My guess is that he has taken over this realm and is now able to control his soul energy for longer than three minutes. I must be cautious as my timer has already started,* Ohr finished his thought.

Souldarkness emerged from The Son's side of the portal, and at that moment of its closing all of the dark souls that were in Palaleon had fully taken over their human hosts.

The Council of Swordmasters, which now included The Son, got up to their feet and realized what they had to do. In order for them to save Ohr, they had to gather all the dark souls that inhabited Palaleon and bring them to the portal. Transferring them in a gourd that The Mother gave to The Son was their best bet to ensure success. The gourd was created in the Soul Realm, and was found on Draefast by The Mother years ago when she was hiding from Hoshek. She had stored water in it even though its greater purpose had eluded her. When she and The Son met after their long absence, she gave it to him as a gift, but a gift to be returned to her when they reunite for the second time. The Son lifted the gourd from his belt and as he did May noticed writing underneath. *Sluos eseht dehtrib taht mlaeR eht ni degrof saw ti sa slips krad gnirutpac fo elbapac*

271

cigamluoS morf edam si siht. As she awkwardly read the words out loud, The Son grinned.

"It's in reverse." The Son stated. "It really says: 'This is made from Soulmagic capable of capturing dark souls as it was forged in the Realm that birthed these souls.' We will capture the dark souls using this and bring them to the portal. If we release the dark souls at the portal while thrusting our swords at the portal, I bet it will open."

May replied, "Yes, the combination of the beings from the realm and our Soulmagic should grant us access into the Soul Realm so we can retrieve our friend."

Lehavah, May, and Ehven had no reason not to believe The Son. Ohr was gone. Even if he had previously believed that The Son was a threat, he was not the biggest one at this moment. Since Nahvel left the physical universe, the only darkness was sprouted from The Son, so the dark souls that left the Soul Realm were not at their peak strength as for when they were in the Soul Realm.

Lehavah and May created a portal for the Swordmasters to travel through to go to Aestercrat to begin collecting dark souls. When they were done on Aestercrat, Lehavah and May made a new portal to Vastrilio. Upon exiting, they saw dark souls infiltrating the bodies of the people, including the loyalists. Ehven and The Son watch as the loyalists were frantically running around before entering a sedated state due to a new being overtaking their mind and body. The four Swordmasters tried their best to sneak around the planet and collect as many dark souls as they could. Eventually they made it towards Lehavah's parents' apartment building. Lehavah opened the door to the apartment and saw that her parents were aimlessly walking around with a dark shadow under their eyes indicating the dark souls had taken over. She knew her parents did not respect her since the fire years ago, but they were still her family and she wanted to help. Before her parents could inform the other dark souls of Lehavah and May's presence, the Swordmasters looked at one another and concluded that they needed to knock them out in order to obtain the dark souls without mentally hurting Lehavah's parents. Lehavah ran in front of her parents to distract them. They made an inaudible noise and proceeded to grab her. As she embraced them, knowing she might be corrupted May and Ehven went behind her parents and hit them on the head with the hilt of their swords. The Son then opened the gourd and Lehavah tapped her sword on her parents' chests and pulled the dark souls out. This motion consumed a lot of Lehavah's Soulmagic. She then moved the dark souls into the gourd and The Son closed it. Her parents awoke. Now that the dark souls left their bodies, they became immune to the Shroud. They staggered over to their daughter, as their minds were now regaining control of their bodies. "We are so sorry for the way we treated you in your childhood. We are glad you have made friends, a new family that respects you. Just know that from now on we will always be here for you. Please forgive us."

Lehavah nodded, then turned around and ran to Ehven. She was crying. She did not want to show her weak side to anyone else, but she felt she could share her feelings with Ehven. They quietly embraced. The tender moment did not last long, however, for the Swordmasters realized they were in a hurry as dark souls started surrounding their area. May then created a portal to her homeworld and everyone jumped through the opening.

They landed outside the village where May found her brother's dead body. This was her own nightmare, going back to the place that caused her so much pain. A place where she had nobody and where the villagers around her hated her since they blamed her for Im's death. The Swordmasters noticed villagers with dark lines under their eyes that drooped down beneath their ears.

"The people here are dark souls. Find cover!" The Son told everyone.

They snuck around the village each individually knocking out people, tapping their swords on the people's chests and tossing the gourd or one another to collect the dark souls. Once the people regained consciousness, the Shrouds' effect dissipated from their minds. Each villager came up to May and apologized for ostracizing her. One villager went to her and said, "I can't say I understand how you feel losing all of your family, but I want you to know that I believe that you did not kill your brother. The Shroud was telling me you did and so I mindlessly believed it. I truly am sorry. This village is your home. We are all your family. I apologize on behalf of everyone here."

Relieved, May looked at him and replied, "Thank you that really means a lot."

As the people were still gathered in the center of the village The Son stated, "We will do our best to get rid of the darkness around your planet so that everything will go back to a more peaceful time." The people began to cheer as May. She felt her Soulmagic becoming depleted, since she had not rested for a while, but managed to open a portal with Lehavah's help. The Council was now heading back to Draefast.

274

While the Swordmasters were collecting the dark souls in The Son's gourd, Ohr and his grandfather were having the fight of their lives in the Soul Realm which was now fully corrupted in darkness. Upon falling into the Soul Realm, Nahvel encased his shoes in Souldarkness, and landed unharmed in the Soul Realm. He proceeded to unsheathe his sword. Ohr had used Soulmagic out of his hands creating wind that would weaken the impact of his fall. Nahvel ran over to Ohr and swung his sword at him. As Ohr dodged the attack, Nahvel's sword slashed right through his throne, shattering it into pieces. Ohr began his defensive strategy, dodging each swing from his grandfather. He noticed that Nahvel was keen on defending the right side of his body, so this is where Ohr attempted to jab him with the tips of his fingers. Suddenly Ohr felt as more of his Soullight Attribute Soulmagic escaped his body. *My three minutes are up. Not only do I have to focus on fighting my grandfather, but I have to find a way to keep my soul energy at bay. I do not need my inner darkness taking over my body at this moment. Breathe.* Ohr was partaking in two fights at once. One was occurring outside his body and the other within.

Nahvel, reading his grandson's movements, anticipated his next strike and began intensely protecting his weakest point while maintaining offensive sword stances. Ohr leaped backwards to maintain distance from Nahvel. He took this opportunity to close his eyes, inhale, and then intensely exhale. He projected himself inside of his soul and pushed the darkness out. It took all of his strength but now as he opened his eyes Ohr noticed that his hands were glowing white. *I have let go of my darkness and released it from my body. Now I feel that I am overexerting my soul but that can't be helped for the time being.*

Hopefully the Swordmasters will be here soon. Ohr looked up and noticed Nahvel jumping towards him. Dark souls had emerged from the ground and went after Ohr. He was able to create a gigantic beam of light from his hands blasting some away, but there were just too many of them. *I feel much weaker after using that last attack. I must have run out of my Soullight Attribute completely by now, even with the soul boost from earlier. That took a lot out of me, too. I have to continue to buy time.* He couldn't fight his grandfather and the dark souls all by himself. As the dark souls surrounded Ohr, Nahvel walked behind them parting them with his sword and walked to his grandson. "Why are you doing this?" Ohr shouted. "First you kill my brother and now you attempt to destroy Palaleon. Why?"

"The answer is simple, my child. If I cannot rule Palaleon, then I will rule the Soul Realm and have my dark souls corrupt your universe creating a space for the Soul Realm to engulf each planet, thus turning my new Palaleon into a dark plain that I will rule over," Nahvel revealed menacingly.

"I won't let that happen, and my friends, the new Council, will find a way to get here and help me stop you! For your goal to be completed, you would kill off the rest of your kin. You truly are a disgrace to the Council of Swordmasters," Ohr sternly replied.

Nahvel thrust his sword at Ohr, but Ohr used his remaining Soulwind Sub-Attribute to summon wind encasing his palms. Ohr clasped the sword with both of his hands and started to push it and his grandfather backwards, taking steps forward to keep his grandfather from regaining his balance.

All of a sudden, Ohr saw the Soul Realm portal open, and four figures emerged. *They made it and just in time. The Son's soul energy feels different. I can fell his inner light combating his inner darkness not swaying his soul. The Souldarkness Attribute is living inside of him but it is at bay somehow. Wherever he ran off to, was the place he needed to go in order for him to clear his mind and make his own decision regarding his destiny. He truly has made me proud,* Ohr thought to himself. Nahvel used the distraction as an opportunity to regain control of his sword and knocked Ohr to the ground. The Son looked out into the vast Soul Realm and spotted his mentor on the ground with Nahvel looming above. The Son could tell that the amount of Soulmagic Ohr possessed was almost totally drained from fending off Nahvel and the dark souls. Since the portal opened with a beam of light entering the Soul Realm all of the dark souls dispersed, moving farther and farther away from Nahvel and Ohr.

Ohr was about to be killed. If his grandfather were able to absorb his soul, Nahvel would be the most powerful being to ever exist and would be able to create his version of Palaleon. Just as Nahvel put his sword to his grandson's throat, the new Councilmembers made their move. With quick-thinking they all flung their swords at Nahvel. Upon seeing the new Council of Swordmasters arrive in the Soul Realm, Nahvel realized his original plan would not work, so he would need to act fast to enact his backup plan. First, he was going to kill his grandson to end this generation's Council. He poured most of his Souldarkness Attribute into his strike, thinking that it would also turn his sword into his version of the Planetary Sword. However, that was not the case.

Ohr extended his arm and each of the Councilmember's swords returned to its original shard. The Son's sword produced both the white and black shard. All of the shards then merged into one thus creating the Planetary Sword. The Planetary

Sword was a large double-edged sword with the five Attribute insignias engraved down the center and five circles carved into the bottom portion of the blade representing the different planets. Ohr closed his eyes as he felt his grandfather's sword on his throat. His grandfather extended his arms, locking his elbows. The smile on Nahvel's face exhibited his enjoyment for he believed this act would see to the end of the Council of Swordmasters, along with extinguishing all light in Palaleon.

Nahvel went for his killing strike, but was too late. As the tip of his sword inched closer to Ohr's throat, Ohr gripped the Planetary Sword and let out a scream as he put all his remaining Soulmagic and each Attribute he controlled into it making him able to sway time. Having his soul energy flowing within the sword gave him more of a connection to it than any other Councilmember who was able to wield it before him. He had complete control of time, and was able to slow it down, making it easy for him to stand back up. He was out of range of his grandfather's attack now, and unharmed. Ohr then returned time back to its normal pace. His grandfather, now realizing he had thrust his sword in the dirt of the Soul Realm, was frozen in disbelief. He thought he had killed his grandson, but upon turning around realized that Ohr was behind him. Ohr took a deep breath and with one swift stroke of the Planetary Sword decapitated his grandfather. As his head was falling onto the dirt, Nahvel's hand touched Ohr's leg, poisoning him with the remainder of the Souldarkness Attribute that exited his body. This was too much for Ohr to handle especially after wielding the Planetary Sword for the first time. The poison was burning through his flesh. Nahvel's soul diminished, leaving Hoshek's tattered headless body on the ground.

The Son ran over and placed his hands over his mentor. Some of the Souldarkness started escaping Ohr's body and was latching onto The Son. He took as much as he could into his own body since he had built a tolerance for it. After that, May took out one of her Ice Tablets to refer back to how she was able to heal animals on Crateolios. After rereading exactly how she did it, May was then able to heal Ohr enough without being poisoned herself. She had to stop healing him abruptly since she saw the poison moving to her hands. She had hoped that he could begin to self-heal. Ohr's body not only took a toll from Nahvel's poisonous Souldarkness Attribute ability, but also from controlling the Planetary Sword and the Time Attribute. The Planetary Sword then broke back into the Councilmembers original swords. The Son then placed one hand on his chest and with his other hand holding his sword he pierced Ohr in the chest to transfer the piece of Ohr's soul that resided inside himself. Once the last piece of Ohr's soul traveled back into his body all of his wounds healed including the mark The Son had just left him, and the Souldarkness poison completely escaped his body disintegrating as it touched the air. The Son heard Ohr whisper, "It seems that you have now saved me much like how I save you from the Purple Fire years ago. Thank you for returning this piece of my soul back to me."

As The Son nodded, his pupils and hair turned back to their original black color.

Instead of his body staying at the age of 56, It reverted to how he looked when he was 47 years old. This age was significant because it was how old Ohr was when he first fought his brother and lost a piece of himself in the process. He looked younger but still felt the growing pains as if he were in his older body. He was indeed more agile now but concluded that if he spent more time using the Time Attribute, his body would continuously succumb to the negative effects of time.

Ohr then gripped his grandfather's sword and pulled it out of the dirt. The dark sword was consumed by Ohr's pure Soulmagic causing it to break into shards. He gave pieces of it to each Councilmember for safekeeping. They all then headed to the portal to leave the Soul Realm. As Ohr walked through he also held onto his brother's body, as he wanted to bury it on Draefast. Before The Son stepped through the portal, he felt some sort of connection to the Soul Realm, and vowed to watch over it in the future.

The Obsessors of Souldarkness had felt the Souldarkness essence from their master disappear. They were lost now, and with nothing to do they made a drastic decision. They traveled to the exact location in the Soul Realm where their master died, and each closed their eyes. They focused on the excessive amounts of the Souldarkness Attribute that was flowing through their bodies. As one of the Obessors opened his eyes, he noticed a glowing crack in the ground from where Hoshek's body had dropped as Ohr cut Nahvel's head off. He then pointed his sword at the crack and the other Obsessors began to pour their Souldarkness Attribute into him, as they believed this crack to be a crack in time. By cutting it open more with the Obsessor's sword they could all travel back in time and warn Nahvel of his eventual death.

"How could the Council of Swordmasters miss this,

especially since that man took his body?" one of the Obsessors asked of the other.

"Maybe we created this." As all five of the Obsessors further inspected this crack it started to intensely glow, then they all got sucked as if it were a portal to another time. Along with the Obsessors, other souls both dark and pure in the Soul Realm also got absorbed into the crack. It was generated from residue where Ohr used the Time Attribute, and where the Obsessors conducted their Souldarkness Attribute ritual thus messing with time. The Daughter's dark soul was all alone traveling throughout and clinging to the Soul Realm until she made her way over the crack and got sucked in. The crack cleansed her soul from being a dark soul back to her normal self, and she finally had her body back as she noticed so did the other souls around her. But where were they?

After the Grand Battle

All of the remaining dark souls in Palaleon detached from the humans and returned to the Soul Realm where they belonged. Since The Son thrust his sword encased in Souldarkness at the portal last forcefully opening it, he became in command of the Soul Realm portal. He made it so anyone with Souldarkness Attribute abilities could open it but if he entered the ruin just by unsheathing his sword the portal would react and open for however long The Son wanted it too.

The Council stayed on Draefast with The Son since they all needed to build new ships. They crafted each ship using the combination of one another's Attributes. Their Soulmagic would act as fuel. This would make them the fastest ships in Palaleon and invisible to the average human's eye.

During their time on Draefast, The Son brought Ohr to where he buried The Father, so that Ohr could bury Hoshek next to him. Before Ohr began his burial preparations he raised his palm up to the sky. The Son, in turn, raised his sword towards the sky. Ohr's palm glowed a bright white and The Son's sword glistened black. Ohr released a beam of Soullight to the center of the universe and The Son shot a blast of Souldarkness next to Ohr's light. The light and darkness intertwined and spread through each planet touching the souls of each human. Their memories of Hoshek, Nahvel, The Dark Warrior, and the dark souls faded. They were replaced with a calming sensation that everything had been and was peaceful. The Son erased any form of Souldarkness that lingered within their souls, so even their dreams would be free of nightmarish thoughts. Memories of flight and planetary travel were restored in those born before Hoshek's rule, and for people born during Hoshek's rule The Son and Ohr unlocked knowledge within them so they learned how to fly ships.

Once they were done The Son opened his mouth to asked Ohr a question. "Is it possible to revive my father? My mother told me that you were once famed for healing people, but can you restore life?"

Ohr had finished covering Hoshek's body with dirt when he replied. "I am afraid that bringing life back from the dead is just a myth passed down from the original Council until now." He paused. "If it is not a myth then I am just not lucky enough to find the Tale that holds the secrets to resurrection." Ohr thought to himself, *Maybe the reason the Tale became lost is due to the fact that the Legendary Beasts sensed future chaos, so they hid it where no one could find it.* As Ohr thought this, a white scroll appeared in his hands. He looked up and a White Warbler was flying overhead. "That is another one of the Legendary Beasts," Ohr told The Son as they both gazed at the bird. "I suppose they believe that we restored order to Palaleon, so now this Tale can be brought out of hiding." Ohr continued to unravel it and noticed the names beneath the title of the Tale. "Life rejuvenation, by Ohtav and Hosra." His ancestors were the ones who had written this Tale, the same people who he and his brother were named after. *It is interesting that this Tale is coming to me today of all days. Today also happens to be Hoshek's birthday,* Ohr thought to himself as he held tightly onto the parchment. Ohr then stated, "According to this Tale we could only bring back your father since the body that would be receiving life needs to be whole, and my brother's head is detached from the rest of his body. Are you sure you want to try and bring your father back? We would need to simultaneously stab his chest with both of our swords and equally distribute some of my Soullight Attribute and some of your Souldarkness Attribute to revitalize his soul." Ohr stated as he looked over at The Son.

The Son then looked at his mentor and replied, "I do not think it is such a smart idea, since we don't know if he will come back as the Dark Warrior or my father. I would like to just have him as memories inside my head. Plus, I have his sword to always remember him by."

Ohr nodded, "I agree. It is best to keep both my brother and your father's past buried in the ground, but we will make sure to never forget them, and to teach their stories to our successors."

The Son looked at Ohr and said, "I think it's best if the head of our Council of Swordmasters holds onto that Tale."

Ohr replied, "Thank you. Without your help we would never have been able to free Palaleon, and for that I am truly appreciative."

As the Council completed their ships, the White Warbler appeared again to Ehven. He took it as a sign for them to go to Aestercrat.

The new Council of Swordmasters flew to Aestercrat. They found a plot of land where they would start to build a Grand Sanctuary where they would meet from time to time. The Grand Sanctuary would also hold all of the Tales that the Councilmembers collected and studied from in order to teach future Swordmasters. Ehven created the outline of the Sanctuary and made statue guards out of Counterrock that would be triggered to attack anyone who wasn't trained in the use of Soulmagic. Each room in the Grand Sanctuary was separated by the different Attributes and had their respective Legendary Beast insignia etched into the doors. Different Tales were stored in different rooms according to their relationship with each Attribute. The door to the room for the Soulfire Attribute was on fire, so only someone who studied Soulfire could open it. There were ice spikes above the Soulwater Attribute door and the only people that could enter that room without dying were the ones able to turn the ice spikes into water. Much like the Soulwater Attribute door above the Soulrock Attribute door was a boulder that would drop on anyone who dare entered. If the person who was trying to enter the room was able to slice through the boulder with their sword turning it into dirt the door would unlock. Once the door to the Soullight Attribute room opened, the person entering was blasted with a gust of wind while blinded by a beam of light. If the person was able to dodge the wind while their eyes were closed and then absorb the beam of light with their palms the light would dim and that was the person's que to open their eyes. After that they would be safe to walk around the room and read Soullight Tale. The last chamber on the left side of the Grand Sanctuary was for the room holding knowledge of the Souldarkness Attribute and acted as a resting place for The Son. If a person of no formal stature went through, then they would become severely burned by Purple Fire. Ehven, May, Lehavah, The Son, and Ohr were all immune to the effects from the doors and rooms since they helped create the defense mechanism. They were the only ones able to travel between each room without being harmed, until they would train their successors to become immune. The defenses were put in place to protect the sacred Tales that would help one control their Soulmagic, along with their Attribute.

This Council of Swordmasters would take up a responsibility that was seen years before and that was planetary travel between the people of Palaleon. People on each planet started to build ships much like their ancestors so that they could explore the new worlds, find new homes, and trade with one another. With their sense of curiosity of the universe restored, now more than ever, the Council needed to keep everyone safe. The Council eradicated grunt control over towns, villages, and cities around Palaleon, freeing the people. Some of Hoshek's grunts had fled to the Soul Realm once their master had perished, going into hiding to escape the Swordmasters.

After The Son helped the others build the Grand Sanctuary,

he officially took on the title of the Souldarkness Attribute wielder of the Council of Swordmasters. Now that the Council was complete, the members could further the task of maintaining peace throughout Palaleon. The Council of Swordmasters informed the people of a new form of leadership. This was a government system that would be put in place for the benefit of the people. Once the governing system was in place, and the people were getting accustomed to it, the Swordmasters were able to retire to their homeworlds. This new system was democratic instead of tyrannical. Everyone affected by the Shroud had regained their free will and rebuilt their villages, towns, and cities. The castles on each planet had turned to meeting places for the leaders of each village, town, and city on the planet. This is where the new rules for a democratic lifestyle would be born. Some people felt lost without a ruler. The Council knew they had to step in and help govern the planets, and by helping the people know that they could live in unity, without having someone rule over them. The Swordmasters had become each planet's delegate and met on Aestercrat when there was trouble on a planet that could affect other planets. While The Son was fully committed as a Councilmember, he also had time for a side project. He began to draw up plans for his own training base on his homeworld, Draefast. He wanted it to be connected to his home, which he would rebuild where his old family hut was. The other Councilmembers went to their homeworlds on their ships and started the search for successors. The Son was the only one not thinking about a successor at this time.

The Son believed that now was the best time to complete his new mission, which was to try and free the "pure" from the Soul Realm. Doing this would allow them to return to their bodies and live in the peaceful Palaleon. He got the idea for his mission after coming to the realization that his sister was trapped somewhere in the Soul Realm, and so he wanted to do everything he could to try to free her. Dark souls, and the remainder of the grunts who were still on Palaleon, would still be banished to the Soul Realm, but would now be fully watched over by The Son. As he entered the Soul Realm by unsheathing his sword, The Son noticed that it was quiet, almost as if none of the souls that he had banished to the realm days ago were there. He summoned the White Hyrax which yawned and then disappeared. To the Legendary Beast nothing was wrong … yet. The Son then left the Soul Realm and sheathed his sword, closing the portal behind him to go tend to his other Council duties.

After Nahvel's defeat, the Shroud disappeared along with the darkness throughout the universe. The Son was in control of the Souldarkness Attribute now and wanted to change how the Attribute was viewed. Through studying the old Tales, he mastered new abilities, including how to use his Attribute without being tempted by his inner darkness. The Son learned that the original meaning behind Souldarkness was that the one who commanded it would have their soul corrupted by its power. He was able to command both Purple Fire or Purple Lightning from his sword controlling the intensity of each attack and where they would land with precision. He would then go on to learn how to conceal his sword into a grey shard which was the combination of both the black and white shard forms, so that it would be more efficient to carry. During the first of many Council meetings, he was able to teach this ability to the other Councilmembers since all of their swords originated from shards. This would make it easier for each Councilmember so they could willingly transform their swords. Ohr was so proud of the man The Son had become.

As the first official meeting ended, each Councilmember held hands and used a little bit of their Soulmagic stemming deep within their souls to transfer a bit of their Attribute to one another creating an eternal bond. Each of them looked at their left inner forearms as they felt a burning sensation. "The power from this bond we share left a scar on each of our left inner forearms. This scar represents everything we just went through as a Council and how our collective vision will change the future of this universe for the better," Ohr stated.

"Do you feel that? I feel like my soul has been reawakened. I feel me Attribute coursing through my veins as if I don't need a..." The Son then rubbed his right thumb against his four fingers and created a bolt of Purple Lighting which shot upwards and then disappeared.

"I guess we do not need our swords anymore to use our Attributes," Ehven stated.

"Nevertheless, I would recommend that you still carry it on your person until you fully grasp your new powers," Ohr replied to all.

"Oh, by the way I have figured out how to control my Souldarkness Attribute and not become tempted by its corruption," The Son said. "Since I am the only person in Palaleon that knows how to use the Souldarkness Attribute I will rewrite it in Tales for the future Councilmembers as a branch of Soulmagic and its own Attribute. I also read in a Tale recently that, 'There is no light without darkness and no darkness without light but that does not mean one needs to overpower the other. They can coexist as one.' Let us not forget that when we are teaching our future successors. The soul is everyone's own individual driving force. Nothing is as black or white in this universe as it seems and the proof behind that is Hoshek. In order for us to maintain peace and unity we must remember the lessons we learned from our journeys - together and separate - and pass down those teachings."

The sixth Council of Swordmasters was unlike any prior Council. Not only did they successfully free the people from mind corruption and two villainous tyrants, but through their teamwork they discovered that their abilities seemed limitless.

The Son looked to the door of the Sanctuary room they were in and noticed five beasts standing there and on top of the White Hyrax was his mother. *I do not know how long they have been there or how they got here, but I am glad my mother is here.* The Son then looked at Ohr and continued to speak to everyone. "As Ohr taught me on our journey the original Council named their Attributes after the element they could command because of their unique connection to their soul. Thus Soullight, Souldarkness, Soulfire, Soulwater, Soulrock and all of the Sub-Attributes were born from the Soulmagic given to our predecessors by the Legendary Beasts. Up until now these abilities could only be used through the use of a sword, but the bond we created now goes beyond our sword and directly to our individual Attribute's. We have also created a bond with each other through our shared turmoil and the want to protect everything close to us. Now that we have come together and learned how to conjure this ability from our bodies, why don't we name it Soulattribute."

May responded, "I like the sound of that. Soulattribute. It combines our soul, the source of our abilities with the power we control outside our own bodies." Lehavah and Ehven then nodded in agreement.

"My mother actually gave these abilities that name while she was still alive. I have learned through meditation how to use it and can train each of you," Ohr stated.

"That would be great," each of the Councilmembers said in unison.

The Councilmembers still carried their swords with them since they knew they could not fully rely on their Soulattribute as it was a new concept to them. Each Councilmember would go on to learn how to use their Soulattribute to the best of their ability. Ehven was able to control rocks, wood, and metal through his soul from his palms. Lehavah was able to control fire and lightning, and create bursts of both the Attribute and Sub-Attribute. Her power much like the others was generated through her soul and then extended through her hands instead of her sword. May was able to control water's flow and create shards of ice to shoot around her body. Ohr was able to call upon the Soulwind Sub-Attribute from his soul and could now shoot wind out of his palms like his mother. He was also able to emit bursts of light out of his body towards any direction. On top of being able to use his own Attribute, Ohr could do anything Ehven, Lehavah, and May could while using their Soulattributes. It was more difficult for him to fully control the Souldarkness Attribute like The Son, but he could do it for moments at a time. The Son was now able to emit darkness much like how Ohr could do it with the light, on top of controlling Purple Lighting, and Purple Fire from his palms.

May and Lehavah waved to the others as they were getting ready to go back home. The White Warbler circled above them, then quickly dove. As it descended, it shrunk in size, and gently landed onto Ehven's shoulder. Ehven and the White Warbler had quickly created a bond with one another after the Councilmembers created their Soulattributes. Ehven was even able to summon the White Warbler through the sword ritual, showing how powerful the Legendary Beast's connection was with him. When he summoned the White Warbler, it would watch over him from the skies and become very protective of him, making a noise every time it sensed danger.

The White Ocelot appeared and motioned to Lehavah. She got on its back and entered the portal to Vastrilio. Another portal opened and water started spewing out. May noticed that White Manta Ray was inching closer and closer to the portal. She walked over, jumped on its back, and was sucked into the portal as if it were a current pulling her back home. Besides The Son, the others thought about where on their homeworlds they would find and train their successors.

The Son and The Mother then headed back to Draefast, as the White Hyrax bent its head down as a way to signal to The Son that it was time to go. *The others left their ships on Aestercrat, I guess they found a new way of travel through their bond with the Legendary Beasts. I will stay here with Ehven for a bit and train to better master my Soulattribute. Maybe the ships can be passed down to our successors. Now that's a thought.* Ohr began sparring with Ehven so that they could both become more in tune with their Soulattributes.

As the portal opened back on Draefast, The Son and The Mother appeared back to what remained of his family's hut.

He then whispered to the White Hyrax, and it brought The Mother back to her home. The Son planned on building a new home and base on the same dirt where his original home once stood. Hoshek City and castle were now changing. In fact, the city was re-named Takuma. It was becoming a city without corruption, and a place that fostered equality among all people, much like the rest of the towns and villages which were now freed from grunt occupation. The tiers of the city adjacent to the castle were no longer based on a scale of classism that Hoshek had created in order to have his loyalists close to him. Anyone could live anywhere as this was a fresh start for the people and the city. Those who once followed Hoshek had become less greedy through watching The Son, making them appreciate everybody around them. All the villages were safe thanks to The Son. He would occasionally make public appearances, but most days he spent alone visiting the ruins inside the castle. After the grand battle, he had moved the portal to the Soul Realm from Hoshek's chambers back to its original place, the ruin. As he walked close to it unsheathing his sword, it opened, and he entered to look for his sister. When he felt his Souldarkness Attribute reacting to his surroundings and heightening his power to yet uncontrollable levels he left and closed the portal behind him. The Son was the only person on Draefast to know exactly where the portal was, and how to get to it. Before people began congregating in the castle, The Son destroyed the entry point from the castle to any of the old secret passageways that rested in between the tiers. He could only get to it from the grate that he and his father went through to enter the castle years ago. He took trips entering the city and spending time throughout the various tiers before leaving to go to the grate. Sometimes he just sat next to the portal and read from old Tales or practiced stances to flesh out new Souldarkness Soulattribute abilities.

The Son frequently met with The Mother at her new home in one of the rebuilt villages and learned details about her past. She told him "My origin begins at my birth on Draefast. I was born into a loving and caring family. We were not wealthy and did not live in Hosheks city. In fact, we lived in one of the villages westward on the outskirts of one of the dark forests. I was born around the time Hoshek came to power, but oddly enough, I was not impacted by the Shroud. I watched my parents act mindlessly along with the people around me. I had to act dull in order to get by. That was until I met your father, and left my home."

The Son replied, "Wow your childhood sounded rough. I am sorry you had to grow up at the beginning of Hoshek's rule." The Son put his hand on his satchel and felt the gourd's shape.

"Oh, by the way, here is the gourd you gave me. It actually helped us defeat Nahvel, since we were able to catch the dark souls in them," The Son stated.

"Dark souls? Nahvel?" The Mother looked puzzled.

"You're telling me you did not see people running rampant around here as if they were encased in a shadowy darkness?"

"No, I guess I did not. While you went off fighting, I remained at home, and only went out when it was necessary to do so. Once the Shroud disappeared, I knew it was safe to live my life again," The Mother replied.

"Also, Nahvel was Hoshek and Ohr's grandfather. Apparently, he was puppeteering Hoshek the entire time. Ohr ended up killing him, thus restoring peace," The Son commented.

"Ah. I see. Well, I am glad you are safe now," The Mother said.

The Son then left his mother's home and began walking toward one of the dark forests. He grasped his sword and was able to traverse through time to visit the sword's previous owner, his father. The Son followed the journey of the sword. He learned that when his father was young, he was given to Hoshek by his parents as an offering for safety. Hoshek made The Father one of the early grunts by removing his soul and nurturing his body with Souldarkness, then returning his soul back into the body. Hoshek thought the process had worked on this young man, and that he was now under his rule. He did not know that, in fact, The Father's soul was too strong, so the soul-morphing failed. The Father was able to release himself from Hoshek's grasp. He fled into the forest. As he came to terms with who he was and his true purpose of not being Hoshek's pet, his body transformed from a grunt's body to an older version of the body he was in when given to Hoshek by his parents. Then suddenly, a man appeared from behind a tree and stopped him to talk. "You made a wise choice for leaving the city. You will live a far better life secluded from everything. Since you are different, I was wondering if I could see your soul." He then motioned for The Father to unbutton his shirt.

The Father looked in confusion. A man just appeared from thin air and asked to see his soul. "Who are you?"

"I am one of the very first beings of this universe. I can make it so you live the rest of your life in peace, but you must promise to never go back to Hoshek City."

The Father, intrigued by this man's offer replied, "I promise," even though he had no intent on keeping his promise.

The Father then removed his shirt, and the man extended his pointer finger towards The Father's chest. A white string started to emerge from his body and fell into the man's hand. "Your soul is very special. Do you mind if I keep this portion and replicate it for my studies?"

"It's already out of my body and I feel fine so I guess you can." The Father said. The man then vanished. Looking down to the ground where he stood, The Father saw a shape in the dirt resembling a lion's paw. This string, and the others the man went on creating, became the Merchant's original lute strings. The lute then turned into the two swords both of which made their way to The Son's hand at some point along his journey. Having a piece of The Father's soul on The Son at all times, acts as a memento and a way The Father can be with The Son even in his absence.

After this encounter, The Father referred to himself as the Soul Grunt, the one who escaped Hoshek. Eventually, The Father met The Mother in a village while boasting to others that he was able to flee Hoshek's grasp. While other villagers did not care for his attitude and behavior, The Mother found him to be quite engaging. She introduced herself and they instantly fell in love, deciding on starting a family. As The Father went on about his past to The Mother, he realized that she was very accepting of him. The only thing she asked was for him to never repeat it to anyone ever again. She did not want her family to be targeted and felt that if The Father told others about his past then it would be easier for Hoshek to find them. Only when the family felt that Hoshek was finally catching up to them, did they deem it necessary to have weapons to protect themselves with. Once The Son and The Father had stolen the swords, they had created a target on themselves. Once The Father went back to Hoshek City, his fate was sealed.

During the night of the Purple Fire, when Hoshek bent down to turn over the body of The Father, he noticed a familiar face. It was his prized grunt, the one that got away. Elated at his find, Hoshek decided to carry The Father's body out of the Purple Fire and transform him into the Dark Warrior.

The combination of a mortal female and a Soul Grunt is what made The Son special, for his soul had been different from others since the day of his birth. This is what made him not only Attribute worthy, but also destined him to be the one to change the future view of the Souldarkness Attribute as a whole. Locating and stealing the swords was no coincidence, The Son and The Father were connected to them.

The Mother and The Son would meet a few times during the rebuilding period on Draefast, to discuss if they had heard any word about The Daughter's soul. The Mother would search other planets, while The Son would search Draefast and continue to search the Soul Realm, but needed a way to remain in the realm for a longer period of time without becoming corrupted by his own darkness.

The Son created his very own Soulattribute ability. He traveled to the Waterfall of Light where he unleashed all of his Souldarkness Soulattribute as he submerged himself in the water, thus momentarily separating his soul from his inner darkness. His body turned into a Shroud as he reabsorbed his soul leaving a phantom version of himself created by his inner darkness under the water. The Son dueled his inner darkness, until he conquered it, and reabsorbed it into his body. Instead of succumbing to this darkness, he took command of it which changed his fate from his predecessors. His inner self was stronger than his darkness, thus his inner light was able to shine brighter. The Son had now unlocked full command of his Souldarkness Attribute and would never be tempted by it again. He tested this ability back at the Soul Realm where he was able to travel the vast plains for days as opposed to mere minutes without having to exit and re-enter. He had also compiled all of the notes he had taken and adventures he went on with Ohr. The Son burned the edges of the parchment using Purple Fire so the pieces would stick together and never tear. He also etched over his writing using Purple Fire on the tip of his quill so the words would remain on the page until the end of time. He did this so the future generations of Swordmasters would understand more about the struggles of holding such a power, and that the choices one makes not only affects them, but everyone around them. The Son titled his Tale, *Two: The Tale of Light and Darkness*. To write this Tale he had to make it a story, so he compiled his information into third person, and all his knowledge about Hoshek and the Dark Warrior was gained from passages he found in the castle on Draefast that was written by none other than Hoshek. It came to The Son's attention that at the end of Hoshek's life he knew that his grandfather would try to double cross him, but in his arrogance believed he would outsmart and defeat his grandfather.

The new Council of Swordmasters swore to meet every three years to discuss official business, but each Councilmember welcomed one another to travel to their home planet and be a guest in their home for as long as they wanted.

The Son and Ohr reconnected on Draefast two years after

the first new Council of Swordmasters meeting. It was time for Ohr to return The Son's ship to him, and he had finally found a way to use a pulley system from his own ship to carry The Son's. He did not summon the White Lion, so it did not join him on this journey. Instead, it continued its Legendary Beast duties while roaming freely throughout space.

Ohr landed both ships as The Son exited his base. He went to greet his mentor as they walked to the front steps. Ohr had never seen The Son's base. He was in awe of how matured The Son had become. "This is where…"

The Son interrupted Ohr as he spoke. "This is where we first met, and where you pulled me out of the Purple Fire."

Ohr replied shockingly, "So I take it your memory is fully restored then."

"Yes it is, and since it has been I have learned more about myself, along with reading through Tales of the Souldarkness Swordmasters who came before me," The Son proclaimed.

"You are different from them. You have a kinder soul," Ohr stated.

"I can thank your training for that," The Son said. After a pause, he continued, "I never knew how truly powerful your brother was in with the Souldarkness Attribute."

"My brother got corrupted, but before that he never meant to harm anyone," Ohr replied. "He was just lost." The Son then handed Ohr writings that he found in the ruins of Hoshek's castle. The Son knew that the parchments belonged to Ohr, and he had already taken notes from it for his Tale. Ohr and The Son did one final task before Ohr left.

They glanced up at The Son's base and walked inside. Together they removed a piece of Counterrock that was in one of the walls and put the Tale inside the wall. Both Ohr and The Son used their Soulattributes to repair the wall making it seem like a piece was not removed moments prior, so nobody unworthy could find the Tale. The Son summoned the White Hyrax and asked it to guard the Tale. The Son looked at Ohr and said, "Hopefully one day, someone who is worthy will find it and learn about the past. Hopefully we will have prevented more chaos by then."

"I feel that placing the White Hyrax in charge is a smart idea since the one who will find this Tale will be someone similar to you and will need to learn from your teachings how to defeat their enemy. The White Hyrax has always been and will always be your guardian much like how the White Lion is mine. When our souls pass on to their next venture it is important for the future Council - whether in fifty years or eighty years - to gain the knowledge they need, from people they can trust," Ohr replied. Those who were worthy of finding and reading this Tale would be directed to it by the White Hyrax.

After hiding the Tale, The Son said goodbye to Ohr. The old mentor then boarded his ship and traveled into the vast space of Palaleon, as night drew into Draefast's skies. The Son glanced to his right and noticed a lute laying on the ground next to him. *This is that same instrument that Merchant was playing years ago when Ohr and I saw him,* he recalled. The Son knelt to pick it up. It felt comfortable in his hands, like it was specially designed to the contours of his hands and fingers. He started strumming; it came naturally to him. He then started singing the words he remembered the Merchant sing years prior, while altering a few of them.

I come out here daily
Dusk till dawn
To reiterate about our past
Now that it's back
From times old that which I sing
The Council of Swordmasters survived again
To reteach everyone the ways of peace
Unity we had until the darkness came to be
Now that it is gone
We remember everything and are thankful for
those around us
We woke up
Yes, we did
We woke up
And now the Merchant can rest

As he was singing and playing the lute, he felt a strange sensation in his fingers. A breeze whistled in his ear and The Son looked up from what he was doing. He noticed a figure walking on a hill in the distance as the sun was setting. The figure winked, then transformed into a four-legged beast and ran away. "That looked like the...." The Son concluded aloud. He shrugged his shoulders and finished the song. He then put the lute down and went back inside. *I wonder why it is here. Maybe the lute has a special connection to that beast's soul or mine. Well, that's a question to be answered tomorrow.*

It was dark out now, and he was able to close his eyes and get the rest he needed.

For now, everything was peaceful, yet The Soul Realm's unexplored vast plains still exist with hints of darkness, so The Son knew that this is where the next chapter in his life will take place.

Epilogue

The Son woke up from what seemed to be a long slumber. He got out of his bed, looked around, and couldn't believe his eyes. He was in his old family hut, in his ten-year-old body. *Was all that just happened a dream?* he thought. Then he heard a voice calling for him. "Son, it's time for breakfast." He recognized the voice of his father. The Son walked toward the door, but before he made it to that side of his room, he stepped on what seemed to be a loose floorboard. He called to his father, "I will be right there." He moved the floorboard to find something wrapped in a blanket with a note on top. "You will need this on your next venture. Hopefully it will bring you to the answers you seek." *That is odd there is no name on this note.* The Son opened the blanket which revealed the sword from his dream. The Son was really confused. *It must not be real, or is it. How am I here with my father? Was the Soul Realm real or just a place in my dream? Who wrote me that note? This must be a trick. Maybe I am trapped in the Soul Realm or some new dimension yet to be explored. Maybe we lost against Ohr's grandfather and this is all a part of the future that he is in command of,* The Son thought. Nevertheless, he was glad to have this new time with his family, at least for now.

The Son finally replied to his Father, "Coming father". Leaving his room, he then closed his bedroom door and headed to the kitchen for breakfast.

The End

OHR FAMILY TREE

Ohtav - *spouse*
\
Second Council Leader - *spouse*   Hosra - *spouse*
\   \
Third Council Leader - *spouse*   Second Council Darkness Wielder - *spouse*
\   \
Fourth Council Leader (Gathran's Mom)------Gathran's Dad   Third Council Darkness Wielder - *spouse*
\   \
Gathran---------Malikaya   Fourth Council Darkness Wielder (Nahvel)
\
Ohr and Hoshek